SHADOW
LIFE

SHADOW
LIFE

For Jody,
In the hope
you enjoy
this story,
Michael.

a novel by

Michael
Decter

Cormorant Books

The publisher gratefully acknowledges the support of the Canada Council
for the Arts and the Ontario Arts Council for its publishing program.
We acknowledge the financial support of the Government of Canada through
the Canada Book Fund (CBF) for our publishing activities, and the
Government of Ontario through Ontario Creates, an agency of the Ontario
Ministry of Culture, and the Ontario Book Publishing Tax Credit Program.

LIBRARY AND ARCHIVES CANADA CATALOGUING IN PUBLICATION

Title: Shadow life / a novel by Michael Decter.
Names: Decter, Michael, author.
Identifiers: Canadiana (print) 20220215405 | Canadiana (ebook) 20220215413 |
ISBN 9781770866676 (softcover) | ISBN 9781770866683 (HTML)
Classification: LCC PS8607.E4235 S53 2022 | DDC C813/.6—dc23

United States Library of Congress Control Number: 2022935822

Cover image and design: Angel Guerra / Archetype
Interior text design: Tannice Goddard, tannicegdesigns.ca
Manufactured by Houghton Boston in Saskatoon, Saskatchewan in September, 2022.

Printed using paper from a responsible and sustainable resource,
including a mix of virgin fibres and recycled materials.

Printed and bound in Canada.

CORMORANT BOOKS INC.
260 SPADINA AVENUE, SUITE 502, TORONTO, ON M5T 2E4
www.cormorantbooks.com

For my remarkable children, Riel and Geneviève.

*And for all those who wonder from time to time,
as does Matthew, from whence they have truly come.*

BOOK ONE

MATTHEW UNRAVELLED

Turning and turning in the widening gyre,
the falcon cannot hear the falconer;
things fall apart; the center cannot hold.
Mere anarchy is loosed upon the world.
The blood-dimmed tide is loosed, and everywhere
the ceremony of innocence is drowned…

W. B. Yeats, *The Second Coming*

The world is what it is – those who are nothing or allow themselves
to become nothing have no place in it.

V.S. Naipaul, *A Bend in the River*

CHAPTER ONE

THE VERDICT

THE COURT CLERK READ each of the charges as she had done four months earlier when the jury selection for this trial began.

"Henry Dawson. You are charged with one count of murder. You are charged with one count of statutory rape. You are charged with one count of kidnap. You are charged with one count of forcible confinement."

Matthew Rice rose in the jury box and faced the judge.

"Your Honour, as foreperson of this jury, it is my duty to report that the jury is unable to reach a unanimous verdict on any of the charges."

A thin, ghastly smile spread over the defendant's face. It was a cruel and victorious grin. Matthew turned away from the defendant Henry Dawson, angry to his core. And defeated. His anger did not blunt or diminish the sense of failure that overwhelmed him.

"I have no choice but to declare a hung jury," the judge said, solemnly. "You are dismissed with the thanks of the court for the time and effort you have expended as jurors."

He then declared a mistrial, before turning to the lawyers for the prosecution. "Does the Crown wish to seek time to consider its position on a new trial?"

"No, Your Honour. The Crown will not seek a new trial."

The judge sat silent for a moment before he declared, "The defendant is free to go."

Matthew's hands developed a mild tremor. He could not bear to look at the mother of the murdered child. He could not shut his ears to her cries of anguish and loss that echoed through the courtroom. His own heart broke. Matt's eyes filled with tears. He and the other jurors followed the court constable back to the jury room to collect their belongings. He knew he had failed to convict a guilty man, the killer of a child. His head was reeling, searching for the rational world and not finding it.

The jurors were escorted into the sub-basement of the court-house and sent to their Sunday night homes in taxicabs, some individually and some sharing the ride. Matt found nothing to say to his fellow juror in the cab; each sat in silence as the city passed by, lost in his own thoughts. The streets of Toronto had never seemed so barren and cold.

He called his lawyer friend Harris when he reached home.

"I heard. Hung jury," Harris said immediately.

"It was…," began Matt.

"We can't discuss jury deliberations," Harris interrupted. "Criminal Code offence under section 649."

"I know," Matt replied. "I only wanted to say it was horrible to fail to deliver a verdict. Gut-wrenchingly horrible."

"Get some sleep and try to put it behind you. You did your best and that's all any of us can ever do."

"Thanks. I could use some sleep."

Matt hung up, then immediately dialled his daughter. "Sarah, I'm finished the trial. We did not reach a verdict. Hung jury. It needed to be unanimous."

"Are you all right, Papa?" she asked.

"Very tired. Need a lot of sleep."

"Are you going to be all right?"

"I'm always all right. No worrying."

"Go to bed and call me tomorrow."

Matt choked up. "Love you, Sarah."

"Love you too."

Matt couldn't reach his son Gabriel, but left a voicemail. He remembered Gabriel was travelling and likely on a plane.

He poured a glass of his best Scotch. He sat and sipped it slowly, trying to push the horror of the last seven days of the jury deliberations out of his mind. Forget the deliberations that had gone sideways.

He remembered a line from Yeats, but not clearly. *What hour of terror comes to test the soul.* Matt felt his hour of terror closing in. He did not sleep until first light. His morning became a twilight, deprived of real sleep; nightmares took full reign when he eventually closed his eyes. The precious little sleep did nothing to trammel up the worries of the day; it darkened and poisoned them. Matt knew in the deepest part of his soul that he had failed. He knew that his long life of success had run aground on this fatal shoal of abject failure. And he knew he was wounded.

When he reached the point of total exhaustion, he knew that his only refuge would be his cottage on the island in Georgian Bay. It was his Fortress of Solitude; it was the place he could rest, far away from the night noises and the lights and sirens of the city. Quarry Island had proven to be the place he could sleep when troubled. And he hoped it could heal what was broken within him.

CHAPTER TWO

QUARRY ISLAND

MATTHEW WATCHED THE BRILLIANT red sunset over Beausoleil Island and recited the sailors' warning silently to himself. *Red sky at night, sailors delight. Red sky at morn, sailors be warned.*

Lake Huron's Georgian Bay has always been known for its fierce west winds. This Sunday afternoon was no different. The temperature had dropped steadily throughout the morning, defying its usual pattern. At dawn, it was near freezing, and by noon, seven degrees colder. It had snowed the previous day. Not a lot — just enough remained on the ground to tell you that the air was certainly cold.

Dawn had broken with grey, dark overcast clouds. By noon, the steady wind was fifty kilometres an hour with fierce gusts to sixty. The waves in the Bay had begun to build into large rolling, cresting waves. Gusts whipped foam off the white-capped waves. For an inland body of water, a mere lake, the waves were huge — often described by alarmed newcomers as "ocean-sized."

With mounting concern, Matt watched his much-loved Limestone boat thrash violently on its mooring. Constructed of a dense, bright orange plastic, the mooring buoy featured an iron ring on its top where the line clipped on. Below the water, an identical iron ring attached the buoy via a steel link chain to a cement block on the sandy lake bottom. To Matthew's uninformed gaze, the set-up still seemed sturdy, but when he'd bought the Limestone, his neighbour Harris warned that he'd probably need to change the mooring to something considerably more solid.

"That old rig is not up to the heavier boat," Harris bellowed. "And you really need to put a name on the Limestone. Looks naked without one."

"Maybe I'll call it the Busted Flush," Matthew replied.

"Good idea. Then I can sue you for theft of intellectual property on behalf of the literary estate of John D. MacDonald."

Matthew snorted. "There must be thousands of boats named the Busted Flush."

"More work for me! Class-action territory."

Despite Matt's repeated requests to Buck at the marina, a heavier mooring block had not yet arrived. The marina ran on country, not city, time. In the schema of the locals, Harris and Matt were "city idiots." City idiots were to be resisted for intruding their annoying city urgency into the more measured pace of the country. There were no New York minutes in Honey Harbour, only the gentle pace of people more at ease with the daily and seasonal clock of nature.

All morning, Matt had glanced out the window towards the lake. The Limestone rose and fell on the white-capped waves. His friend Don, who was visiting from Winnipeg and an avid photographer, had hiked to the back of the island to photograph the abundant and colourful birds and flowers. Thirty minutes after Don departed, Matt looked again out the front window, but this time his boat wasn't where it should be. Still attached to the orange buoy, yes, but instead of bobbing up and down at its mooring place, the Limestone was now being driven by large waves and high winds parallel the beach to the east. The buoy had clearly broken free from the steel link chain and the cement mooring block.

Later, Matt would learn that it was not the small size of the cement block but the advancing age of the buoy that caused the calamity. The metal fitting below the waterline had given way, leaving his boat adrift on the stormy lake.

The jagged rocky shore of the Canadian Shield lay less than three kilometres to the east. Three-billion-year-old rocks only slightly softened by millennia of wind and water; his cherished Limestone would be reduced to pieces.

Matt raced out the door. His first thought was to get help, but there was no one on the deserted beach. He sprinted east, his deck shoes sinking into the soft sand as he ran. Despite the awkward footing, he began to make some ground on the boat. Would it drift closer to the beach so that he could swim out, and retrieve it? This is how people drown, he thought as he ran. They go after a boat and swim themselves out to the point of no return. And even if he reached the tow rope, his boat might drag him down the stormy lake to his death.

The May water was frigid, but he kept running along the beach, past the first cottage, the second cottage, the third cottage, rounding the point to the east. He bounced over the large rocks that sheltered the last cottage's dock from the currents. His boat headed steadily further off shore, beginning to move towards the distant ridge of rocky land, the bright orange mooring buoy still attached.

Matt continued to run, fixated on the boat, considering a desperate swim to save it. He found himself suddenly sinking, not through the sand, but slightly deeper. There was movement underfoot. Matt looked down and realized with horror that the ground writhed. Dozens, if not hundreds, of yellow-striped garter snakes crawled around and over his feet and ankles. He jumped out, his hatred of snakes clogging his throat. It wasn't a deep pit, maybe two feet, but completely filled with snake after snake after snake. He sprinted away as fast as he could, but ten yards later he stumbled into an identical replica of the first snake pit. This time, he jumped out and began to watch the ground ahead of him as carefully as he was tracking his boat.

What if the writhing mass had been Massasauga rattlers? Their bite was venomous. Did they also have a breeding pit here? He willed himself not to think about it, and instead focused on his endangered boat. At the eastern end of the island, he saw the Limestone tossed steadily away from Quarry Island's shore, across Severn Sound, and towards the rocks that marked its southeastern shores — towards its destruction.

The cottages Matt ran past were all deserted. He found a small boat tied up around the corner at a dock, with a small outbound motor. He jumped in. Yes, there was gas in its red five-gallon tank. Then he noticed that the boat was padlocked with a heavy chain to the dock to prevent theft. *Damn*, he thought. *I'd just be borrowing it.*

Dejected and frantic, he sprinted back up the beach and saw Harris's wife, Sophie, with her thirty-year old daughter, Laura. They had just been to his cottage looking for him. The wind howled and they were huddled together, backs to the west, against its fury. Out of breath, he gasped and pointed at his boat riding the swollen waves as it disappeared down the sound. *The boat is insured*, thought Matt. *Maybe I should let it go and make a claim.* Then his stubborn inner Matthew reasserted itself. *I will get my boat back*, he decided. *I must.* He hated asking anyone for help.

Unasked, his three neighbours appeared almost immediately. Laura, in a bathing suit and the top half of a wetsuit hastily pulled on. Her boyfriend, Todd, wore a too-large set of hip waders. Only her brother-in-law, David, was properly attired for the frigid water in a full wetsuit. Together, the four waded out to Harris's boat, a twin of his own, only newer and, he would admit reluctantly, much cleaner.

Normally, in calm weather, one person could easily detach a boat from its mooring so the three of them piled into Harris's boat while Matt went to the mooring. It became rapidly clear that in these large waves, Matt couldn't generate enough slack in the mooring line to unhook it. He struggled until his arms ached and his back protested. The two young men got back into the water to help.

With all three of them straining on the mooring line, they managed to dislodge it. Matt realized that even if they caught up with his boat, it was going to be one hell of a journey getting back against the wind and waves. As if to underscore this point, the waves spun the boat, and Matt fell hard in the back, banging his ribs on the hard fiberglass gunwales. It knocked the breath out of him. He lay for a moment on the floor.

Laura called over to him in concern.

"I'm okay," he replied, wincing in pain. "I'm okay."

Laura was unconvinced.

He pulled himself up and stood squarely, attempting to look uninjured. Fearing an early end to mission impossible, he said, "No, no problem, I'm fine."

Even as he said it, Matt knew that at least one of his ribs was cracked, maybe more. He'd experienced cracked ribs before — once sailing, and twice skiing. He knew the drill. His breathing became laboured. Each breath was agony, a sharp and deep stabbing pain. He had no time to worry about this now.

Ribs heal. He knew to take shallow breaths — to keep the pain at bay. Shallow breaths. He tightened the life jacket straps to keep his ribs from moving. The movement generated another sharp, stabbing pain. The life jacket would have to do until his ribs could be properly taped. I've lost so much, he thought. I can't lose the boat too. I lose things and people because I am not careful with them.

Laura drove the boat with determination, her hands steady on the wheel. The throttle at half speed. No heroics from Laura, but a deep respect for the treachery of the lake with its many reefs and shoals. Her gaze was unblinking. The boat made steady, if slow, progress. His boat was running quickly with the wind along the sandy beach of the island. Matt had always been afraid of the tip of the island; his one trip down there had ended in a chewed-up propeller. He knew there were many rocks and reefs to the east, but he didn't know exactly where they were precisely. He hoped Laura did.

The fierce wind was from behind them, throwing spray from the top of the waves on them. Gusts tore at their clothing, chilling him to his broken bones, the cold making it yet harder to breathe. In this howling wind, with a high-pressure area moving in, the lake grew steadily more turbulent and the waters grey beneath the dark clouds. Matt's ribs ached under his life jacket

Matt estimated his boat was very close to the rocky shore three kilometres away. But distances on water are deceiving and the waves obscured his view. Their propeller touched a rock; they held their collective breath. A broken propeller and it would be game over. They only began to breathe again when they did not hear any further noise of metal on rock. The battered propeller blade would have a notch, but it wasn't destroyed. Not yet anyhow.

Laura guided the boat toward the north.

"Rocks to the left. Turn to the right, to the east a bit," Todd shouted over the wind.

Laura shook her head. "We're past the rocks," she said, moving east.

Matt stayed silent. Not knowing the rocks in this area of the lake, and not having anything useful to contribute, he quietly prayed Laura didn't take the boat into rocks that would tear off their propeller, leaving them in the same position as his own boat — drifting without control down the lake. Transformed from rescuers to needing rescue.

Even if they did reach his Limestone, it was unclear how they'd get it back. Too heavy to pull or to tow in the lake's churn, Matt would need to get aboard and start it. Running it back under power was the only way, providing the prop was undamaged.

Laura drove the boat across what seemed to be deeper water, slowly and carefully closing the distance to the drifting boat. Matt began to game-plan his actual transfer from one boat to the other, realizing how treacherous it would be. The waves rolled the boat up and down nearly three metres each time. He signalled to Todd to join him at the front.

"We both need to jump into my boat," Matt said in a low voice, not wanting to alarm the others. "I'll try to start the engine and drive us away from the rocks."

Todd nodded. "What's my mission?"

Matt looked hard at Todd's hip waders, which sloshed as he moved. They'd filled with water while they were trying to get the boat off the mooring. There was no way to empty them. If Todd missed jumping from one boat to the other with Matt, he would sink like a stone. There'd be no saving him.

"Climb out on the deck of my boat and get the line. If I can't start the engine Laura will need to tow us."

"Got it."

Matt leaned in closer to Todd, speaking to him as firmly and quietly as he could. "Don't fucking miss. If you sink in those hip waders, you drown. Grab the boat when we get out there, and get inside after you land."

Todd gave him the thumbs up. "I won't miss."

The two boats were very close now. As Matt's Limestone drifted, powerless on the large rolling waves, it rose and fell by at least three metres. Todd jumped first; landing heavily on the deck of Matt's drifting boat, grabbing the seats to stop from being pulled overboard. Matt followed. As he landed, his ribs sent such a sharp pain to his brain that for a brief moment he thought he'd lose consciousness. Matt looked up to see the rocks looming. They had only minutes to get the boat in motion.

Todd wrestled with the mooring line and the buoy. He pulled both aboard so they wouldn't get tangled in the propeller. Matt quickly turned the power on, switched the blower on, and really couldn't wait five seconds, let alone five minutes. If there was a build-up of gas vapour and the engine compartment blew, it would be a spectacular end to their harrowing rescue mission.

Thankfully, the engine not only started but caught quickly. Matt idled it in neutral, as long as he could to warm it so that it would heat and not stall. Todd pointed at the looming rocks along the shore. "Getting close."

Matt rammed the throttle forward, praying the engine wouldn't stall. He pulled it back, thrust it forward, engaging the gears and, through them, the propeller. When the engine didn't stall, Matt gave it enough throttle to slowly move into the heavy waves. He swung the helm until the boat turned, heading back for home, now four kilometres away. The wind howled and the waves rolled — not running with them, but against them. The Limestone was a sturdy, heavy boat with a deep V-hull, designed to take on a big swell. Yet, these waves were so large they broke up and over the bow of the boat.

Matt turned on the windshield wipers so he could make out the shape of the boat ahead of him. He decided to hold back a couple of hundred metres. "Just follow them slowly back across the lake," he mumbled to himself, shaking from the cold.

As they came towards the southeast corner of Quarry Island, Laura took her boat too close to shore. Matt couldn't hear the propeller being torn up, but he saw them spin the boat back hard to escape the rocks. Matt stayed out, going where they should've been, not where she did. Later, he'd see the propeller — what was left of it — and realize they'd come home, propelled by a whirling blob of metal, the blades bent and torn by their earlier encounter with the rock. He knew he owed his neighbours a new propellor as well as the rescue of his boat.

Even attaching both boats to the Harris moorings proved a challenge. Their arms, cold and exhausted, were unequal to the task. They had to run the boat up to create enough slack and then hope that the buoy would hold against the still-massive waves.

When Matt eventually reached his cottage, he shook so badly

he could barely tear off his soaking wet clothes, let alone walk the meagre distance to find a towel. Instead, he simply climbed wet into warmer, dry clothes. With trembling hands, then with grim determination, he poured a large, heavy glass of Scotch. He could barely lift it to his lips.

Damn Quarry Island, he thought. *Never let your guard down. It tests you all the time.*

He'd nearly lost his boat; they all had nearly lost their lives. The embers in the fireplace responded to crumpled newspapers, kindling, and, eventually, one big log, then two others. The fire became a huge blaze to warm the stones of his cottage and his cracked ribs.

His friend Don not yet back from his photographic safari to the back side of the island, Matt sipped the Scotch and stared at the framed picture of Pierre Elliott Trudeau on the cottage wall. It was the campaign photo of Trudeau in 1974 in his gunslinger pose, a gift from a Liberal friend.

When Trudeau was then a young man, fully twenty years before he would become Canada's prime minister, he took a canoe trip on the Mackenzie River to where it reached the Arctic Ocean. Naked, he had waded into the frigid waters where the fresh river waters met the salt of the Arctic Ocean. The poet Frank Scott would later write about this moment, he was "a man testing his strength/against the strength of his country," capturing in poetry the essence of Canada's northern magus.

The quotation was printed under the photo. Matt thought to himself how he and Laura and David and Todd had all tested their strength this day, against the strength of the nation, against the strength of the elements, the cold, the water, the wind. They'd returned, if not triumphant, alive and with his boat reclaimed from the storm. *This stubborn testing was what defined Canadians,* Matt thought, *not author Pierre Berton's oft quoted assertion that Canadians were people who knew how to make love in a canoe.*

Today had been a warning. Matt knew it. A warning to be more careful to test his moorings, to be less trusting of his moorings. The jury deliberation and verdict had damaged his trust in the logical world, undermined his confidence, and frayed his own moorings. Trials were not meant to render injustices.

Before today, did he have Trudeau's courage to test his strength against the strength of his nation? He felt spent and unravelled too often these days, devoid of courage. *Still,* he thought, *I got the Limestone back.*

Then he took a deep, prideful breath, and his cracked ribs reminded him with an agonizing stab that his harsh northern nation rarely surrendered anything without a fight.

Harris arrived to see how Matt was, agreeing to stay for a glass of red wine. He scrutinized the bottle of red Matthew selected, before gently nodding his approval. Matt found himself sharing with Harris not only wine but his overwhelming sense of failure. Harris would not brook Matt's interpretation of the trial outcome as failure.

"Sometimes the evidence is just not enough. You cannot make yourself a martyr to this trial. You have too much to contribute," declared Harris.

"It feels like I failed that murdered girl and her family. Hard to shake that feeling."

An hour later, Harris headed home for bed or dinner — Matthew wasn't certain which. As Harris departed, along the winding path through the poison ivy to his own cottage, Don came walking back into the living room.

"I got some great photos of the fields of trilliums," Don said. He paused, noticing the trail of wet clothing from the porch door towards the bathroom. "Did I miss anything?"

Matt poured him a large Scotch. "Some real adventures on the high seas."

They drank enough Scotch into the evening that their planned morning return to Toronto was delayed until the middle of the next day. Matt did not discuss the trial with Don. He decided that he could safely burden Harris, but not Don. Harris was a creature of courtrooms and trials and, yes, juries. Don was not.

CHAPTER THREE

CIVIC DUTY

THE CALL TO CIVIC duty in the form of being on a jury had arrived to Matt in an innocent but official-looking envelope. He was surprised to see an envelope from the Attorney General and even more so when he saw it contained a summons for jury duty. Heading along the beach, he had found Harris seated on the old wood chair on his dock

"You should do it!" Harris thundered with enthusiasm, clutching the summons in the air. "It'll be fascinating."

"Really? Everyone else I know will tell me to find a way to be excused as I did the last time I got a summons."

"But think of the experience."

"Have you ever served on a jury?"

Harris shook his head. "I wish I could, but all lawyers are barred from jury duty."

Matt took the summons back and stared at it for a long moment. "I've always had an affection for public service. I guess jury duty is just another form of it. Besides, I might get rejected."

Harris chuckled. "Not bloody likely. They'll be glad to have you. Let me see that summons again?"

Matt handed it back.

Harris stared at it intently for a minute before looking up. "Judge is Shawn McDouglas."

"Do you know him?" Matt asked.

"Best judge on the Superior Court. Tough-minded but fair and smart. He knows his law and knows his juries. He won't let you escape."

Matt thanked Harris and walked slowly back to his cottage. Seated in the screened porch, he smoothed out the summons on the long oak table. He thought about what Harris said. It might well be an interesting experience. He might never have another opportunity. And, besides, it truly was his civic duty.

Events had been slowly grinding away at his attachment to the city over the previous few years. The tectonic plates of his beliefs and Toronto's civic realities ground against each other. The summer when the temperature stayed over thirty degrees centigrade for forty long days. The summer when smog alerts were issued nearly every day — fifteen alerts covering fifty-three days. The summer when the UV index proclaimed every morning that sunlight itself had become a hazard to health. The energy minister begged the public to turn down their air conditioning to conserve electricity. Toronto the Good had become Toronto the Unpleasant, the Unbearable, the Uncoolable. The city that he loved. The city that he'd spent thirty years coming to terms with seemed to have turned on him at every corner and in every way, both large and small.

This morning, he had not waded ashore for the old green canoe to ferry his stuff from the Limestone. Instead, he'd waded ashore carrying all of his gear in one awkward struggle. Distracted, Matt neglected to put on the green rubber shoes he wore to protect his feet from the rocks and the sharp zebra mussels that covered them. By the time he reached the beach, his feet were cut and bleeding. Life with a thousand cuts he thought. Small price to pay for getting his boat back. His feet would heal.

Increasingly, Matt had startled his children by talking about the crumbling of a society he'd once been so proud of, once been such a participant in. As his son would say, "You were big in the government when I was little, Pops."

It all seemed so manageable then. And to be slipping away, now. "That was before," came to mean that was when it worked for Matt. When he had purpose and when he got things done.

On that boat training day, a few summers previous, when Sarah steered towards the distant island with its two distinct trees, she found the second buoy before Matt. As she turned the Limestone to port, Sarah pointed. "Buoy number two," she said.

"Three to go," he'd replied.

They pointed out buoy number three together at exactly the same time. Laughing.

The water had been too shallow to drag the Limestone all the way into the dock. Matt waded ashore and floated the canoe out to the mooring buoy. Together, Matt and Sarah had loaded the grocery bags, their clothing bags, and everything else into the canoe and towed it ashore together.

That weekend, they sailed and swam. Matt cooked thick steaks with the dry spiced Barbarian restaurant steak seasoning Sarah loved. She even listened to his *Best of The Guess Who* CD without protest, a CD he played repeatedly in the soft evenings as Georgian Bay storms subsided. For a Winnipegger of the 1960s, the sweet voice of Burton Cummings claimed the heart.

But Gabriel and Sarah were young adults now, with their own lives to live, and increasingly Matt had found himself alone at the cottage, listening to The Guess Who, memories of Winnipeg flooding back, including the time he'd hired the predecessor band to The Guess Who, Chad Allen and the Expressions, to play his junior high school sock hop. He took to googling his birth year, 1952, searching for the course code of his life. What began as a mild curiosity gradually transformed itself from interest to pursuit, and then, at a pace, to hunger, to compulsion, and finally, full-blown weekend obsession. The depressing Bob Dylan lyrics that he played endlessly at university were more apt than Matt would like to admit.

Matt also began buying the literature of 1952, preferably first editions with their sense of history and occasion. He wanted to see how each book actually looked in 1952, when it first arrived, not in subsequent editions. At first, the purist in Matt's character caused him to search in his favourite used bookstores. He did the rounds, after work and on weekends, and carted them to the cottage.

When his bookshelf began to bend and overflow, he hired a local carpenter from Port Severn to build him a room in the basement, where stored his gradually burgeoning 1952 collection.

The purist in Matt gave way to an urge to possess the books sooner, so he began to search relentlessly online, ordering them from bookstores all over the world. Like the colours of the book jackets, 1952 was for him a kaleidoscope of looming import.

He marvelled at the post-World War II explosion of major literary works. Ernest Hemingway published *The Old Man and the Sea* in 1952; John Steinbeck *East of Eden*; Anne Frank's *Diary of a Young Girl*. By the time of publication of her diary, Anne Frank had been dead half as long as the only sixteen years she'd lived. Her belief — that people, at their core, are good at heart — haunted him.

Matt learned that in 1953, the Irish Government banned books by both Hemingway and Steinbeck. The powers that ruled Catholic Ireland declared Hemingway's books to be immoral. In a double reproach, Steinbeck's works were deemed both immoral and subversive. Anne Frank's story, the murderous obscenity of the Nazis, was not banned in Ireland. Perhaps, the Catholicism of the Irish rendered them more comfortable with death than with life.

His father, Daniel, had read one book each day for most of his life as did E.L. Doctorow. Doctorow's first job had been to synopsize books, all westerns, for the movie studio that employed him. The experience drove him to write his first novel, *Welcome to Hard Times*, first published in 1952. Although the reader, conditioned to expect good to triumph over evil, particularly in westerns, awaits the moment, when the white-hat-wearing hero emerges to defeat the Bad Man from Bodie. Instead, the Bad Man completely destroys the town, its spirit and its soul, as well as its buildings. Evil triumphs.

One day his son Gabriel, on a rare cottage visit, was looking by the shed for a gas can, and pulled up a tarp. Later, he confronted his father. "Pops, there are twenty cans of propane for the barbeque, all brand new, all shiny, and all full. What the hell is up? Don't you know how dangerous it is to store propane in a basement?"

"I told you, if things get bad in the city, you can come up here. We've got enough barbeque fuel to last us three years. By then, things will be fixed or not fixable," Matthew said.

"What would we eat?" Gabriel demanded. "The squirrels? The chipmunks?"

Matt had no answer. Watching the look of genuine fear cross Gabriel's face, he turned to weak humour. "Relax, the tanks were on sale. I got a great bargain. We won't be cooking the chipmunks. We'll have a freezer full of food."

Matt knew that Gabriel and Sarah were worried. Was their father losing it? Was this what happened to everyone his age? He overhead them agree to look for danger signs and to report to each other. Then, as children in their twenties inevitably do, his children got busy living and left him largely alone. They'd promise to come to the cottage and then find reasons to remain in the city. They possessed the elusiveness of their age.

Matt's obsession expanded beyond a mere utilitarian impulse. Beyond enough propane for the barbeque. He thought about comfort. One day, he cleaned out all the twelve-year-old, fifteen-year-old, and one bottle of eighteen-year-old Glenlivet at the modest Honey Harbour liquor store. *If things go badly*, he thought, *at least I'll have my favourite Scotch.*

He stored that in the basement, in a corner of his archive room, which he took to locking. Matt rationalized that this would keep anyone from stealing the high-speed printer and computer he had carted up to the island, although in fact, the computer was a laptop that he took back and forth. But the real reason he locked the basement room was because he was afraid that someone would stumble onto it.

Matt's attempts to hide his growing obsessions were undercut by the curiosity of his daughter, Sarah. In her efforts to confirm the existence of the many tanks of propane first discovered by her brother, she found the solar panels Matt purchased after seeing a television ad from Canadian Tire. He had the batteries to go with them.

"It's time we had a talk, Pops," Sarah said.

Matthew was not ready to reveal to his children the full extent of his obsession. In a few years, his pension would provide more than he needed. He hadn't told them yet that he'd explored how to run the water system at the cottage in the cold depths of winter. A simple copper line run down the middle of the water into the pipe to the beach well and then hooked up to a low-level electric current would keep the water in the pipe from freezing. A bit of an electric current through the copper wire caused it to heat up and would allow the water system to operate in the winter even at negative forty degrees. Matt now cut firewood for one hour each day, explaining it away when asked about the three cords of wood already stacked carefully behind the cabin.

"Clearing the deadfall," he remarked when asked. Eventually, he'd need to tell them he planned to stay through the winter on the island. But not yet. It would erode their remaining confidence in his sanity. Matt thought vaguely about Thoreau in his cabin, but that seemed so long ago, in a simpler time and a shorter hike from Boston.

Apparently, Sigmund Freud believed that all children are denied the full status and maturity of adults until their parents are dead.

Even then, it took a long time to outgrow the parental phantoms. His own parents, Daniel and Beth, were a particularly powerful presence even now, decades after their deaths. Perhaps Freud was not wrong about absolutely everything, as many revisionists asserted. He remembered how fiercely Daniel had driven him to win, "98 but of 100? What happened to the other 2 points?" Why not perfect? That was the message. If only you worked hard enough you could get 100 out of 100. After all, Matthew well knew that Daniel had scored 100 percent throughout his student days. He'd been bumped up one full school year.

Beth was completely different. She wanted her children to go to art galleries, to symphonies, to the theatre, and to develop their cultural knowledge and artistic talents. She insisted on piano lessons for all of them. Such was the clash between his parents. But not all of it. Once when he was young, Matthew had crawled down the stairs to the landing at the sound of their raised voices, he got a glimpse of a darker struggle between them.

"You have always favoured Matthew. He can do no wrong."

"He is the oldest child, the first born."

"The others are your children too. Give them some of the attention you reserve for Matthew."

"I do."

"You do not."

Their conversation deepened into anger.

"You are a liar."

"Don't you dare say that word to me, Daniel Rice. You just can't face the truth of your behaviour."

The next sound Matthew heard was the front door of their house opening and then slamming shut.

Daniel had left. Beth was silent. Matthew fled back to the safety of his bedroom.

CHAPTER FOUR

JURY SELECTION

ONCE MATT DECIDED THAT this call to jury duty was indeed his civic responsibility, he informed his colleagues and the mayor.

"I can call the judge," the mayor had joked. Matthew laughed weakly. Politicians who called judges were out of work quite quickly under Canadian laws and norms.

He had arrived at the courthouse early. He suspected there would be a long line of prospective jurors each bearing a summons, and there was. Three hundred prospective jurors had also received summons identical to the one Matthew held in his hand. The security check required an airport-type scanning with removal of coats, phones and pocket contents. Plastic trays carried the items to be scrutinized through a primitive version of the airport scanners. There were two lines. One was for prospective jurors. The second and shorter, faster line was reserved for those already serving.

His cohort gathered in a large, high-ceilinged courtroom to be selected or rejected. The raised position of the judge reinforced the formality of the court, as did the wood panelling and multiple wood railings. The jury box on the judge's right was even slightly elevated. The prisoners' box was positioned behind the lawyers and directly faced the judge. Flags added to the grandeur and majesty of the court.

A court constable shepherded the prospective jurors into long benches and answered their questions.

"How long will this trial be?" one elderly man asked.

The constable smiled. "You'll find that in the judicial system, time is fluid."

An answer worthy of the philosopher Yoda, Matt thought. Later he'd discover the wisdom of the court constable's answer.

Sitting on the long wooden bench, one of a dozen rows of such benches, Matthew waited patiently for something to happen. After about thirty minutes, the large man seated beside him in a leather jacket with motorcycle gang patches, tapped not very gently on his shoulder. "Do you know if this is a criminal trial or a civil trial?"

"No idea," Matthew replied.

A few minutes later, all six doors to the courtroom opened simultaneously, each one admitting a Toronto Police Constable sporting bullet proof vest and gun holster. Their prisoner, clearly the defendant, was led in by two other armed police and told to sit in the prisoner's box. He was a tall man, formally dressed in a dark grey suit, white shirt and dark blue tie. He looked like thousands of office workers that Matthew passed every day on the way to his own office. Ordinary. Matt wondered what this man could have done to earn such an armed presence?

He tapped his gruff seatmate firmly on the shoulder. "Criminal," he offered.

His fellow prospective juror nodded, slowly, large black beard nearly grazing Matt's face. "No shit, Sherlock."

The defendant stood while the charges were read by the Court Clerk. He was older, but not elderly or frail. *Perhaps fifty-seven or fifty-eight. Could even be early sixties*, Matthew thought. Suit neatly pressed. Cuffs on the pants. Average height.

The judge's voice was formal and direct. "Henry Dawson. You are charged with one count of murder. You are charged with one count of statutory rape. You are charged with one count of kidnap. You are charged with one count of forcible confinement."

Matt shuddered as one charge was read after another. Murder. Statutory rape. Forcible confinement. A hammer of dreadfulness brought down in quick succession.

"How do you plead to the charge of murder?"

The defendant's voice was emotionless. "Not guilty."

"How do you plead to the charge of statutory rape?"

"Not guilty."

"And how do you plead on the charge of kidnap?"

"Not guilty."

"And how do you plead on the charge of forcible confinement?"

"Not guilty."

Matt's thoughts tried to run away from the extremity of the charges, one side of his brain seeking escape from the horror, the other side of his brain, the curious side, taking it all in.

The formal proceedings carried on as Matt and the other prospective jurors sat riveted in their seats. A full list of witnesses was read to the courtroom; some were clearly police officers, others were medical experts. A dozen or more were not readily identifiable by title or occupation. The name of the Crown attorney, Catherine Brown, was read into the record, as was the defence counsel's, James Blackstone, and his much younger assistant counsel, Kelly McPherson.

Matthew slowly absorbed the exchanges taking place, mind focused on the charge of statutory rape. That meant the victim had to be under the age of consent. A child? *And everywhere the ceremony of innocence is drowned.* He stared at the grey-suited defendant, the average-looking man; his mind drifted back to the summer and the escaped Penetang patient with the axe.

The judge looked out over the heads of the prospective jurors. He seemed to be searching for something, but it wasn't clear what. "There are two stages to jury selection," he said, finally. "In the first stage, I'll hear from those who believe themselves to be ineligible for jury duty. To be ineligible, you must be younger than eighteen, not a resident of the City of Toronto, or unable to understand or speak English. If you seek to be excused on any other grounds, this is not the time to make those grounds known to me. There will be a second round in which each prospective juror will have a chance to present any valid reasons which would cause them to face hardship if they were to be chosen for jury duty. Save those pleadings until the second round.

"If you believe yourself to be ineligible based only on any of these three criteria, please make your way to the microphone and I will hear from you on the eligibility question."

Only a handful of the three hundred prospective jurors assembled made their way to the microphone. The first one claimed a lack of proficiency in English.

"So, it is your position that you are incapable of understanding the trial in English and communicating in English?" the judge asked.

The man very hesitantly nodded. "Yes, English not good."

"You are excused." The judge paused, then continued in a stern tone. "I heard you conversing with the court constable fluently in English. I will excuse you, but I will excuse you because you are dishonest, not because you're incapable of understanding English. I do not want a dishonest juror on my jury."

A collective shudder ran through the crowd. No one wanted to incur the wrath of this judge. Several people returned to their seats on the long wooden benches, pleadings unspoken.

"Are there any other potential jurors wishing to be excused on the basis of the three possible eligibility criteria — that you do not live in the city of Toronto, that you under the age of eighteen, or that you cannot speak or understand English?" Judge McDouglas continued, "Also, if you know any of the people named as witnesses or the defendant or the lawyers here present, either Crown or defence, come forward and let me know how you know them."

This invitation produced a modest line of nine or ten prospective jurors. After a series of questions from the judge, most of the line were dismissed from the jury pool on the grounds that they might know or have known one of the witnesses.

"Don't know if it's the same Larry Simon that I went to high school with?"

"How old would your Larry Simon be?" asked the Judge.

"About fifty-eight or fifty-nine now," replied the prospective juror.

"You are excused," declared the Judge.

There was a low rumble in the court room as other prospective jurors pulled papers from their pockets, some of them making their way to the court official standing below and to the right of the judge.

Judge McDouglas spoke sharply to the room. "Now is not the time to present your requests to be excused. Hold on to those letters; they'll be useful when I interview you individually. For right now, you'll be divided into groups. Each group will come forward over the next two days to be selected or not selected for jury duty."

Matthew glanced around the courtroom. The judge had success-fully shut down further would-be escapees from round one. The next step of the process began swiftly and strangely for an activity in the digital age. Officials brought forward a varnished wood tumbling box. Into it, they placed individual numbers representing each of the jurors. Then, in an action that reminded Matthew of Harry Potter and the sorting hat, they spun the hexagonal wood box and began to draw out jury numbers one at a time.

Jurors were reassigned to smaller groups and given times to be present for stage two of jury selection. Groups A, B, and C were directed to remain in the courtroom. Group D, in which Matthew had landed, was sent away for the day to return at nine o'clock

Friday morning. They'd be individually scrutinized then, and if so inclined, attempt escape from jury duty.

Matt's original jury summons was seized, then handed back with D10 printed at the top. Clearly, the court system was not committing any of its process to machines.

Judge McDouglas wasn't finished yet. "If you believe that serving on the jury will cause significant harm to you, then you should bring a letter with you when you are interviewed by myself and both Crown and defence counsel," he said, sternly. "Your letter should state the grounds which you put forward for consideration. I remind you that the rule of law, trial by a jury of your fellow citizens, and therefore jury duty are among the crucial foundations of our democratic society."

He took a drink of water before continuing. "Juries are as important as democratically elected governments. They ensure our democracy. Therefore, jury duty is a civic duty of each and every one of us."

Matt shuffled out with the rest of Group D, returning to his office amidst the modernist towers of Toronto City Hall, which always struck him as being modelled on the shape of early flying saucers. Several hours later he returned home, the impending trial forefront in his mind.

His house overlooked one of Toronto's deep ravines. The dense trees and quiet of its nature usually comforted him, but that night, his dreams were dark and troubled. The stresses of his job at City Hall mingled together with anxiety about jury duty and the nature of the crimes on trial. He woke over and over, worries and fears bleeding into his dreams and his waking consciousness.

Promptly at eight thirty the next morning, an exhausted Matt joined the line-up at the courthouse entrance to pass through the metal detector one more time. Signs directed him to a courtroom on the sixth floor. It was less imposing than the one from the day previous.

When Group D's turn arrived, Matt and the other prospective jurors were lined up in the corridor by the court constable. He took each one individually into the court room where they were positioned in the witness box to be questioned.

The first questions came from the Judge. "Do you know the defendant or any of the counsel involved in this case?"

"Not personally, no," Matt replied.

"Do you have any reservations about your ability to serve as a juror and come to your verdict based solely on the evidence at trial?"

"No reservations, Your Honour."

Matthew produced a written list of City of Toronto Council meetings and committee meetings that he'd miss as result of jury duty.

The judge was unmoved. "I can see how your absence might harm others," he said. "The absence of your advice and so on. But I do not see how it would harm you."

Matt had added a line to the end of his letter, which read, *I believe jury duty is a civic duty, therefore if you decide that I should be a juror, I will serve to the best of my ability and without fear or favour.*

The judge looked up at Matt when he got there and nodded. Then, it was the Crown prosecutor and the defence counsel's turn to grill him. Turning to counsel, the judge offered them each a chance to ask questions. There was only one question for Matt, from James Blackstone, lead defence counsel.

"Do you harbour any negative feelings towards those accused of a crime that would prevent you from rendering a fair verdict in this trial?"

Matt was answered firmly. "I have no negative feelings towards those who are accused. I believe I am fully capable of rendering a fair verdict."

The judge asked Matt to look into the eyes of the defendant, catching him off-guard. He gave his best unblinking stare, with neither a smile or a scowl on his face. The defendant returned his stare. He, too, had the right to veto jury selection. The moment passed without any reaction. Matt shivered internally without revealing his unease.

Harris had been right; Matt was selected for jury duty. He was told to report to the courthouse the next morning at nine AM, along with the eleven other jurors selected and two substitute jurors. Once again, his original summons was seized; Juror #9 now printed in ink at the top next to D10. The summons and photo ID would be necessary to pass through the security check and metal detector at the courthouse entrance for the duration of the trial.

Matt was both excited and filled with dread as he walked back to his office from the courthouse. The nature of the crime was horrific. He imagined his own daughter when she was much younger being seized and it filled him with rage. But he also felt strongly that he needed to embrace his democratic responsibilities. If he did not step up to serve, who would? He was now a juror; Juror Number 9. Where would this journey lead him? How long would this trial take to complete? The court constable's answer came back to him. *You will find in the judicial system that time is a fluid concept.* What the hell did that mean? Some Zen courthouse nonsense, he suspected.

Matt awoke covered in sweat. His thin T-shirt was soaked. For several moments he became completely disoriented. Why was he at his cottage? Where was the courthouse? And then it came back to him as though a sledgehammer to his soul. The trial had ended. He had failed. The killer had walked free. He was reliving that failure. Matt knew that there would be no way of moving forward until his dream mind finished its painful review of every moment of the trial.

CHAPTER FIVE

THE TRIAL

MATTHEW FOUND THAT THE trial had its daily rituals. Each morning at nine, the jurors were directed to meet at the top of the escalator on the second floor of the courthouse. Once all were present, the court constable lined them up in the hallway by their numbers. No names, no deviation in the ritual. Always in the same order by number. It reminded Matt of an oddly inappropriate yet apt song fragment about numbers and names, but he could not remember it exactly.

A murder trial struck Matt as an odd time and place to remember a line from a long-ago song. But there it was bouncing around in his head every time they lined up.

The court constable explained the daily rituals of the courthouse. Orders for coffee, tea, and snacks would be taken before the trial began either in line or in the jury room. Those refreshments would be delivered to the jury room at the midmorning break — a stark room with one small microwave plugged into the only outlet in the room, and a fridge where they were allowed to keep snacks if they wanted to bring their own. At lunch, though, the constable said, they had to leave the building and eat elsewhere. Staying inside the courthouse was not permitted. In the lower-level cafeteria, jurors might encounter witnesses or defence counsel, so lunch was not permitted there.

Four times each day the jurors left the jury room to enter the courtroom. The ritual never varied. Two cheerful court constables would knock on the jury room door. When they were given the all clear, they'd unlock the door. As for the jurors, they were lined up with juror number one placed at the head of the line and juror number twelve at the back. All other jurors sorted themselves in order. Matt rapidly discovered, as juror number nine, that all he needed to do was remember the backside of juror number eight to secure his proper place in line. Until all jurors were lined up properly, the courtroom door remained closed.

When the courtroom door opened, they filed in. The first six jurors took the front row, thus facing the side of the witness box and the left side of the judge. The second six jurors, including Matt, took the higher back row. If the jurors looked to their left, they saw first the Crown counsel, then the defence counsel and behind them, the accused who sat with a police constable in an adjacent seat. The rest of the courtroom was occupied by people Matt supposed to be journalists, family of the victim, and perhaps family of the accused. And, as they would learn later, classes of high school students.

The jury box chairs had an upholstered, well-padded seat, much to Matt's relief. A large, black binder greeted each juror. They quickly learned that the binders served a dual purpose. Lined paper for their note taking partially filled the binders; that was their first and primary role. As the jurors would discover, the binders also received evidence — photos from the crime scene, autopsy reports, agreements on facts signed by the lawyers and other documents related to the evidence throughout the course of the trial. As the binder filled, Matt came to regard it with a mix of curiosity and dread.

The diversity of the jury mirrored Matt's daily Toronto life. He and his fellow jurors could have been plucked out of the subway. Their ages ranged from eighteen to seventy; there were seven women and five men; there were four Asians, three African-Canadians and five whites. Their occupations ranged from teacher to unemployed electrician, from journalist to two healthcare workers.

The trial opened with His Honour explaining the importance and process of a jury trial. "I am not the only judge in this court-room. You, the jury, are judges too."

Judge McDouglas paused while the jurors absorbed this revela-tion. "I'm the judge of the law and you're the judges of the facts," he continued. "The only evidence you may rely upon is evidence that is tested in this court proceeding. You are not to read about the trial in the newspapers or to watch any news about this trial on television. And, in particular, you must not search the internet for any information about the trial or any person involved in it."

Matt already knew not to look and he had resisted the temp-tation. He scrutinized each of his fellow jurors as the judge spoke. He wondered if they had been as careful. Certainly, there'd been opportunity between the reading of the charges and jury finalization.

"The fundamental basis of a fair trial by jury is that all the facts you consider must be tested in this proceeding by both the Crown counsel and counsel for the defendant," the judge contin-ued. "Before you enter jury deliberations, I will present my charge to the jury. I will explain the law as it pertains to the facts of this trial. Now I will ask the Crown to present their case."

The two Crown attorneys were both women Matt judged to be mid-career. He could only imagine the horrific crimes they had dealt with. The darkness that was like a poisoned river running through the city, visible only in the headlines and easily avoided by most residents.

They began by calling their witnesses, who were largely foren-sic experts. They testified about the evidence that proved that the little girl had been murdered, that she had been raped, and how her murder had been carried out. While the experts spoke in technical terms, the impact on the jurors was not muted by the language. They were silent when they returned to the jury room. Numbed from the horrific death of a small child and the cruelty inflicted on her.

In the early going, most of the Crown testimony was given by police witnesses. It was factual. The daughter had disappeared from a public park while she was in a public washroom. No more than five minutes passed after the mother last saw her and the logged time of the first desperate 911 call.

Agreed Statements of Facts were introduced midway through the trial. These statements were agreed between the prosecutors and defence counsel. They reduced the scope of witnesses and in some cases spared the jury and the grieving family from testimony on details of the girl's murder. The specific cause of death was part of this. These statements were often in the clinical language of forensic experts and the coroner. Cause of death was rupture of the aorta; literally the six-year-old was stabbed to death with a fatal wound to her tiny beating heart. No matter the horror of their content, each Agreed Statement of Facts had three holes punched in it so as to fit into the black binder held by each juror on their laps or at their feet.

One woman suddenly rose and bolted from the court as that part of the statement was read into the record. Matt felt sick to his stomach. Later he learned that it was the victim's mother.

Camera locations and the videos obtained from those cameras provided a central element of the trial for both prosecution and defence. Many hours of jury time were spent in the courtroom while one or other of the lawyers used the video to amplify their point of view on how events unfolded that fatal afternoon.

The key prosecution witness was a homeless man who spent his nights at Seaton House. He described with unusual accuracy the clothing worn by both the victim and the defendant. "The little girl had on a pink dress, cotton I think, maybe just below her knees, the hem. The skirt length was just below her knees."

"And the man who took her from the park?" asked the prosecutor. "Can you describe him?"

"He was tall and wore a suit. He had cuffs on his trousers. He had expensive, black shoes — brogues, not oxfords."

"And where were you sitting, sir, when you saw the man leading the girl out of the park?"

"Just there on the small hill. I had a view of the path and the park exit."

Defence counsel were brutal with the park witness. "You, sir, are an alcoholic? Admit it?" began the interrogation.

At first, the witness tried to fight back, but he was overwhelmed by the continuing verbal assault from the defence attorney. "You, sir, you are a cocaine addict."

Not a question, a declaration.

"You assaulted your own mother, sir. Did you assault your own mother?"

"Whatever you say, yes." He paused and looked down at the floor. "Whatever you say, yes."

By the third question, the witness, a man of thirty years of age, was curled up in the chair almost in the fetal position. His answers became a repetition. He was a beaten man and a damaged witness.

"Whatever you say, yes."

Defence counsel brutalized the witness, sneering at his answers. It descended from there. Yes, the witness had been an alcoholic, but one of the police officers had had the wisdom to conduct a breathalyzer test on the man. He was cold sober the day of the abduction and murder. Zero blood alcohol content.

There was no video of the accused in the park. There was an Agreed Statement of Facts that the defendant was in the vicinity of the park at the time of the abduction. A storefront camera captured him two blocks away. Crown and defence sparred over the video.

The child's body was found in an abandoned warehouse building, a five-minute walk from the park. She was inside a small room a few feet in that may have been used by the security when the building was still in active use as a warehouse.

The knife, later identified as the murder weapon, was found in a community garden bed six months later by a gardener tilling the beds for new plantings in the spring. Because of the length of time that had passed and with the knife being buried in the earth, there were no useable fingerprints. However, forensic experts matched the knife blade to the slash marks on the victim's tiny throat and to the fatal stab wound to her heart.

The most horrific day of the trial came with the autopsy report. An Agreed Statement was entered into evidence and distributed to the jury.

There were no photos of the murdered girl's body. Somehow, that made it worse. Matthew's imagination took the horrific clinical language of the autopsy — the lacerations, the crushed larynx, the bruising to so many body parts — and transformed it into a photograph in his mind. The image haunted him as mercilessly as the killer had hunted this little girl. Unlike the autopsy report that could be contained within the black binder and left in the courthouse, Matthew carted the mental image inside his head everywhere he went, every hour of the day and night. His dreams were haunted by it. Sleep, when it came, did not "knit up the ravelled sleeve of care." Macbeth had it wrong.

The trial consisted of long periods of tedious and detailed testimony punctuated by truly awful revelations about the crime committed. The juxtaposition of intense emotions and then boredom was difficult for Matt to reconcile. He slept poorly for the three months the trial consumed. After the first week of rushing to the office before and after court, and racing back to his office each lunch break, he realized there was no way he could continue like that. He needed to take a leave of absence from his job at City Hall. The trial required his full concentration.

It also became apparent to him that one hour in court was gruelling in a way his work was not. The stress of the constant battle between prosecution and defence; the stark horror of the crimes against an innocent young girl and the tedium of the end-less detail of evidence overwhelmed and exhausted him. The trial existed as a battle between two competing explanations of the same evidence. At stake were the fate of the defendant and justice for the dead girl.

Matt and the other jurors were routinely reminded that the rules were strictly enforced. The jury could deliberate on the evidence and the verdict only after all of the evidence had been heard. They were not to discuss the trial with anyone else, or with each other during the trial itself, only after the presentation of evidence concluded and the judge made his charge. Looking at any media coverage was strictly prohibited.

Their jury room rituals included smoke breaks as two jurors were smokers. Initially, the jury's assigned court constable would only allow the smokers to go outside with all the jurors brought downstairs too, so that they could stay within view of each other. Eventually, the jury convinced the court constable that the non-smoking jurors could safely remain locked in the jury room with one court constable, while the other constable escorted the two imbibers outside to the official smoking area and then safely returned them.

There was chatter among the jurors, but not about the trial specifics or the evidence presented. Instead, they tried to find a phil-osophical basis for what they were expected to do as jurors — to be the judges of the evidence. The burden of their responsibilities seemed to Matt a constant weight on each of them personally and as a group — impossible to escape, carried in both the body and the soul.

In the early weeks of the trial, one of the jurors quoted William Blackstone, a famous English jurist and legal scholar: "It is better that ten guilty persons escape than one innocent suffer." As the trial dragged on, defence counsel displayed a near contempt for police witnesses. This provoked another juror to counter with a quote from English writer and journalist George Orwell. "People sleep peacefully in their beds at night only because rough men stand ready to do violence on their behalf."

Views hardened; there was a brutality to the cross-examination of witnesses. Matthew, and he believed many of the other jurors, did not support the extent to which defence counsel bullied prosecution witnesses. Their collective respect for the rough men and women who served grew. But this view was not universally shared by the entire jury, as he would later learn.

After three months in the courtroom, the last evidence was finally presented by the defence counsel, followed by summations of both the Crown prosecutor and defence counsel. The judge adjourned the trial for the day. He advised jurors that the last step prior to the jury being sequestered for deliberations would be his charge to them, which he'd commence the next morning.

"I expect that reading my charge to you in which I will explain the law that applies and review, in an objective manner, the evidence called by both prosecution and defence will take a full day and a half. Then you will be sequestered for your jury deliberations."

He paused while the jurors absorbed this new reality.

Time is fluid in the criminal justice system, Matt thought. *That constable was right.*

"You will need to bring the things you need for sequestration — changes of clothing, any medications — and the constable will direct you further on this matter," the judge added.

As they sat in the jury room waiting to be escorted out of the courthouse for the night, one of the jurors asked, "Sequestered? What does that mean?"

"Locked up in a hotel. Brought back to the courthouse for deliberations and then locked up again each night until we reach a verdict," replied another juror.

"Reach a unanimous verdict on each of the charges," added a third.

Two days later, after the judge's charge had been delivered with exceedingly careful detail, it was time for deliberations to start. The jury entered a new jury room, larger than the last and with padded seats. The court constable had delivered a box with all the exhibits of evidence presented at trial, which sat accusingly on the jury table in front of them.

The little murdered girl's dress weighed heavily on Matt. In what kind of world did a child go to the park and end up murdered? He knew the answer and he resisted it. In our world, in our city. That was the answer he could not bear.

Matthew was elected by his fellow jurors as foreperson. It was not a job he wanted, but he was willing to accept it to try to finish the trial. The jury deliberated for three days. The impasse emerged gradually. Eleven jurors came on board with a guilty verdict by the end of day two. They'd reviewed in detail all of the evidence presented and when tested, eleven of the twelve were ready to convict. One was not. The entirety of the third day was reviewing all of the evidence to try to satisfy the hold-out juror.

"Does anyone have a view on how we should proceed?" Matt said, frustrated, but trying not to show it. "We've reviewed all the evidence in detail. For most of us, the more we review, the more confidence we have in a guilty verdict. But one of us looks at exactly the same evidence and sees flaws. Do I have that right, juror number three?"

"I have doubt about the testimony of the witnesses," she replied. "They each described the man differently. Different heights? Different weights? That troubles me."

"I'm not going to let that guilty bastard walk because you have doubt," one of the men on the jury exploded. "Let's vote and get this over with."

The hold-out juror started sobbing.

"We have to arrive at a unanimous verdict," Matt intervened.

"Freely and unanimously. We can't bully one of the jurors and call that unanimous. Let's take a break and try again."

Still at loggerheads, the jury decided to send a letter to the judge at the end of the third day of deliberations. In it, they asked several questions pertaining to the proper definition of "beyond reasonable doubt." This was the point of impasse for the holdout juror. Where precisely between "probable" and "absolute" lay "beyond a reasonable doubt."

The judge was constructive and sympathetic to the jury. However, all he could do was reread sections of his one hundred twenty-seven-page charge to them. While his words comforted Matthew and ten others, they didn't solve the problem for the one holdout. After another full day of jury deliberations, it became painfully clear that unanimity was impossible. Thinking back, Matt knew the exact moment he suddenly realized that the jury had slipped away. He remembered looking around the table at the sense of defeat, betrayal, exhaustion — eleven people who believed that the guilt of the defendant had been proven, and one who did not.

The jury reassembled in the same seats in the jury box where they'd spent three months painfully listening to evidence, diligently taking notes. The guilty man — the murderer — sat in the prisoners' box staring at them.

Matthew knew the jury system held a unanimous decision of the jury as a sacred tenet, yet he wondered how many guilty murderers had been set free by a single hold-out juror.

CHAPTER SIX

THE AFTERMATH

AT THREE IN THE morning, Matthew heard loud banging noises from outside. Thinking it likely the raccoons at his large, plastic garbage bin in the alleyway beside the front door, he nevertheless got up and went downstairs. The trial had taken its toll.

The noise had awakened Matt from the recurring dream where he was back in the jury box reading the verdict. When he first awoke, he could feel the hush of the courtroom as he stood in the jury box reading the admission of failure, the hung jury. Even after he realized he was dreaming, the sobbing of the victim's mother haunted him. Her cries had shaken not only her thin body but also the hearts and consciences of all those in the court.

Matt knew he'd never forget the mother's anguish. Nor would he ever forgive the hold-out juror who hung the jury — hung his jury — who had prevented this devastated mother from obtaining what small measure of closure a guilty verdict would have brought.

Two weeks after the trial concluded, Matthew picked up his ringing phone just as he saw the headline in the morning paper. He knew her voice. She was the lone juror. The one who had let the child-killer go free. Now, two weeks later, he had killed again. Another young girl dead. The killer they had turned loose, arrested. This time there was no doubt. The jury had freed him, but the police must have kept close watch. *But not close enough to save this young child*, Matt thought, anguished at the turn of events.

He knew it was the hold-out juror even before he heard her hysterical sobs. "We killed her. We killed her."

Matthew said nothing. He waited.

Then she broke. "I killed her. I killed her —"

Matthew cut her off. "Yes, the unspeakable monster we let go has killed another innocent young girl."

"I let him go. I hung the jury."

Matt let the silence hang between them like the sword of Damocles. He would not absolve her. To his enormous surprise, what he heard next was not sobbing but her professional voice. Steady, if not calm. It had suddenly returned, perhaps because her sobbing and hysteria had failed to move him. And, then he heard that voice say, "Would you like to talk?"

An involuntary shudder ran through his body before anger filled him to an instant boiling point. "Talk won't bring that little girl back to life. Save your talk for someone who still wants you to find a way home."

Matthew hung up. When his own sobbing stopped, he sat, drained, on the couch staring at a television he could not bring himself to turn on.

Harris called. When Matthew heard his voice he felt momentarily buoyed, hoping that Harris would say something to make sense of this tragedy.

"There are no words for this, Matthew, no words at all."

"She just called me, the hold-out juror. She wanted to talk. I had no words for her."

"How could you have?" Then, as always, the kind heart of Harris made itself known. "She must be devastated."

Matt shook his head from side to side, as if Harris could see through the phone. It wasn't time yet for sympathy. "I appreciate your call."

After a long, unbroken silence, he heard Harris hang up.

That moment of reading the brief statement was burnt into Matthew's memory. With all of his soul, he wanted to have read a different series of answers.

"On the charge of murder?"

"Guilty."

"On the charge of kidnapping?"

"Guilty."

"On the charge of forcible confinement?"

"Guilty."

"On the charge of rape."

"Guilty."

Would he ever forgive himself? What if he had gone back to the judge one more time? Another letter to the judge for greater clarity? Could he have brought the hold-out juror on board with another careful walk through the full body of evidence?

Matthew poured over the trial and deliberations again in minute detail. There was no denying the unshakeable truth that they — he and his fellow jurors — had freed a guilty man to kill again. Another innocent young girl violated and brutally murdered.

Nothing Matt could say or think would ever erase that truth or lift that burden. His soul would bear that scar for the rest of his life.

In a daze, he went outside. As he got to the sidewalk, he ran into his neighbour to the north, who held the morning paper up, folded to the story about the murder. They'd joked previously they were the only two subscribers in Toronto who still got a print paper delivered. "Was this the trial you were on?"

"Yes," Matthew replied, cautiously, not knowing what to expect.

"They should throw this child murderer in general population. They'll deal with him."

Matthew said nothing.

His neighbour stared at him. "You know in your heart you agree. I know you agree with me because I can see it in your eyes," he shouted, walking away much faster than Matthew could follow. Matthew slowly walked one block to the subway, before turning back home. Did he want the murderer put in general population to be killed? He remembered arguments between his parents. His father, Daniel, favoured the Old Testament, An Eye for An Eye. Beth, his mother, believed the commandment Thou Shalt Not Kill extended to the state as well as individuals. Matthew had leaned towards his mother's view, but in the wake of the trial, he wavered. He emailed the office to stay he wasn't coming back in today after all. Instead, he poured a large Scotch for breakfast, and sat in front of his fireplace, thinking about the words of JFK. "All that is necessary for evil to prevail is for good men to do nothing." Had he done nothing, he wondered. What more could he have done?

Matt returned to work three weeks after the trial ended, a week after the second killing. At first, he felt the comfort of the familiar, but something had profoundly changed.

A month went by slowly and Matt did not regain his former self. Most of the time he seemed lost in a daydream. He rarely spoke at senior staff meetings. He nodded his head and his managers took his gesture as agreement with what had been proposed.

Early in his fifth week back, Matt lost his temper in a meeting about the police department budget. Although a compromise was obviously being worked out at the political level, Matt waded in, furiously absent the calm good humour that had characterized his persona as public servant.

"We have uniformed police officers doing data entry. We have a rising murder rate in our city. Time for the Chief and the Police Services Board to step up. We need officers on the street. We need to bring back some effective version of stops. How many more innocent children must die because we are incapable of some real backbone?"

After his angry words, Matt stormed out of his office slamming the tall, heavy wood door behind him. The echo of the slammed door followed him down the corridor. He took the stairs down. Outside the door, he sat on a bench and stared at the courthouse across the plaza. Tears filled his eyes. He went home on the TTC and crawled into bed.

His assistant called the next morning. She was a little awkward. "Morning, boss."

"Morning, Stephanie. What's up?"

"I have the Director of Human Resources here. She wants a brief word with you."

"Please seat her in the small boardroom and put the call through to her there."

Matt spoke as soon as he heard the line open. "Susan, what's up? Another harassment suit involving a councillor and his assistant? Will they never learn?"

"Actually, Matthew, this call is about you. No one's accusing you of anything. We're all worried about the toll the trial has taken on you. The mayor thinks you might need a leave to recover."

Matt harrumphed. "Likely wants me out of the way so he can flog another strange transit plan to the premier and prime minister."

"I support what's proposed," Susan said, tone firm and filled with concern. "You've been through hell, and you need time to heal. You are ...," she hesitated, "not yourself."

Matt was now fully aware, and curious. "What do you want me to do?"

"You have an appointment with a Dr. Bergman. He'll make a recommendation. Stephanie has the details."

Matt began to protest and was cut off by a now more vehement Susan. "For heaven's sake, Matt, you are our greatest advocate for treating mental health seriously. Set an example for everyone who admires you and go get help."

There was a long moment of silence. "You're right, Susan. Thank you for going to bat for me."

The next day, Matthew entered the inner office of Dr. Joseph Bergman, Psychiatrist. A man of about forty-five with a neatly trimmed beard and well-tailored suit, rose out of his chair, came around his desk and extended his hand.

"Dr. Joseph Bergman. You may call me Joe."

"Matthew Rice," he said, as he shook the doctor's hand. "Call me Matt. My family and friends, and those who help me, call me Matt."

"You will be mostly helping yourself, Matt. If you're willing to do the work." Dr. Bergman hesitated and then added. "I'll do everything I can to help you do that work. Please take a seat."

The doctor gestured at two leather, high-backed chairs arranged across a coffee table from each other. No couch, Matt noted. They sat.

"Let me get a few basics established, Matt. How old are you?"

"Sixty years old this month."

"Family?"

"I have a son who's twenty-eight and a daughter twenty-five. I'm divorced but on good terms with their mother."

"And you work at the City of Toronto?"

"Yes. I'm the Chief Administrative Officer. It's often called the City Manager."

"And your current status?"

"I'm on an administrative leave because of jury duty." Matt hesitated, eyes tearing up. "It was my first jury in a murder trial. A six-year-old girl was murdered. The trial went badly. I'm having trouble getting past it."

"Tell me about it?"

Matt didn't speak for a long time, and then once he began, he found the words rushing forward of their own volition. "We spent weeks and weeks hearing witnesses, but the only witness who saw the abduction was not fully reliable."

"How did you feel about the daily activities of the trial?"

"The horror of the violent crime gave way to a repetitive numbness. Maybe I was protecting myself."

"Perhaps you needed to take it all in more slowly," Joseph offered. "How about your fellow jurors?"

"The jury deliberations are secret. It is a criminal code offence to disclose," Matt said, in a rush, mimicking Harris. "But I can talk about the trial itself, it was public."

"Okay."

"I was the jury foreman, now they call it jury foreperson. It was my duty to get to a verdict. I failed. Hung jury, they call it. The defendant went free."

Now, Matt's tears began in earnest. Joseph pushed a box of Kleenex across the table. Matt took a wad of tissues to dry his eyes and blow his nose.

"You probably read about the trial," Matt said, when he finally regained his composure. "The man we freed killed again. Another little girl."

"I did read about it. But I want to hear from you how it affected you. Was it a kidnapping in a park?"

"That one, yes," Matt replied. "The one where the jury failed to convict and set the killer lose to kill again."

"Was it quite recently?"

"Seven weeks ago."

"How have you been? Are you able to return to your normal activities?"

"No." Matt paused. "I can't sleep. I lie in bed thinking about the trial and about the second little girl who was murdered. I'm afraid to sleep because the trial occupies my dreams and transforms them into nightmares." Matt reached for the Kleenex again even before it could be offered. "Since we let the monster out to kill again," he mumbled.

"Matt, let me be unusually direct for a first meeting. You have likely spent your whole life taking responsibility. That's why you run the city. You can't bear the burden of this yourself. Did you do your best?"

"My best wasn't good enough. It was our job to make certain that the jury judged the evidence. We all had that burden."

"And you met your burden."

"I did what I could for seven long days to get to unanimous verdicts. The judge sent us back twice in those seven days. I failed. The killer walked free to murder another child."

"That's our system of justice. You did your job. I'm not asking, but I don't believe you are the juror or one of the jurors that hung the jury."

Matt remained silent.

"Let us try to move forward," Joseph said. "What are you experiencing in addition to the problems sleeping?"

"I have a recurring nightmare where the child being kidnapped is my own daughter. I see the man in the grey suit leading the girl out of the park and the girl turns and it's my Sarah," Matt sobbed. "I try to follow, but my feet won't move. They're encased in cement and he takes her just as he took those two other girls."

The psychiatrist nodded. "Keep going."

"I had one other episode. It was in daytime. I was driving and stopped at a corner. I looked into a park and saw a young girl in pink. I don't know how long I was in a dream state, but when I came out of it there were twenty cars behind me all honking. It must have been several minutes."

The doctor's kind expression was almost more than Matt could bear. "Do you know what Post Traumatic Stress Disorder is, Matt?"

"I know soldiers, police, and other first responders get PTSD. But I was only on a jury."

"I'm not inclined to put labels on patient problems without fully understanding them. PTSD covers quite a wide range of experiences and, yes, you may be suffering from that condition. But the real issue is how to get you through this. You've suffered a trauma and need to recover."

"What do I do to heal? How do I get myself back? I am not myself. I am angry. I experience severe mood swings. I weep uncontrollably at times."

"Do you have a place where you are calm and can rest?"

"I have a cottage on Georgian Bay, on an island near Honey Harbour."

"You should spend time there. I'm recommending a six-month medical leave. We need to meet, either in person or by phone, every two weeks to discuss your progress."

"Do you think the City will approve a medical leave?"

"I'm more worried about you than I am about them. You need to get through this and City Hall is not the place that you will heal. I don't need a PhD to understand that, Matt."

"Any other advice? Meds?"

"I view drugs as a secondary measure. If you don't sleep at this island cottage of yours, then I'll prescribe a sedative. For now, I have some advice that you may find odd, but I've had success with it."

"Please. I'm a little desperate."

"Fair enough. I suggest that before you go to sleep at night you read or tell yourself a happy story. It can be reading a children's story out loud or telling yourself a story of some happy event in your own life."

"How will that help?"

"Other patients report that while the happy story does not immediately displace the nightmares, it does get intermingled with them. The happy dilutes the sad and that helps. Try and do it every night until you see me again. We'll see if it helps."

Matt nodded slowly. "I will try. Thank you, Doctor."

Two weeks later Matt called Dr. Bergman from his cottage. "Is it still a good time to speak, Doctor?"

"Yes, it is the time we arranged for your appointment."

"Sorry not to be there in person."

"No need to apologize, although a very Canadian way to start."

"Well, being at the cottage is helping. I sleep better here."

"Tell me about your day. Do you have a routine?"

"I wake up with the sun and go to sleep when it gets dark. I'm sleeping nine or ten hours a night"

"Good."

"Much better than the city."

"And the nightmares?"

"I took your advice. I'm reading Dr. Seuss before bed. It's helping. Some nights I still have bad nightmares, but not as bad as before."

"What do you do during the day?"

"Clearing the deadfall on the property in the mornings with a small, electric chainsaw. I have an acre of land surrounding the cottage and with the fierce winds on Georgian Bay there is always deadfall. Trees get knocked down."

"And in the evenings?"

"I make a fire and read and listen to jazz and old rock-and-roll. The Guess Who."

"How many years have you been working, Matthew?"

"Nearly forty. Started right after college and never stopped."

Dr. Bergman continued his questions and Matt his answers for an hour. They covered Matthew's children, his marriage and divorce, his parents. Not deep, but broad was the pattern of the questioning.

"Our time is up for today, Matt, shall we talk again in two weeks?"

"Yes, Doctor. I would like that. Do you have any advice?"

"Yes, be careful with that chainsaw. Wear thick gloves and protective gear. Goggles. Don't forget goggles. You can't be too careful with a chainsaw. Even a small one."

"Thank you, Doctor. I'll be careful."

CHAPTER SEVEN

A TROUBLED TIME

THE FOLLOWING WEEKEND, MATT stopped at the service centre just north of Canada's Wonderland to fill his hybrid SUV. His windshield had a layer of encrusted mosquitoes that the wipers could not scrape off. He chose the full-service lane. His SUV was loaded with supplies: food, Scotch, and an unread book a day for six months; such was the diet of an island survivalist.

The attendant made conversation as he pumped the gas and then scraped the windshield. "Heading north?"

Matt nodded. "Up to Georgian Bay."

"Quite a storm last month."

"I nearly lost my boat. Broke loose. We chased it across the Bay."

"Where's your cottage?" inquired the attendant.

"I get off at Honey Harbour. Cottage is on Quarry Island in Severn Sound."

"Is that near Penetang?"

The attendant pulled the nozzle out. "Better be careful. One of those nut jobs escaped last night. Took a rowboat and an axe. News says he's armed and dangerous."

"A patient with mental health issues is not a nut job," Matthew said, trying to hide his discomfort at the idea that one of the criminally insane from the secure facility re-branded as Waypoint Centre, but still known colloquially as Penetang, had escaped. Penetang, the mental health hospital, asylum for the insane; it'd been called many things over the years by the local community and beyond. For the worst of the criminal offenders, those who killed their children or chopped up their wives, it was meant to be like the Hotel California — you can check in but you can never leave. Someone had missed the memo. All of the horror of the trial came back to Matthew. He only came out of his daze when the attendant spoke.

"Want the oil checked?"

Matt worried that he'd been a bit abrupt with the attendant, but he wanted to get going before traffic piled up further, not engage in a lengthy debate about mental health and criminal trials. "Not necessary. It was changed last week."

The attendant disappeared, returning quickly with a paper receipt for him to sign.

"Thanks," Matt said, pocketing his copy of the receipt.

"Watch out for the axe murderer, my friend. You never know."

"Will do," Matthew replied as he drove off, the likelihood that the escaped patient might row over to Quarry Island, or at least get blown there by the prevailing winds, now on his mind.

Matt settled into the flow, the stop-start rhythm of the traffic. Barrie was less than an hour north of Toronto, early morning or late at night. At rush hour, the drive expanded to ninety minutes and on long weekends in summer, two to three hours was not unusual. Just north of Barrie, the great ribbon of four-lane black-top divided. Georgian Bay drivers exited to a highway ambiguously named 69 or 400, Matt was never quite certain. Perhaps it had two numbers to confuse the GPS. The divided highway, whatever its number, headed towards Sudbury while those holding out for Muskoka took Highway 11 to the northeast.

Those destined for Georgian Bay, or simply "The Bay" as it was dubbed by the faithful, held themselves to be hardy survivors, sailors. They were a tough, weather-hardened crew who defied bad weather and storms. They sketched an easy caricature of the Muskoka-bound as effete, golf-and-tennis-loving, white-shoed, country-club types. Much injustice was done in such categorization, but there was also a modicum of truth, at least in Matt's view.

For those on islands in the Bay, the drive up Highway 400 was only the beginning of their journey. After dodging aggressive drivers for hours, those hardier Bay people would arrive at their particular marina, dozens of which lined the inlets and harbours. The marina parking lots filled each summer Friday and the boat slips emptied. On Sundays, the flow reversed. If winds or storms barred the way to the thousands of islands dotted with cottages, then the real work lay ahead.

Matt thought back to one stormy Saturday, shortly after buying the cottage, when he and his daughter, Sarah, left the marina in their shallow, five-metre Rinker. The boat stood nearly on its end, fighting the wind and waves.

Above the howl, Matt shouted at Sarah. "If we go over, don't try to swim for shore. Hang onto the boat. Your life jacket will keep you afloat."

The wind howled louder. The boat plunged. "What the hell are we doing out here, Papa?" Sarah yelled back.

"Good question," he answered, spinning the Rinker in the face of the furious storm, even as the waves that stood the boat vertically on its transom threatened to upend it. "We return in fairer weather."

That winter, encouraged by his neighbour Harris, he bought the Limestone. The Kings of the Bay — both the Limestone and Harris.

Today, a bright early-morning sun danced across the wind-rippled water. There was a careful ritual for Matt to starting his boat, backing it out of its slip and navigating across to Quarry Island. Quarry was roughly triangular in shape, with three shores, each two kilometres in length. Seventeen cottages lined the southern sandy shore, facing the large island-dotted bay towards the town of Midland. When the light struck the limestone buildings in Midland, they appeared magically closer. The other two shores of Quarry Island were uninhabitable by cottagers, but the shallow, marshy habitat proved perfect for a pair of magnificent trumpeter swans as well as a myriad of lesser birds, ducks, loons, and cormorants.

Many reefs, shoals, and individual rocks lay between the marina and Quarry. Matt's boat was moored at a small floating dock at the very back of the marina, his slot far too small for the Limestone, but the only one available given his relative newness; he'd been there a mere twelve years. Those who had stored their boats at this particular marina for thirty years, like Harris, had the prized slips.

Matt had learned, through painful trial and error, to manoeuvre his boat gingerly through the shallow and rocky channel from his slip to the larger, deeper lake. He'd also learned to keep the propeller unit tilted most of the way up until he passed the last slip and reached the end of the docks and open water. Individual rocks in the channel were marked with Javex bottles, their plastic whiteness stained yellow by the sun and lake. Other rocks he'd learned about the hard way, by banging them with his propeller. He'd been careful and lucky — and learned from each rock only once.

Matt's ritual of starting the Limestone was precise. He devoted a day early on to teaching his children. His son, Gabriel, absorbed it all without showing emotion or frustration. Sarah, on the other hand, was sullen in the face of his relentless and detailed instructions. "Do you think I'm stupid?" she snapped.

"No," he replied, calmly. "You're highly intelligent, and that's why you need to master the detail of the boat."

This didn't win Sarah over. She stared at him, while he continued to lecture her on the boat drill.

"There are many steps to be followed in careful sequence." He paused. "Five minutes of running the blower to exit any gas fumes that might have built up in the engine compartment."

Matt fished the key out from where he kept it, not well hidden, under the seat. He showed Sarah how to turn on the power circuit with the big orange knob under the dash — two clicks clockwise — and set the blower fan to running. "If there was evidence of recent rain," Matt said, "put on the bilge pump."

He made several trips to the car and back with groceries, wine, and bags of books and papers, deliberately allowing the blower time to do its job. Only then did he start the boat, first by pushing the throttle forward in neutral and then turning the key.

"If you hurry and the engine's too cold, it'll conk out on us, leaving us adrift in the channel." He pointed at Sarah over the rumbling engine. "Untie the two lines from the metal rings on the dock. Flip in the fat white bumpers."

Once she'd done that, Matt indicated for Sarah to come join him. "Ease back the throttle," he instructed. "This is a single lever throttle and gearshift. To shift the gear, you push sharply backwards into reverse, like this. It only takes five to ten seconds for the boat to gain momentum, so ease the throttle back to neutral and spin the steering wheel so that as the boat comes out of the slip, it's pointed along the tips of the six floated docks."

He stood back, handing her the wheel spot. "Careful of the docks."

She glared at him and spun the wheel, turning the corner precisely, hands steady and certain, engine noisy and echoing off the side of the channel and the adjacent boats.

As they came out of the narrow, shallow channel and moved into deeper water, Matt let Sarah know it was time to fully lower the propellor.

Sarah glared at him. "I just did."

Matt thought, *she is really stubborn.* Then he smiled. *Just like me. Why do children inherit their parents' flaws and not their virtues?*

"Aim the bow of the boat for the blue cottage across the other side. Keep the boat between the green and red sets of buoys right down the centre of the channel."

Matt stared intently for the black and yellow striped buoy that marked the turn to starboard into the deeper main channel out to the big lake. Success lay in the detail of the voyage, especially in waters as changeable and dangerous as Georgian Bay.

Harris, a veteran of nearly thirty years on the lake, had been Matt's original guide on his first trips through the reefs and shoals. So certain was Matt that Harris had gone to starboard at the black and yellow marker, that on his first solo trip, Matt, with the original smaller Rinker boat, had swung to the right of the yellow and black channel marker and demolished his propeller on a very large rock.

Buck, from the marina, had towed Matt and his disabled boat into the dock with a bemused look on his face. "There's a big rock to the right of that marker," Buck said, as they passed the collision site. "On the other side, there's twelve feet of clear, deep water."

The violent, unexpected destruction of one propeller was enough to imprint this particular lesson of the lake on Matt's brain. He vowed to veer left of the yellow-and-black-striped buoy without fail.

Gingerly, he raised this point with Harris, who had come to give him a ride back to Quarry while his own boat was in the repair dock. They roared their way back to the island, directly across where Matt knew the propeller-smashing rock lay.

"Apparently," he said to Harris, "there's a big rock about here and twelve feet of water on the other side of that yellow-and-black-striped buoy."

Harris nodded his head, in a thoughtful way. "I've hit that rock a few times," he said, and continued directly across the place where Matt knew, with certainty, rocky disaster lurked.

Matt braced for the impact. The boat roared across the treacherous water. They hit nothing.

Harris had also introduced Matt to the Russian who repaired propellers in a tiny little machine shop on the far end of Port Severn. The shop was a marvel; no bigger than a dozen feet in either direction, and yet a room that seemed to contain hundreds, if not thousands, of propellers. They hung from the ceiling, were fastened to the walls, and, where there were shelves, they were stacked up. Every size, shape, and variety. New, old, some still bearing the scars of encounters with rocks.

The Russian, Harris said, had served in the army and fought the retreating Germans all the way into Berlin. Then, in the chaos, he managed to disappear. After two years of wandering the forests of Germany, he found his way to Canada with no reason to go back to mother Russia. His entire family had perished in the siege of Stalingrad.

The Russian accepted Matt's mangled propeller. "Two weeks," he grunted.

This allowed Harris to expand upon his "General Theory" of the propeller and Georgian Bay. "You need to own three propellers for your boat. One is on the shaft, driving the boat. Keep the second prop safely tucked away in the front of the boat wrapped in a cloth, to be used as your replacement after you hit a rock." Harris paused. "The third propeller will be with the Russian until you need it."

To Harris's orderly mind, this meant that when one hit a rock, one always had the replacement propeller handy. Then one needed to make a trip to the Russian to retrieve the previously damaged propeller now repaired and drop off the newly damaged one. Completely logical.

The only difficult moment for Matt was when Harris introduced him to the Russian. "Matt had a big job in the government."

Distrust bordering on fear flashed across the Russian's face. Catching the look, Matt understood it was a look borne of decades of survival in a violent world with shifting allegiances and fatal consequences to those lacking a nimble response. A world where government meant Stalin and gulags and death.

"Not the tax department. Health. I ran the Health Ministry," Matt said.

The Russian looked instantly relieved. Harris chuckled.

This morning, Matt continued down around the outside of the treacherous big rock, taking the channel. He came out toward the main channel dead ahead and faced Beausoleil Island with its National Park, its campers, and its famous Eastern Massasauga rattlesnakes. Matt questioned the wisdom of the campers. Apparently, the campsites were surrounded by woodchips, and Massasauga rattlesnakes preferred not to traverse the woodchips to enter the tents. This seemed a bit thin to Matt. What about Darwin? What about evolution? What about the first Massasauga rattler to have a new attitude toward woodchips — an evolved attitude?

Later, as he sat on the heavy red chair on his dock reading and enjoying the warmth of the sun, Matt heard the distinct noise of an aircraft. As it drew closer, he knew that it was a helicopter. It began flying in low circles over the island.

"Looking for the rowboat and the escapee," he said aloud, with only the breeze to hear him.

A few hours later, Harris appeared carrying a bottle of Scotch. "They found the rowboat overturned on the west end of the island. OPP boats are searching for the body."

"Best keep the doors locked in the event he didn't drown."

"Hopefully if he survived, his axe is at the bottom of Georgian Bay. Join me in a Scotch."

"So long as you don't drown the Scotch in water,' Matt said, as he grabbed two glasses from the kitchen.

Harris poured out a healthy amount into each one, then settled back into the couch. "Now that you have some time to reflect, handicap for me working for the province versus working for the city?"

Matt shrugged. "Working for the city is vastly different. Harder in many ways."

"How so?"

"At the province, senior public servants and deputy ministers were more insulated from day-to-day politics. You brief the minister every morning, but it's the minster who answers in Question Period. You accompany your minister to cabinet committees and Cabinet itself, but the minister's expected to present the new policy or program at Cabinet, in the Legislative Assembly and in public. It's orderly."

"And City Hall?" Harris asked.

"Even very senior officials can get a rough ride at a public committee meeting. Our head of public works was presenting a twenty-year plan for the sewer system — billions of dollars at stake — when he was interrupted."

"By who?"

"A councillor with more volume than content. Demanded that he come with him to inspect a leaking pipe in his constituency. Right then." Matt took a long pull of the Scotch. "The councillor has enough clout to get the sewer plan put off to the next meeting and to drag the head of Public Works off to deal with what's essentially a constituent issue. That would never happen in provincial government."

"Fascinating," Harris said, "to have had senior roles in both governments and witnessed the difference."

"But with the province, I actually ran the health ministry. Made real decisions that impacted millions of lives. At the city, I spend most of my time watching big, important issues get shoved aside by councillors focussed on minutiae. Not all councillors. There are a few really good ones."

"How about the mayor?" asked Harris.

"Solid. Comes in early every day and does what he can to inject some sanity into the circus." He paused. "Weak mayor system. He has very little real power. Not like a premier who has real power."

Matt lapsed into contemplation as Harris finished his glass of Scotch. "Might I borrow your chainsaw," Harris said, as he stood to leave. "I had a tree blow down on the side deck."

"Of course. It's in the basement. Let's go get it."

In the cellar, Matt gathered up the chainsaw, chain guard, and oil. Out of the corner of his eye, he saw Harris examine a neatly stacked row of open cardboard boxes.

"Planning a major party, Matt?"

Matt shrugged. "Just supplies."

"Case of Scotch?"

"There are two cases of Sancerre as well."

Harris was too used to cross-examining witnesses to be easily fooled. "You planning a longer stay up here, Matt?"

"Not planning," Matt said, self-conscious at articulating half-baked thoughts. plans. "Just wondering what the winter would be like up here."

"You would freeze your nuts off!" declared Harris. "Georgian Bay is dangerous at the best of times. You'd need more than two cases of Scotch to survive the winter.

"Is this still the aftermath of the trial?" he added more gently.

"Likely, yes," replied Matt. "I want to run away from it all, but it follows me."

Outside, Harris took the chainsaw and headed back to his cottage along the narrow trail cut through the woods, carefully groomed to eliminate the poison ivy that grew plentifully on Quarry Island.

Later, after another Scotch, Matt climbed into bed, listening to CBC radio, as the news of the world crashed over him. Twelve children killed in Gaza. ISIS insurgents torturing women and children who refused to convert to their idea of Islam. Forest fires ravaging California, Greece, Portugal, Australia, and Spain. Hundreds killed in flash flooding in China. Another mass shooting in an American high school. And on it flowed.

The only relief was the final item, traditional humour to relieve the horrors of the world. Cat with head stuck in birdhouse evades capture. Still at large in Brandon, Manitoba.

Even the mental image of a cat prowling the parks and alleys of Brandon with a birdhouse on his head was insufficient to offset the horrors that had preceded it. Matt fell into a troubled sleep, dreaming of the river of death and disease and pain that flowed hourly from his radio. In the morning, the news reported that a body had been recovered in Georgian Bay overnight. No mention was made of the axe.

CHAPTER EIGHT

SMALL CHANGES

SAINT JIM REIGNED AS the patron saint of the Quarry Island cottages due to his prowess as a handyman. A retired engineer, Jim came when the toilets cracked from the carelessness of cottagers who failed to fully drain them for winter and put in the antifreeze. He came when boat batteries died. The good news about the island cottagers was they only made the same mistake once. So usually one cracked toilet, one burst pump, one shattered length of pipe, was enough. But with fifteen islanders, it was still a relatively long list of one-time problems.

Matt's experiences, though, had been annual. No matter how carefully he drained the cottage's water system, no matter how much time he took to make sure every tap was open, it seemed he always missed something. Through the years, he'd experienced the destruction of his toilet, one pump, and the spray attachment for his kitchen sink. The annihilation of the spray attachment was particularly spectacular. Bits of its exploded plastic were spread all over the kitchen when he arrived in the spring to open the cottage for the season. The expansion of water that had previously frozen in the minus 30-degree temperature of a Quarry Island winter was impressive.

Matt hadn't settled easily into his first summer on the island. His very first night at the new cottage, he was awakened six times by a tapping noise, as if someone was knocking on the window, two knocks, sometimes three. Each time he got up to check the windows and the doors, searching the cottage with increasing anxiety. His active imagination transformed these instances into the foundation for a grand nightmare. Only in the morning did he discover that the demon that disrupted his sleep was the large oak tree that overhung his cottage. The tapping noise was produced by acorns dropping on the deck. It was ironic that the innocence of an oak tree in nature could deprive him of a good night's sleep while the wail of endless ambulance sirens in Toronto no longer woke him.

On days when Matt sailed his small catamaran on the blue-grey waters of Georgian Bay, he thought, *I am a sailor.* Before he considered the other parts of himself — the economist, the public servant, the father — he thought, *I am a sailor.* He considered this declaration with pride. He moved quickly to qualify the kind of sailor he'd become in any discussion of the subject. "I am a lake sailor, a sailor of small boats, a wet sailor most of the time," he'd say.

On this cool morning, Matt tended a failing fire in the big field-stone fireplace, thinking of his drive to Quarry. Out of Summerhill, south on Yonge, left onto Rosedale Valley Road, left again onto the Bayview extension, and then onto the Don Valley Parkway North exit onto the 407 Toll Road, then north again onto Highway 400 up to Highway 69 to Muskoka Road #5, left along Baxter Loop Road and into the marina, on a potholed gravel road that rocked his vehicle from side to side.

His father had had this same obsession with the details of directions. Perhaps that is why Daniel had chosen to become a surgeon. The precision of it. Daniel always gave detailed directions, so detailed that recipients of these directions often felt he took them to be fools. This approach was simply precautionary on Daniel's part, in case the person he was addressing actually was a fool. In Daniel's view of the world, the population of fools, while outnum-

SHADOW LIFE | 65

bered by the population of bastards, represented a sizeable group. Better to be safe than sorry when giving directions.

"To get to the cottage," Daniel would say, "you drive exactly one hundred miles due east, on the Trans-Canada Highway — Highway 1. Then you take the turnoff for West Hawk Lake." Even twenty-five years after his father's death, Matt could still hear Daniel's voice giving him directions.

Simple enough, you can only miss the turnoff if you are completely stupid since there's a large green highway sign with letters four feet high announcing the West Hawk Lake exit as directly as possible. If you're particularly worried about a lapse of memory or the sudden onset of idiocy, you get a seven-minute warning at Falcon Lake.

After passing that exit you are exactly seven miles, and if travelling the requisite sixty miles per, seven minutes from the West Hawk Lake exit. You get a further saving in the form of the one-kilometre warning sign to prepare you for the unexpectedly easy task of exiting. You then travel under the Trans-Canada Highway by means of an underpass. It's imperative you honk the car horn under the underpass. It makes a resounding echo. No Daniel-driven car in thirty years passed under the highway without honking.

"You're not quite there yet," Daniel would note patiently, paternally, but intent on the detail of his driving directions. Long before MapQuest, there was Daniel. "You still have three turns to go. At the first stop, where the exit road from the highway joins what had been its predecessor, now the old highway, you turn right. Stop first. There is a stop sign. Jack's Place is a further landmark. It will be on your right at the turn. Descend the big hill, past the Trans-Canada restaurant owned by the Reicherts, past the campground entrance, the park ranger's log house, and the CBC cabins."

Daniel's voice resonated in Matt's memory. "After traversing the top of the public beach, you reach the first cottage sideroad, marked Crescent Beach Road. Here you turn left. You now reach the gravel portion of your journey, fortunately a mere few hundred yards in length. I still know the cottages by their original owners' names: Dr. Samuel Joyce, the Macphersons, the Smiths, the McDaniels. At Lot Ten Crescent Beach Road, you turn right into a long sloping driveway. Avoid the large rock, known to cause serious damage to the cars of unwary motorists. At last, you'll see the actual cottage."

His late father had held one lifelong credo about driving: never swerve to avoid dogs. Too many dead or maimed drivers result from such false heroism. Daniel had plenty of examples among his medical patients. "Your family needs you to stay alive. Run over the damn dog."

Daniel felt very differently about deer and moose. These animals were much taller than dogs. The effect of hitting a deer or moose at any speed could be fatal as they were just tall enough to come over the hood and smash through the windshield into the passenger compartment. "Brake for deer, brake for moose. Run over the damn dog."

Harsh life lessons for survival were Daniel's special gift to his children. Oddly, Matt thought, the driving distance to his own cottage was exactly the same hundred miles that measured Daniel's drive from Winnipeg to West Hawk Lake so many decades before. Coincidence? Or were the hundred miles deeply coded in his genes?

Now, forty years later and a thousand miles from his childhood, Matt's reverie was disturbed by Harris who came by to enquire about sailing. Matt agreed instantly. There was a brilliant blue sky and a brisk — almost too brisk — wind. Fabulous conditions for a sail on the Bay.

Matt had grown up sailing and racing single-hulled boats. His family owned a Fireball, also a seventeen-foot mono hull, but a very fast boat. Matt had taught children to sail in Cadets and raced in Albacores. All of these were single-hulled boats. There are subtle differences to the twin-hulled catamaran he now owned, particularly in the heavy winds of Georgian Bay. These differences must be learned, not from books, but from the actual experience of sailing. And, after this day, he would qualify even further that he should be considered a simple small boat lake sailor of single-hull boats.

The twin slender white hulls of Matt's Hobie Getaway catamaran were each five metres long, set two metres apart. In front of the tall black aluminum mast, a tough black mesh stretched on a tubular frame to form the trampoline like-front deck. Behind the mast, the floor was a turquoise blue canvas. Above the twin hulls, two wings cantilevered out to the sides almost half a metre above the hull. The wings doubled as back rests and seats, depending on the fierceness of the winds. The tall black mast swivelled as the colourful sails tugged it from side to side. Twin rudders attached to a single tiller at the stern. A long, slender tiller extension allowed the catamaran to be steered while sitting on the wing out over the water.

This was Matt's catamaran, his pride and summer joy. The day his wallet went to the bottom of Georgian Bay was the first and only time it capsized.

A stiff wind gusted to thirty-five knots as Matt and Harris set sail from the beach, the Hobie Cat flying across Georgian Bay. At speed, the twin rudders fought Matt's grip on the tiller. A rooster tail, a spout of water, followed the cat, thrown skyward by the force of the boat's rudders.

"Metre-high rooster tail," Matt yelled to Harris, pointing backwards. Harris sat forward, enjoying the swift ride.

Just then, Matt noticed, as the boat heeled, that the lower hull, the one fully in the water, began to dig its prow into the top of the larger waves. As his brain processed the reality that the front of the boat, which was hitting waves and beginning to dig in, would slow while there was nothing to slow the back, the lower hull's prow went suddenly underwater.

The back of the catamaran careened forward at fifteen knots, but the front of the catamaran had stopped dead. When an irresistible force meets an immovable object, something has to give. What gave way was the catamaran's trajectory. The cat pitch-poled end-over-end, sending Harris and Matt flying through the air into the turquoise waters of the Bay. In this brief period of unanticipated flight, Harris's sunglasses were irretrievably lost. Matt's wallet came out of his pocket and followed the sunglasses to the bottom. Neither Harris nor Matt sustained injuries, despite the violence of the crash.

The catamaran turned turtle, completely upside down in sailing terms. After a long struggle, they climbed the slippery hull and righted it. They sailed back to shore.

Sophie, Harris's wife, had been watching from the dock with great anxiety. Once it became clear they'd survived, she greeted them as conquering heroes back from the deadly grip of the waters, though Matt still worried that in her darker moments she considered him a hazard to Harris's continued existence.

Matt knew the drill on a lost wallet. He put in the call to his bank to have the credit cards cancelled and new ones issued. He did a form email, later that day, once he was dry and warm, on his laptop computer. The email that could go to each of the points programs, Aeroplan, Air Miles, and so on, that had populated his wallet. He knew he had a backup social insurance card at home, but he would need to send off a letter to replace his driver's licence.

The most important item that he needed to replace was his birth certificate. For many years, he'd carried that battered birth certificate, card-sized and protected with plastic, in his wallet. He'd been meaning to order the long-form version — a copy of which he'd never had — as his passport was due to expire within the year, and the requirements had changed.

So, he felt, although a frustrating nuisance, the loss of the wallet was not catastrophic. He crafted a simple email to Vital Statistics in Manitoba, requesting a new birth certificate, and sent it.

A few weeks later, a response appeared with the familiar green

Government of Manitoba logo — the government he had served for a significant portion of his career, including a five-year stint as Clerk of the Executive Council and Cabinet Secretary. Just gazing at the the logo made Matt feel familiar, comfortable, even proud. It wasn't until he opened the email and read the brief letter, that a cloud of uncertainty descended over him.

First, annoyance, merely annoyance. This was, after all, the government he'd worked in under three separate premiers and yet here was a little letter, a form letter, proclaiming that Vital Statistics had no record of his birth. This had to be some administrative screw up. Matt's uncertainties began to boil up into anger. Surely, they would have remembered who he was, that he had, in fact, signed every cabinet document in the government for five years, authenticating that the cabinet had indeed raised the speed limit on this highway, or made a decision to enter into a legal agreement, or passed that Order-in-Council. Much of his time in government had been spent signing things. It was particularly annoying to him now to see a letter back to him through a mere director that they had no record of his birth.

He wrote back as polite a letter as he could manage to the Deputy Minister for Community Services, who was also responsible for the Bureau of Vital Statistics. Catherine was a protégé of his. Her career started on his watch at the Cabinet Office. He simply asked her to look into this and to see if they couldn't turn up some record of his birth. Matt noted that he had, until his sailboat capsized, carried a very official document issued by her department that was in fact his birth certificate. Every five years the Government of Canada issued Matt a new passport based on this birth certificate, now lost, and the submission of his previous passport.

He penned, on the bottom of his mildly formal letter, a personal note to his protégé: *My dear Catherine: Hope things are well. Sorry to trouble you, but this former public servant could use your help in establishing that the undersigned was actually born in the City of*

Winnipeg in the Province of Manitoba, in the year 1952, on the day of September 25th. Your friend, who is alive and would appreciate having his birth certificate in hand so he can prove his existence to the relevant authorities!

As he sent the email, he imagined the consternation that it would cause when it arrived. Catherine was one of the most detail-oriented public officials he'd ever worked with and one of the most conscientious. He smiled, as he could imagine her summoning the head of the Bureau of Vital Statistics. "Of all the goddamned birth certificates to screw up, you have to screw up the one for my former boss. Look at this goddamned email."

Later that day, Matt handed Harris a glass of Sancerre as he joined him on the sandy beach. They sat in heavy red wooden chairs. A brown umbrella shaded them from most of the sun's rays. Harris wanted to know more about Winnipeg; he was propelled by a vast curiosity about the world and had a way of asking insightful questions that gently prodded Matt's stories.

"What's this about major flooding in Manitoba? Is Winnipeg in danger?" Harris asked.

"Winnipeg sits on a vast flood plain with clay underneath," Matt said, always happy to talk about the city of his birth. "Given the frigid winters, the ground is still frozen in the spring for the run off. But underneath the soil is a layer of clay that stops the water from being absorbed, so there's nowhere for the snow to melt and rain to be absorbed. The Red River is a winding, twisting riverbed that runs through the heart of Winnipeg, draining several states as well as southern Manitoba. Once in a generation, it mounts a serious effort to wash away the city."

"Like now?"

Matt refused to be drawn immediately to the contemporary. First, he had a story to tell. "In 1950, a huge flood overflowed the banks of the Red River even though those banks had been reinforced with millions of sandbags, and devastated Winnipeg. After that, the search was on for a means of better protecting the city from future floods.

"Duff Roblin became Manitoba's Premier in 1957," Matt continued. "One of Duff's goals was to dig the Great Floodway. Prime Minister Diefenbaker put federal money in. Imagine that, a visionary partnership for the long-term; not the kind of thing that seems possible in politics anymore. By the time the floodway opened in 1968, more earth had been moved to create it than to create the Panama Canal. They called it Duff's Ditch."

Matt paused. Harris nodded at him to continue.

"A term of derision for what had been an enormous undertaking," Matt continued. "But, forty years later in 1997 when Winnipeg was in danger and the floodway saved the city, only then was Roblin properly honoured. Absent Duff's Ditch, the City of Winnipeg would have been washed down the Red River. Sixty-three million and some visionary leadership to save billions of dollars and untold human misery."

Matt paused again for another drink, longer this time. "Only forty years since premiers and prime ministers were builders and leaders. Before they became slaves to polls, the twenty-four-hour news cycle, and gotcha journalism."

"You're sounding more than a little dark, Matt."

Matt's head snapped up. He looked at his friend. "I can't fully weather the world falling apart, or maybe I just listen to too much news."

"Maybe a little bit of both," Harris said, putting his hand on Matt's arm. "But take it easy. I don't want you going down some dark rabbit hole. You have too many good stories I still want to hear."

Matt's preoccupation lasted after Harris's departure. His thoughts drifted back to his father. For Daniel, Medicare had the same visionary quality as the Floodway. True, it carried no water of a literal sort, but it did shield all Canadians from the ravages of far more common disasters, that of illness or injury. When physician payments were insured by governments, Daniel rejoiced. Matt could hear his father's voice as clearly as if he had been sitting there. "Think of it. I never have to ask a patient for money again."

Daniel delighted in the freedom of it. He loved his unrestrained ability to provide care based upon the needs of his patients and not financial considerations. "I don't care if they ever raise the fee schedule," Daniel would declare when fee negotiations with the government loomed. "They pay me for every patient. No bad debts. We don't need a raise. If doctors want more money, we can just work harder and see more patients sooner."

Matt gazed out at the water, thinking of his father's idealism and prairie determinism, contrasted against his own fatigue and wariness. There seemed no sense of genuine urgency left in Canada. The puffed-up indignation and phony inadequacy of the Parliamentary Question Period dominated the body politic. National purpose had ebbed away. It was as though a giant mosquito had punctured his skin and sucked out all of his red blood. For Matt, this fatigue could not cover the anger he directed at himself over the trial. He had failed.

Climbing listlessly into bed that night, he reread W.B. Yeats. *The best lacked all conviction, while the worst were filled with a passionate intensity.*

Was this a recurring theme in human existence or a feeling that overtook one with the passage of one's own life? Matt considered this likely unanswerable question as he willed sleep to descend.

Matt hadn't intended to take his wallet sailing, only Harris. But in the rush to get the catamaran in the water, and to get Harris aboard, he simply forgot to take his wallet out of his pocket.

Matt had struggled since the trial to find a new balance. To regain his sense of himself: the self that had succeeded for almost forty years. And now another test would be his to grapple with, but Matt did not yet know it.

BOOK TWO

THE QUEST

No man steps in the same river twice, for it is not the same river and he is not the same man.

Heraclitus

CHAPTER NINE

GHOST

MATT SAT AT THE long, light oak table in the screened-in porch of his cottage. Appended to the east side, the porch was lined with long cedar boards, elevated four feet above the ground. Between the height and the screens on all three sides, it was the perfect place to capture the breeze.

Harris loved that room and, in particular, the vast expanse of low hemlock bushes that bordered it to the north, stretching out like a dark green carpet towards the east.

"Don't cut that hemlock. It never grows back," Harris had declared one evening.

"Just enough for a cup of tea?" Matt joked.

The truth is, Matt loved the room too. It was the most peaceful place he knew. When he read at the oak table, a calm serenity settled upon him, the dark green expanse of hemlocks and the surrounding forest a living green and peaceful cocoon. The waters on the sandy beach could be heard from the screen porch.

Matt was now one month into his six-month leave of absence, and here, in the stillness of the island, he continued to struggle to come to terms with the trial and the nightmares that haunted him.

Sitting in his airy cocoon, examining the email, Matt reviewed the latest letter in the ongoing correspondence from Manitoba. The writer of the letter continued to insist that no record of his birth had been found. Matt was somewhat annoyed, but not astonished, by the failure of the Government of Manitoba to produce a proper birth certificate. More upsetting was the absence of any record of his birth. Was he disappearing from his birth forward? Already disconnected from his job and his routine, from a sense of solid footing in the world, Matt stared down at his hands on the oak table, expecting them somehow to become translucent before his very eyes.

His next email to his previous protégé was more detailed.

Dear Catherine: I'm puzzled and mildly frustrated by the inability of Vital Statistics to produce my birth certificate. In the interest of assisting their work, here is as much detail as I can provide. My birth date is September 25, 1952. I was born at the Women's Pavilion of what was then the Winnipeg General Hospital and is now the Health Sciences Centre. I was delivered into this world by obstetrician Dr. Bowman, one of the twins, both leading obstetricians who did pioneering work on blue babies. Apparently, I weighed a little over ten pounds

My mother, Beth Martha Sinclair, worked as a nurse at the Winnipeg General Hospital and my father, Daniel Harry Rice was an orthopedic surgeon at that same hospital. Sinclair was my mother's maiden name. Both my parents were born in Winnipeg. I have the requisite baby photos. As I'm sure baby photos will not aid your cause, I will not forward them. The reality is that for the past sixty years, all government agencies have relied on the birth certificate, which, had I not lost it in a sailing accident, would still be in the wallet in my pocket. Now it resides in that same wallet somewhere at the bottom of Georgian Bay. I enclose a copy of the relevant page of my Canadian passport confirming my birth date.

I do hope that this additional information will aid the search of the records. I know that there was significant disruption to Vital Statistics in the Great Flood of 1950 but given that my birth was

SHADOW LIFE | 77

*two years after the flood, I'm hoping that the record of my entry
into this planet escaped its ravages. I trust that, knowing me as you
do, that you will restore me to a legal existence. Yours sincerely,
Matthew Harry Rice.* He added a postscript. *P.S. Since 9/11 getting a passport renewed
is very difficult without a birth certificate. I would sleep more
comfortably if I did have an actual record of my birth in my posses-
sion. I'm sure you will understand.* Matt added a P.P.S. *I will be in Winnipeg in a few weeks to visit
and intend to stay for a few days. I wonder if you might have time
for a lunch while I'm in town (my family have already seized all
available dinners).*

Secretly, Matt hoped this invitation to lunch might produce
faster results. Knowing Catherine's pride in her work, he half-ex-
pected that she would show up to lunch and slam a birth certificate
on the table, just to show that she hadn't lost any of her touch in
delivering the goods. That had been their shared credo: Delivering
the Goods.

At the very distant edge of Matt's consciousness, a muted thought
formed and then dissolved. *What if I don't know the truth of my
birth?*

Matt had one other thought as he posted the letters; the Government of Manitoba had not yet moved into the digital age for the
issuing of formal documents. His mother's best friend, Alice Douglas, had originally been a neighbour a couple of doors down when
they still lived on Oak Street. She remained, through all the years
he could remember, his mother's closet friend. Widowed in World
War II — her young husband had died on the beaches of Nor-
mandy — she never remarried, instead supporting her family as a
single mother by teaching at the University of Manitoba. Alice and
Beth's children grew up together. And unlike his mother, who had
passed away fifteen years earlier, Alice was still alive, into her early
eighties and, on last report, in excellent physical and mental health.

I should see Alice. It's been a long time, he thought. He wanted to say, in his own mind, that it had been only three or four years, but he suspected it had been more like eight or nine. Even thinking of her as Alice posed a challenge for Matt. She'd always been Mrs. Douglas. Alice seemed too familiar. Mrs. Douglas felt more appropriate.

When his mother spoke of her, she would call her Alice, but if she sent Matt over to deliver a note or quart of milk, it was always, "Go and see Mrs. Douglas."

It's time to go and see Mrs. Douglas, Matt thought. Did she still live in that same house on Oak Street, the one with the green trim and white stucco that he'd known as a child? Some things never changed. Other things changed all the time.

Wondering if there might be some clue to his birth amongst his father's papers, or even a copy of his first birth certificate, Matt made a special trip into Toronto to retrieve them, and then carted the boxes to his archive room in the basement of his cottage.

Matt, as the eldest, had served as the executor of his father's estate and kept of all of Daniel's papers from those sorrowful days. There were eight heavy boxes — largely tax records, court documents, and insurance policies. At the time, overwhelmed by loss, he had signed what the lawyers prepared and not looked any deeper. Now he began to go through them systematically and methodically, searching for some clue. Box after box yielded nothing of use. He followed the rise of his father's medical income year by year from the tax returns. For the first time, Matthew learned the cost of the large house that had been home for most of his childhood, as well as the sale price of the much smaller house that predated the arrival of three of his brothers and sisters.

It wasn't until the very last of the musty boxes that Matt found some letters under all the other papers. Most were from his grandmother to his father during the war years. He learned that Daniel's prowess at wartime poker had financed the elimination of the mortgage on his parent's small north Winnipeg home. One was dated 1952, a letter from someone named Phil to Daniel. It referred to a time in London — *that dreadful year, 1952,* Phil wrote. It began with *Thank you for your call with your terrible news,* and ended *Take care of your precious son.*

It appeared to be the only letter from that time; everything else was from earlier or later. Who was Phil? Not even a last name. The letter was written more than sixty years earlier on one of those thin, blue aerograms with a return address of Sydney, Australia.

Matthew read and reread the letter for clues. Phil had obviously been in London with his father, had known him there. Another doctor perhaps? But the letter didn't seem to indicate that; rather, it said something about public service, about Phil joining the Australian Public Service. What terrible news at Christmas of 1952? Why was his father in London? Surely both his parents would have been in Winnipeg. After all, he had been born on the twenty-fifth of September of 1952 in Winnipeg.

It was a tenuous lead, but as Matt viewed his situation, this was the only genuine lead he had. So, with only Phil's address on hand, he wrote a brief letter, a letter that seemed to him a little too formal upon re-reading it, but he left it unchanged.

My name is Matthew Rice. My father was Daniel Rice. I am seeking information about my father in London in 1952. The only lead I have is a letter from someone named Phil, at the address to which I am sending this letter. I would ask that if you have any idea who Phil might be, if he's still alive, or if he has any children who are still alive, that you might be in contact with me. Please pass this letter on to anyone who might be able to help with my search.

Matt ended with his name and post office box address at Honey Harbour. He neglected to include his phone number or email address, but only realized his omission after mailing the letter.

"A full Hail Mary pass," he mumbled to himself. He had little real expectation that over half a century later anyone would reply.

Matt looked in his small postal box in Honey Harbour once a week. Usually, all the letters stuffed inside came from charities seeking donations, or companies offering him new and unwelcome credit cards. Occasionally a real estate agent offered him an island paradise. Situated next to the fabulous basement bakery with rich gooey pecan butter tarts that were his Saturday pleasure, the post office reminded him about his quest. He began to check his post office box more frequently, although it never seemed to contain more than annoying flyers and offers.

His attempts to contact Alice Douglas led to her daughter whose news was unhelpful. Mrs. Douglas had passed away the year before. Her daughter, now a judge, was friendly, but had no memory of Daniel beyond that he'd been a very hard-working surgeon.

A month later, Matt walked into Honey Harbour post office, small box of butter tarts in hand. He was surprised to find a genuine hand-addressed letter in his box. The envelope was adorned with an Australian stamp and Sydney postmark. He sat outside on the park bench to read it, eating a butter tart and glancing at two small boats trying to manoeuvre in the harbour.

My name is David Podger. I received your letter today. You inquire about Phil. Phil (Phillip) Podger is my father. He's not well, now. Indeed, he's quite old and frail, and unable to write this letter himself. He did know your parents in London, in the early 1950s. But he didn't stay in touch with your father after the death of your mother. He's glad to learn that you are alive and well. He'd be willing to talk to you, but he is far too frail to travel himself, and frankly, too ill to easily speak by phone. His health is declining and he coughs a great deal. Conversation is difficult for him now and he's hard to understand by phone. I am afraid if you want to learn anything further from my father, it would require a trip to Sydney. We would welcome you into our home, which is now my home. We care for him here with visiting nurses. He's spoken often about your parents and about the tragedy of your mother's death in London on that Christmas so many years ago. I express my sympathy so many years later. Sincerely, David Podger.

There was a telephone number with a dozen digits including the country code and a full mailing address and email address.

His mother's death in London? Matt's hands trembled as they gripped the letter. Beth had died in Winnipeg and not so many years ago, not in London when he was just a baby. Beth couldn't be his birth mother. Could she? Matthew felt as though the ground beneath his feet had crumbled. He clutched the arms of the park bench.

The fabric of Matt's life that had rent by the simple accident of losing his wallet was now beginning to unravel spectacularly. No wonder Manitoba couldn't find a record of his birth. Who the hell was he? That night, as he sat drinking Scotch, he wondered why he'd never asked his father more about his war years when Daniel was still alive. He'd always loved his father, but equally he'd been afraid of him. Afraid of the anger, of the rages, and the things that triggered the rage. The biggest trigger of all being any reference to World War II. Daniel took any questions as an assault on his war service. Matt didn't dare pursue even the simplest facts about his father's time in London during the war, or after.

Who was this ghost that David Podger called his mother? What was the name of this phantom stranger? Was she from Europe or Canada? Christian or Jewish? The scant details he had were contained in the two letters by the Podgers. His father had apparently married a woman in London; she had borne him a son, Matthew, and she had died on Christmas Day, 1952. The same day as his father's birthday. How? Why?

Matt had to know more. Know everything. A slow-moving idea formed in his mind. Had his father looked into Matt's face and been reminded of the woman he loved and lost? Was that why he lied to him? Replaced the dead mother with Beth, a living one? Were Daniel's rages fuelled by his memories, by his loss? Was Matthew a living reminder of Daniel's lost love?

It was a while before he was steady enough to pilot the boat back across the rocky shoals to the island. He almost steered right instead of left. As soon as he got back to the cottage, Matt started to call his older relatives. Had his father ever said anything to them? Did they know of an earlier marriage? Most replied immediately in the negative, doubting there was anything to be learned. But an elderly uncle in Calgary remembered that yes, there had been a romance in London. She'd been Irish, a Catholic girl from Dublin.

"Norah," he said. "Norah something-Irish." There was no last name to be extracted. No further information. Clearly Matt's father had been no more open with his brothers than he had been with his own son.

Matt was simultaneously exhilarated and unnerved. Exhilarated from the sense of a journey of discovery unfolding before him. But stunned that the circumstances of his birth had been deliberately withheld from him by the two people he trusted the most. His parents had clearly concluded that silence — a lie, really, even in the silence of it — would serve him better than the truth. Was he illegitimate? A bastard son? Had some agreement been reached between his parents? Why would his father not have told him before his death?

Worse than the searing, doubting questions was Matt's isolation. He couldn't bring himself to confide in anyone. Darkness and doubt loomed as a pit before him. Until he had some answers, Matt would need to bear this burden alone.

Could Beth, the woman who raised him, his mother for five decades, not actually have been his birth mother? It seemed highly improbable, but then highly improbable things happened all the time. Were his brothers and sisters only half-siblings? Matt felt the moorings of his life break loose even further. He poured another large Scotch and thought through his childhood anew.

Now that his birth mother and the mother that raised him were separating into two different people, he thought about Beth. The other, his birth mother, remained an elusive concept. But Beth had tucked him in at night; the Catholic mother who knelt beside his bed to pray with him; the mother that comforted him when his tooth ached or fevers gripped him. The mother whose loss he'd mourned deeply on her death, sobbing while eulogizing her at the memorial.

A torrent of moments and images flooded over him. He remembered the family cottage during a bitterly cold Manitoba July. Beth brought his youngest sister to the cottage when she was only ten days old. In those days there was no car, no telephone, no heating beyond the large stone fireplace and Beth with her six children. At eleven years of age, Matthew was the oldest. The temperature kept dropping and a deep chill began to settle over the cottage. At first, Matt organized his younger brothers and sisters to gather birch bark and small twigs from the surrounding forest, but unfortunately, the vast stone fireplace in the very centre of the cottage consumed all that they had gathered in less than an hour. They scoured the woods for larger logs. They dragged all that they could find and chopped them on the huge chopping block in front of the now empty woodshed. Gradually, it dawned on Matt that he needed a larger solution. The temperature continued to drop. A frost forecast accompanied the six o'clock news. Not only frost, but snow and plunging temperatures were also predicted.

"Your father's coming tomorrow with the car," Beth began. "We need to keep the baby warm tonight."

"Yes, mother," was all Matt said. He thought of the tiny baby, his sister, only ten days old.

The days were long on the shore of West Hawk Lake even if the falling temperatures seemed more fall than summer. With the sun setting at ten in the evening, Matt knew he had time. His newly reorganized band of brothers and sisters gathered boxes and coolers filled with more birch bark and kindling. There were large logs, but none of them had the strength to cut them with the dull old swede saw. The axe was even duller and heavy and dangerous to swing. Without sharp tools, cutting a large log would not work.

At nine o'clock, desperate to find an answer that would keep the cottage warm through the night and the baby safe, Matt eyed the chopping block itself. Alone, he was unable to lift it or even move it. It took four of them to topple it onto its side. Then Matt lay twin parallel boards from the front of the woodshed to the cottage door as a ramp.

With the help of his one small sister and two only slightly larger younger brothers, they collectively moved the chopping block. Rocking it, the massive block rolled gradually down the ramp. At their cottage door, there was a short elevation to be overcome. Although only three or four inches, the challenge tested their remaining strength. After several failed attempts to roll the massive chopping block up the small rise, Matt and his next oldest brother lay on their backs and used the greater strength of their legs to move it through the cottage door. Rocking it a tiny bit at first, they gradually achieved a rhythm that eventually led to victory.

After they cleared the door jamb, it was only a short roll to the front of the fireplace. Matt and his brother lay on their backs again. Confident now of their mastery over the chopping block, they heaved it up into the fireplace and onto the grate. It filled the huge fireplace, with barely room to stuff birch bark and kindling around. For the next hour as darkness settled in, Matt and his brother kept stuffing birch barks and kindling around the great log. They waved folded newspapers to create a bellows effect. Gradually, the massive log began to burn. By midnight, when an exhausted Matt dozed off on the sofa nearest to the fireplace, the temperature in the room had risen to a safe level.

The great log burned all night and most of the next day. It warmed the cottage, and the baby, and Matt basked in the gratitude of his mother. When his surgeon father arrived, and the story was fully told, he hugged Matt.

"I liked that chopping block. You will need to help me find a new one," Daniel said. The twinkle in his eye gave away how proud he was of Matt's determination to keep his newest sister warm.

That night subtly altered the fabric of the family. In the chaotic and busy life of a family with a busy surgeon father and six children, Beth made Matthew the first among equals, the junior parent.

For Daniel, Matt was his oldest, his first son; he had always believed that Matt's leadership simply flowed from being the first born.

Beth fought with her husband on this point. "You ignore the others," she shouted at Daniel one day. "It's always Matt do this, Matt do that."

"He is my first born," Daniel replied firmly, as he always did during these arguments. "He is the eldest."

"And you're a first born too. So, no one else matters, is that what you believe? He's your oldest, not your only child. What about letting the others be your children, too?"

This schism shaped Matt's life. For his father, Matt held his affection and support based solely on the timing of his birth. When it came to his mother, Beth, every bit of support needed to be earned. To offset what she perceived as the favouritism shown by Daniel, she became a tough taskmaster. Her efforts to counter Daniel's automatic, almost instinctive, elevation of the first born were largely directed at Daniel, not Matt, but he felt the ongoing tension.

Matt's confused thoughts came back to the present. Back to the idea of finding his ghost mother. So much of his life, his memories, were at risk in this quest. What dreadful secrets awaited him across time and oceans? What further confusions lay ahead?

Matt thought about his favourite insight from Sherlock Holmes, the doctrine of the improbable, as declared to Watson. *How often have I said to you that when you have eliminated the impossible, whatever remains, however improbable, must be the truth.*

Now he realized that the improbable was likely the truth. His birth mother had died in London shortly after his birth. Everything from then on had been a lie — perhaps a gentle lie, a lie to protect him — but, nevertheless, much of who he was and where he had come from had been hidden until this precise moment.

His cellphone rang mid-morning. He did not recognize the incoming call number but answered anyway.

"It's Catherine. How are you, Matthew?"

"This is a surprise. How nice to hear from you."

"It wasn't a polite greeting; I really want to know how you are. I hear the trial was brutal," Catherine said, bluntly but warmly, in her inimitable way. They may not have spoken directly in years, but it was like stepping back into an old, familiar rhythm.

"Yes, it really was. Thank you for asking."

"Takes time to heal, Matt. I have a sister who had jury duty in a long criminal trial. Not as bad as yours but pretty bad. She took a long time to recover. And she got counselling, a lot of counselling."

Catherine asked Matthew, "Before we talk about your birth certificate, could you remind me of a story you told me when you left the Ontario Government and went to work running the City of Toronto."

"Give me a hint?" said Matthew.

"It involved rabbits and hats."

Matthew laughed. "The premier asked why I had been so successful in my public service career."

"And your answer?"

"I told him that my successful public service career had been based on pulling rabbits out of hats, finding money from existing budgets, finding different ways of doing business."

"And when the premier asked why you were leaving for the city?"

"I told him the rabbits got too small and the hats got too large and I couldn't find them anymore. Why do you ask?"

"I am having trouble finding the rabbits."

"Heading for the city?"

"The feds are knocking on my door."

"Worth serious thought."

"If it gets serious, I'll call for your advice."

"Pleased to talk it through."

"Thanks," Catherine replied.

"Any news regarding the birth certificate?" Matt asked, redirecting the conversation.

"Yes, and I didn't want to delay telling you. Our official story is that the document was misfiled. There's a long form birth certificate ready for you. I've arranged for copies to be sent by registered mail, and tomorrow an email copy as well so you have it on your computer."

"Thank you so much, Catherine. That's wonderful news. But why did you say the 'official story'?"

There was the slightest of pauses before Catherine continued, "Something's amiss here, Matt. Several things actually. You need to know that my honest, professional opinion is that your birth certificate, the one we have, is a false document. It'll withstand scrutiny, but it has several unusual features."

Matt's heart began to race. "Do tell," he said, already anticipating the rest.

"Your birth was registered nearly a year late. This is not in itself unusual, but still a long time for parents to wait. But that's not all. The official signature on the birth certificate isn't that of the Director of Vital Statistics, which by all accounts it should be, but

rather the Assistant Deputy Minister of Health. That's unusual."
She paused. "There may be nothing to these oddities, but I wanted
you to know."

"Thank you."

"I'm curious," Catherine continued. "You once told me a story
of coming home from school and your father and his best friend
were planning Manitoba Medicare on your family's dining room
table. If my memory serves me, Andrew Johnson was your father's
best friend."

Matt nodded, as if Catherine were in the room and could see
him, just as clearly as Matt could remember his father and Andrew
Johnson sitting at the family table. "Yes. Yes, he was."

"Well, Andrew Johnson's signature is the one on your late-filed
birth certificate. And it should not be his signature. He was already
too senior to be signing birth certificates."

Matthew knew instantly what had happened. He suspected that
Catherine knew as well. The birth certificate was a forgery; Daniel
and Andrew Johnson cooked it up to hide the true details of his
birth.

Matt breathed deeply before replying. "Thank you, Catherine.
I've just started to learn things that might explain this mystery.
When I'm certain, I'll be back in touch. For now, I'm going to ask
for a raincheck on our lunch. I need to go to Australia rather than
Winnipeg."

"Of course, my friend. I hope you find what you're looking for."

"So do I."

After the call, Matthew had another memory from when he was
in high school. Andrew Johnson was dying of cancer. The disease
had ravaged his tall, proud body. Daniel went each evening to the
Johnson house to inject morphine for the pain. Often, Matt accompanied him. This particular cold winter night Matt started to put
on his coat, but heard Daniel's voice, "Not tonight, Matt. I should
go alone. Andrew is ready to go. I need to help him."

When his father came home, he seemed sad. He sat without a book in front of the fireplace. For a surgeon who never drank, he surprised Matt by pouring himself a sizeable Scotch. Matt sat beside his father. After a few moments of silence, Daniel turned to Matt. "Andrew is gone. He wanted his suffering to end, and I helped him. Many years ago, he helped me when I was suffering. I was finally able to repay him."

With this memory propelling him, Matt phoned David Podger in Australia. After the briefest of pleasantries and an explanation of who he was, Matt went straight to the point. "I'd like to come and see your father."

The reply was short and sad. "You had better come by very soon, then."

As he hung up, Matthew realized he had a scheduled call with Dr. Bergman for which he was wholly unprepared.

He dialled the phone again. "Dr. Bergman, it's Matthew Rice."

"Yes, Matthew. How are you?"

"This has been a very disturbing time in my life."

"The trial?"

"No." Matthew took a deep breath. "I've recently discovered that the woman who raised me and who I believed to be my birth mother may not have been."

Dr. Bergman paused, digesting the information before he spoke again. "How does that make you feel, Matthew?"

"Lost."

"Can you expand on how you feel lost?"

"Like my moorings are broken. As though much of my life has been false. I had a happy childhood. I loved Beth, who raised me, and she loved me. But now I'm filled with doubts."

"What are your doubts about?"

"A birth mother I never knew. A father who lied to me. Or at least never told me the truth."

"How did your father behave towards you normally?"

"He was supportive in a gruff way. If I got ninety-nine percent on an exam, he'd ask where the other one percent went. There was an underlying anger in him."

"Do you have this same anger?"

"Daniel flew into rages. I have spent my life suppressing them. I never wanted to become that part of my father."

"I'd like to talk some more about your father, Matthew. Is that okay?

They spoke for the balance of their hour about Daniel and Matthew's relationship. Matthew alternated between anger and tears. At the end Dr. Bergman said, "Matthew, what you have described was not a happy childhood. You have work to do to sort out the realities of your childhood from the stories you tell about it."

He paused and then added, "You've mentioned that your father only told happy stories about the war. Sailing on the canals with Dutch girls who steered the tiller with their feet. Liberating cases of champagne from the retreating Germans. Yet he was an angry man. A man who you now believe forged your birth certificate. Where might his deception and anger come from? And how has this impacted who you've become as a man? How you experience the world?"

"Thank you, Dr. Bergman," Matt said, slowly. It was a tremendous amount to take in. A lifetime to reconsider. "I'll work to reconsider my childhood and my father."

BEFORE DEPARTING FOR SYDNEY, Matt called David Podger to let him know he was coming. David urged speed. Then Matt googled Phillip Podger. The Australian Foreign Service websites yielded a few results. In the 1950s, Phillip Podger had returned to Australia, not to his native Sydney but to the newly built capital, Canberra, where he joined the Foreign Service. His early postings were hardship postings in the vocabulary of the diplomatic corps: Pakistan,

Ethiopia. Gradually, Phil's star began to rise. By 1964, he was posted as third secretary back to the Australian High Commission in London. Then Washington. Finally, as a full Ambassador to Rome. Matt booked his flight. Air Canada flew Toronto-Vancouver, and then Vancouver-Sydney, but instead he opted to fly Toronto-Hawaii on Air Canada and change to Qantas for the Hawaii-Sydney journey. A nervous flyer, Matt remembered from the Tom Cruise and Dustin Hoffman film, *Rain Man*, that Qantas had never had a crash with fatalities. He wondered if it remained true to the present day. Matt decided not to search out this information; it seemed more comforting to remember Dustin Hoffman's vivid portrayal of the brilliant autistic character, who would only fly on Qantas.

The flight from Toronto to Hawaii was long, but uneventful. After the weary flight change at two in the morning in Honolulu, Matt settled nervously into a window seat near the front of the huge Qantas 747. He disliked flying. No, in truth, he feared flying. He considered the fear odd. He had driven fast, far too fast, across the gravel roads of the prairies in his youth. He had pounded small boats through waves of all sizes for even longer. But the emotions of air experienced in flight unnerved him.

Although not a fair-weather sailor; Matt was, to his core, a fair-weather flyer. At twelve thousand metres on a calm day with a blue sky and steady ride, Matt could breathe almost normally. But let an air pocket or the swirl of high-altitude winds cause even a minor bounce, and Matt began to imagine horrific events. He read somewhere that fear had its roots in imagination. Sometimes, he wished his imagination would recede or abate completely, and leave him in peace.

After the plane climbed to cruising altitude, the pilot came across the speaker system. "Thank you for choosing Qantas tonight, ladies and gentlemen. G'day from the flight deck on behalf of the crew. We're flying over a very large storm. It shouldn't cause us any turbulence. But if you look out the window, you'll see nature's greatest light show. Relax and enjoy the flight. We'll have you in Sydney in nine and a half hours. G'd-day."

Matt raised his window shade and looked out. Dark clouds were illuminated as lightning lit them from underneath. This vast storm extended in every direction as far as he could see, but far below their plane. The pilot had spoken the truth. Matt was watching nature's greatest light show. He sipped a double Scotch and watched for nearly two hours, each lightning bolt illuminating the clouds as though they were vast castles in the sky.

Two hours, Matt thought. *A thousand miles — a thousand-mile storm. How vast is nature? How infinite the mysteries of the universe?*

Matt, although a determined agnostic when on the solid surface of the planet, returned to the Catholicism of his youth at altitude. Bargaining with God was how he thought about his silent negotiations. When turbulence struck, he began to silently recant his indiscretions, his sins, in a Catholic sensibility. He thought long and hard about his life before promising to never sin again. "Let the turbulence end. Let the plane land safely and I will never sin again." No answer was expected or received.

His thoughts again turned to Beth and his ghost mother. What more would he learn in Sydney from Phillip Podger about those fateful months in London so long ago? He settled down and prayed for clarity about his origins.

The turbulence generally abated, but there was an occasional bump. In his heart, Matt knew that one day his prayers about plane safety would not be answered. One day his debt would come due, but not this morning in the bright sunshine of Sydney airport.

CHAPTER TEN

PHILLIP'S CONFESSION

DAVID PODGER OPENED THE door. "Welcome to our home, Matthew," he said. David was the same height as Matt but with blond hair and a broad-faced smile. He offered Matt a drink and after Matt expressed an interest in a tall glass of iced water David went to the kitchen to fetch it. He moved easily and Matt suspected he was a surfer. Matt examined the house. It began with a long, screened veranda that ran the entire front. Inside the walls were covered with many photographs of Phillip Podger with his young family and with the good and the great. Matt imagined the distinguished men in the photos were ambassadors, ministers, prime ministers and presidents from his long diplomatic career. After, delivering the glass of water and relieving him of his suitcase, David escorted Matt into his father's room. "He's awake now and eager to talk to you while he can."

Phil was a very old man lying in a bed that made him seem very small. The cancer had shrunk him to a skeleton, skin tightened against the bones. He seemed pleased to meet Matt, and began to talk almost immediately in a raspy, death-filled voice. His condition removed any necessity for social niceties. There was little time to spare and he knew it.

"Daniel met Norah in London in the war years. She was Irish."

He paused to catch his unreachable breath before shakily continuing. "Her full name was Norah Patricia McCarthy. Born in Skerries, but raised in Dublin. Norah banished herself from Ireland. Her twin sister stayed behind. Your father was Daniel, the son of Jewish immigrants driven out of the Ukraine by the pogroms at the outset to World War I. His parents, your grandparents, Max from Vinnitsa and Edith from Kyiv. Daniel met Norah in the next war. She lit up every room she walked into with her passion for life. They married later, in London, New Year's Day, January 1, 1952."

Phil paused, coughing violently. Matt sat rock solid, worried for this ailing man, mesmerized by what he was learning.

Phil gathered himself to continue. "I was there in the London Registry Office. We were all a bit hungover from partying with the Kiwis the night before. I thought they were joking about the marriage, but Daniel had the licence."

He paused again, gasping for air. "Daniel told me it was a late lunch. Me and two chambermaids served as their witnesses. Two lovers united amidst the ruins of post-war London. The hope of a generation rekindled out of the ashes of Europe."

"What was my mother like?" Matt asked.

"She was a passionate angel, filled with anger about the injustices of the world." Phil pulled himself up in the bed and leaned closer to Matt. "You're clearly their son. You have his build and frame but her beautiful, pale blue eyes."

Phil paused, out of breath again, gasping and coughing. Matt absorbed each new piece of the puzzle with a shock. His life trembled on its false foundations.

David Podger poured his father a glass of water from the green pitcher on the teak table next to the bed. Phil drank, but a long horrible bout of coughing racked his whole body again. It subsided enough for him to speak in one long rush of sentences. "I loved your mother, Matt. I was in love with her before she met Daniel. We were rivals for her affection and he won. Daniel swept her off her feet. He had an intensity that I never had. Yet, your mother remained my best friend."

He coughed again, violently. It took time to subside before he continued. "She wrote to me. I returned to Australia to take up my post with the Foreign Service shortly after they were married. I was broken-hearted but tried not to let it show. I married my high school sweetheart six months later in Sydney. Grace. She moved to Canberra to join me. My beloved Grace died two years ago of cancer. Your mother came to Sydney in the late autumn of 1952. I met her there. Nothing untoward. Just friends."

Tears well up in Matt's eyes.

Phil gasped again for breath, coughs racking his chest between his words. "She was heading for that Japanese boat trip to the Marshall Islands, covering the hydrogen bomb test. She was crazy. I told her she was going to get herself killed." He paused, coughing dreadfully. "But there was no stopping Norah. She had that unbelievable Irish determination and Irish stubbornness. I loved it about her, but I feared for her."

"One last question," Matt implored as Phil, depleted, sank into the pillow. "Is it all right to ask?"

David stepped forward, shaking his head, clearly worried about his father. But Phil rallied himself. "Matt has come a long way. One more, it's all right."

"Do you know why I was never told about my real mother?" Matt asked firmly but in as gentle a voice as he could muster. "Why Daniel hid the truth?"

"I didn't stay in touch, so I can only guess. Daniel was very angry with Norah. For going to the bomb test so soon after you were born. For leaving the baby, leaving you. For coming to see me."

He paused, drawing long, agonizing breaths. "Your father was as stubborn and proud as your mother. He may have left the telling for a long time out of anger and then once the years passed, he probably didn't know how to do it."

He coughed again. This time there was blood on the handkerchief when he put it to the side table.

The old man was exhausted. His son nodded to Matt. They tucked the sheets and covers back up and Phil Podger was asleep before they left the room. The nurse arrived to watch over him.

They sat in silence in the living room for a considerable time as Matt absorbed what he'd learned. He'd come a long way for a short conversation, but there would have been no other way to hear this kind of truth. He needed to see Phil Podger for himself, this one last living link to a mother he hadn't known existed. To look him in the eye and absorb the story. Matt's hands trembled and his voice was unsteady.

"In another life we could have been brothers," David said.

Matt smiled. "I would have liked that." His thoughts turned to his brothers and sisters now rendered into half-brothers and half-sisters by his discovery.

The two men were roughly the same age, there was no blood relation between them and yet there had been a possibility of that at one point. How strange a world where Matt's closest living connection to his birth mother was this remote nearness, her almost-husband, the rival who had loved and failed to win her and his almost-but-for-fate half-brother.

A new nurse arrived to look after Phil. She and David exchanged a few words about his father's condition before David offered Matt a drive back to his hotel.

"Care for a bit of lunch?" David asked, about halfway there.

At Matt's nod, David drove to the Rocks, an area not far from the hotel. "The seafood is excellent, if you're hungry. I reckon you could use a beer."

Matt realized that he was both very hungry and very thirsty. The first pints disappeared quietly and quickly. David proved an excellent host, commanding a mountain of prawns and cool draft beer to accompany it. "Was that useful to you?"

Matt nodded. "Very helpful. He filled in a critical period. Your father may be the last living witness to my own parents' marriage." Then, thinking that "last living" witnesses might be taken badly, he added, "I'm sorry he is so ill."

"Not long for him now," David said quietly. "It will be a mercy when his suffering ends. He's in such pain. The worst is at night. Neither of us sleeps very much."

After lunch, the jetlag caught up with Matt and he crashed as soon as he was back at the hotel. He'd spend only one more day in Australia, taking a quick run through the used bookstores of Sydney before the long flight home. With the change of planes in Hawaii, there were thirty hours of travel to come; ten hours in airports and twenty hours soaring above the earth in the currents of the atmosphere. Twenty hours of sipping Scotch to ward off the fear demons. Twenty hours to think about his next move in this quest. His search for his birth mother, Norah Patricia McCarthy.

Now it was time to go home and continue his search.

"Norah Patricia McCarthy."

He said it aloud. He liked the sound of it.

At last, his ghost mother had a name.

CHAPTER ELEVEN

MEMORIES

AS THE PLANE SOARED in its long journey across the Pacific, Matt's thoughts drifted back to his childhood on West Hawk Lake. The family cottage was nestled nearly one thousand miles to the northwest of Toronto in a rocky valley on an unusual lake that straddled the provincial boundary of Manitoba and Ontario.

Daniel would sit on the dock with young Matt. They would watch the waves and the wind on the water. Daniel explained, "Matt, this is a very deep lake. It's over 450 feet. None of the other nearby lakes are more than 90 feet deep."

"What made it so deep?" Matt asked.

"It remains a mystery," replied Daniel. "Some cottagers believe that a meteorite struck the earth millions of years ago and West Hawk fills the crater the impact made. But it has never been proven scientifically."

"How could it be proved?"

"Not clear that it could be proved," concluded his father.

Over a decade later, while a university student, Matt received a newspaper clipping from Daniel. It showed a drill rig on the winter ice of West Hawk. Daniel's accompanying note read, simply, "scientific proof." The drilling had identified metallic remains which confirmed the meteorite theory.

Beth, who cared more about people than science, told Matthew the stories of the people who lived on the lands around West Hawk Lake, thousands of years before the cottagers.

"Long before you and your brothers and sisters, the Indigenous people took the area around this lake as their home. The Anishinaabe, literally the original people, believe Maito Ahbee, just north of West Hawk Lake, is where life on earth began. Here, it is told in their legend, the Original Man was lowered by rope from the sky. He became the first inhabitant of Turtle Island, so called because after the Great Flood the world had formed on the back of a great turtle."

The six children of Matt's family were not lowered by a rope from the sky. They came in a Pontiac Safari station wagon. For each of them, West Hawk became the centre of their universe. Each June, on the last day of classes his mother Beth, the woman Matt always believed to be his birth mother, arrived at Queenston Elementary School with the white Pontiac. This lumbering station wagon would be loaded to the roof with provisions; bathing suits, snorkels, masks, flippers, jigsaw puzzles, books, and cards. The stuff of cottage life. The younger children had their special safety blankets to ward off marauding black bears.

Beth raised the six children for seventeen glorious summers in a white clapboard cottage on West Hawk. His father, Daniel, gave the cottage to his wife as a gift in the year 1956, Matt's fourth summer of Louis St. Laurent's prime ministership. A decade before the national program of Medicare and fourteen years before the proclamation of the War Measures Act. A time of sweet summers before betrayal and strife.

The cottage is where they grew up, where they learned to swim and sail and play poker and read books and stayed up all night listening for bears in the woods. They built rafts from old dock timbers and took on the mythical pirates of the bay. They were Tom Sawyer and Grey Owl. Wasps stung them, wood slivers pierced their feet and the hot sun of July blistered the skin on their backs. But their skin toughened and their bodies bore the scratches without care. By the end of the summer, they could run as fast as the wind, barefoot, on the rough gravel of Crescent Beach Road without pain. The calluses of summer toughened their feet so that nothing could harm them.

Other, lesser lakes of the adjacent territory owed their existence to the retreating glaciers. They were scooped out of the soft earth that covered the rock. The gravel frozen to the bottom of the melting glaciers sandpapered the other lakes out of the hills and valleys in their path. They were narrow and shallow. Falcon, Caddy, and Star are some of their names. In summer, these lesser lakes warmed quickly in the sun, permitting easy swimming by mid-July.

West Hawk warmed only slowly, if at all. The sheer volume of its icy water refused the sun its rapid impact. Even in mid-August only the top layer of the lake, measured in inches, commended itself to the timid swimmer. Those raised on the lake welcomed its icy grip, knew well the blue-lipped shivering in front of the open fire to regain movement in extremities. West Hawk Lake veterans were a hardy crew. Hypothermia is the natural condition of swimmers, not the exception. A chronic, not acute, condition for the knowing.

Daniel told his young son stories of the fish that lived in West Hawk Lake's black depths. He spoke of huge sturgeon, those primitive, prehistoric fish monsters.

"The plated sturgeon grows to ninety kilos during the hundred years of their life. They share the deep water with twenty kilo lake trout. Determined fishermen troll for these grand trout with four-hundred metres of copper line on large reels," said Daniel.

Matt was impressed although fearful of the large fish when he swam. Daniel loved to sit on the end of the dock and dangle his feet in the cold lake. He let the water cool him through his feet as his own father, Max, had done on the pier at Winnipeg Beach thirty years before. On particularly hot days, Daniel would put on a large life jacket and float near the dock. He was careful to stay where he could touch bottom with his toes. This limited his scope as the depth, nearly three metres at the end of the dock, dropped off sharply. By the middle of the bay, the water was fifty metres deep.

For Daniel, pure joy flowed from the icy waters. The noise of his children swimming, canoeing, and sailing thrilled him. Daniel watched with pride as they revelled in and excelled at these activities that had been beyond the reach of his own working-class childhood.

Daniel never learned to swim. His daughter, Julia, swam for Canada at age ten in an international swim meet in a pool in Pittsburgh. Such was Daniel's determination to have his children exceed both his reach and his grasp.

Matt was consumed with the unresolved mystery of his birth mother. Now she had a name, Norah. While he had her name, there was little else of the ghost yet revealed. She had been gone pretty much as long as he'd been on the planet. He only knew that she had died on Christmas Day, 1952, exactly three months after his birth, in London, England. He knew she had been Irish. And now he knew his father went to his grave without ever saying a single word to Matt about her. He'd have to begin again to come to terms with his father, now dead twenty-two years.

He was working towards accepting that Beth, who had raised them all, her other five birth children and him, was not his biological mother. Was she the biological mother of all the others? Matt desperately needed to know who this other mother had been. What did the truth mean about who he was? And where did that leave his memories of Beth?

Matt felt completely alone. For a time, he was lost in confusion. Confusion and frustration gave way to the same determination that had carried him through a long career. Through the difficulty of the trial. His thoughts returned from 1952 to the present. He began a list of tasks to be done on the paper napkin retrieved from under the last glass of Scotch. When the plane landed in Toronto, he had much to do.

Despite the Scotch and his fitful sleep, Matt summoned enough energy to drive north at dusk to the cottage. He slept soundly for nearly eleven hours that night.

The next morning at eleven AM he called Dr. Bergman.

"Is this still a good time?"

"It is your appointment. How have you been?"

"Busy flying to Australia and back."

"What took you there?"

"The search for my birth mother."

"How's that going?"

"Through some of my father's letters, I was able to track down a close friend of my birth mother's, also a witness at their wedding. My mother was Irish, named Norah Patricia McCarthy. She died shortly after I was born."

"Did you also discover why your father never told you the truth?"

"The dying man I visited in Sydney believed Daniel was too angry and devastated by his wife's death. My mother's death. Daniel returned from England to Canada with the baby me, married his high school sweetheart, and they had five children together."

"How do you feel about learning all this?"

"Completely knocked off my moorings, to be frank. My mood swings from anger to sorrow. I am so angry at my father."

"You have all the reason in the world to mourn and weep for your birth mother even six decades later, Matthew."

They continued until their hour expired.

"Where will your search take you next?"

"Not certain. But at least I have her name to search, although she died decades before the Internet."

"Good luck, Matthew. Talk in two weeks."

CHAPTER TWELVE

PROFESSOR O'CONNELL

A WEEK OF MORNINGS later, Matt rose at first light. To avoid the task of pulling the boat back to the dock, he strapped his clothing bag and computer case to his back and waded out to the Limestone. When he reached it, he threw the clothing bag in, but gently placed the computer bag on the back transom. He then climbed up the ladder into the boat and moved the precious laptop to the safety of the passenger seat.

Once aboard, he let the blower run for the compulsory five minutes to evaporate gas vapours from the engine compartment. Matt wondered if the boat would really blow up if he turned over the engine too early. He couldn't remember anyone's boat blowing up. Matt knew that the old Ontario Provincial Police Limestone 24 had a gas vapour detector, but he hadn't ever used it. Much of the more complicated equipment had been little used since he acquired the boat. *If I were in a hurry*, Matt thought, *I guess I could try the gas vapour detector, that's probably why the OPP has them installed. For use in an emergency.*

Given the stillness of the water, Matt crawled along the bow of the boat, then lay down flat to pull it toward the mooring buoy, arm over arm, heavy line shedding its wetness onto his shirt. He unsnapped the line from the buoy, carefully coiled it on the front deck of the boat. He'd carefully timed his run today to make the marina by eight. If the traffic was moving, this would put him back in Toronto in good time for the drive on to Boston.

Matt's web searches about a female Irish journalist in the early 1950s named Norah Patricia McCarthy had, three days earlier, yielded a footnote about his late mother by esteemed Harvard Professor Niamh O'Connell. Matt was determined to go to see Professor O'Connell at Harvard where she still taught, and which was his own alma mater.

He phoned to make certain that she'd be in her office and willing to see him. A very Irish-sounding secretary answered. "Don't need much of her time, just a question about Norah Patricia McCarthy," Matt said.

After putting him on hold, she returned to confirm an appointment. Matt researched Professor O'Connell as well. There were hundreds of Google hits. In her eighties, she'd been kept on well past retirement. She wrote extensively on Irish history, Irish journalism, and Irish politics in the modern age. In an article some years earlier on twentieth century journalism, O'Connell had written a footnote which read: *Had she lived, Norah Patricia McCarthy might well have been Ireland's Edward R. Murrow.*

This was high praise, indeed, given the iconic stature of Edward R. Murrow as one of the all-time great journalists of the world. The man who had trained Walter Cronkite and a whole generation of American journalists. The same Edward R. Murrow who brought down the vicious and demonic Senator Joseph McCarthy. Matt had read so much about Murrow that he felt elated at the favourable comparison to the mother he never knew.

The route to Boston was long but oddly familiar and comfortable, a faithful friend. Unfortunately, he slept fitfully the night of his arrival. Something about being in Cambridge brought back his university days and the unspeakable terror of sleeping through an exam. He woke several times during the night, each time checking to ensure that he was in fact sixty years old, not twenty, and that he had no exam scheduled that day.

By nine, he had his second coffee, read both the print *New York Times* and as much of the *Wall Street Journal* as he could stomach, and scanned the news online. He re-packed his small case, intending to drive back immediately after his meeting. He'd take his favourite US road, Route 100 through Vermont, stay overnight in Stowe, then spend a long day driving so he'd be back on Georgian Bay the day after. The meeting with Professor O'Connell seemed a faint hope, a Hail Mary pass. In all likelihood, the journey would be a dead end.

Matt walked up the street and across Cambridge Common, as he'd done so many times in his student days. The Littauer Center, where he would find Professor O'Connell, was on the far side. The Common had not changed much in the thirty years since he'd been a student. In fact, it didn't seem to have changed at all except for a few new buildings tucked in and around.

He mounted the same broad stairs — the stairs where he'd stood as a student on the day George Wallace was shot. Matt remembered blurting out the shocking news to the very tall and imposing Professor Galbraith, the most famous living economist at the time, who came down the steps as Matt ascended. Matt didn't know Professor Galbraith; he'd just needed to tell someone.

Galbraith stopped. His head bobbed as he observed the news. "Bad news for him and bad news for us all."

Matt nodded solemnly back. They both knew that shooting Wallace risked martyrdom. Wallace had already lost the presidential nomination, but this would rekindle some faction to believe that Wallace was some kind of saviour, some kind of segregationist messiah instead of the racist Governor of Alabama that he was.

Matt stumbled slightly on the steps and the memory of Galbraith vanished. He was forty years older now, and thirty pounds heavier. Inside the building, he paused to catch his breath before going through a security checkpoint that had not existed in his student days. He took the elevator to the fourth floor for his appointment. Introducing herself as Colleen Callaghan, the secretary ushered Matt into the inner sanctum office of Professor O'Connell. She offered him a coffee in an Irish accent so thick it took him a minute to understand.

"Just water, thanks," he replied. "I've had two coffees already this morning." Undaunted, she brought him both water and another coffee for which, in the end, he was grateful. She leaned in towards Matt and almost whispered, "Her name is pronounced Nee-ev. Most are confused by the Irish spelling."

"Thank you," Matt said, smiling. "I planned to call her Professor O'Connell to escape the peril of mispronouncing her name."

Colleen looked worried. "You must call her Professor O'Connell, regardless."

"No fears. I will."

Professor O'Connell was a woman of modest stature, with grey hair and bright blue eyes. It was the eyes that drew Matt at first. They had game and twinkle, but they also had insight. *Piercing yet kind*, he thought. More arresting than piercing. She wore a magnificent tweed suit, elegantly tailored and rich in its green and violet colours. Her accent was not as heavy as Colleen's — more in the nature of an Irish brogue honed and smoothed and softened by her decades in Boston.

Matt remembered from her biography that she'd taught at Harvard for over forty years, albeit interspersed with visiting professorships back in Ireland and several other places in the world. But for more than three decades, this office had been her intellectual home and sanctuary. And, from the beautiful photographs of Dublin that covered the walls, her very own piece of Ireland.

The Chair Professor O'Connell occupied at Harvard was named for Diarmuid Clancy, an affable and inordinately successful Irish businessman who'd made a fortune in newspapers, and a variety of other businesses. Clancy hadn't actually put up the money; rather, a number of his business colleagues put up the nearly three million dollars to endow the prestigious Diarmuid Clancy chair, to celebrate the occasion of Clancy's retirement from one of his many enterprises.

The Boston Irish were determined to have O'Connell in the position. They resisted all attempts by Harvard's academic authorities to dislodge her, citing her advanced age. The Boston Irish were a particularly formidable group, populating not only the police force, but also, and more importantly, the leadership of many of the major Boston law firms, as well as the judiciary and the State Assembly.

No self-respecting mayor of Boston lacked a claim to Irish blood. It wasn't the Irish Republican Army that worried the Harvard Board of Overseers, but an assault by lethally bright lawyers they themselves had trained over the years. The Boston Irish bar had to a person taken O'Connell's course on Irish history and civilization. She taught each of them the Statute of Westminster, Irish Independence, the works of James Joyce, and the Irish poets — Yeats most prominent among them. All had fallen in love with her and with her passion for Ireland. As a consequence, they'd never let Harvard touch one grey hair on her aging head when it came to this particular tenured and endowed professorship.

Matt knew all of this because he'd read as much as he could find about Professor O'Connell. In an opinion piece penned in the *Boston Globe* after one such attempt to retire the beloved professor had failed spectacularly, the columnist concluded that the only way Niamh O'Connell would ever leave the Clancy Chair was in a coffin. The journalist went on to write that if she ended up in that coffin by any means other than natural causes, the wrath of the Boston Irish legal community towards Harvard would be such as to make the vengeance of the local mafia seem like a walk in the park.

Harvard relented permanently. Professor O'Connell had a lifetime appointment, Harvard's only such lifetime appointment in its three hundred and fifty-year history.

Professor O'Connell looked Matt straight in the eyes and cut to the chase. "You told my assistant you wanted to talk to me about Norah McCarthy," she began. "What is your connection?"

Matt took a gulp of the now most-welcome black coffee that Colleen Callaghan had poured him. "There's so much I need to know. I hardly know where to start."

"I'm eighty-three years old," said O'Connell. "You'd better start somewhere, and soon, because I won't be around forever."

Matt began somewhat unsteadily, taken aback by the directness of the statement. "I-I-I believe —" stuttered Matt. "Ah ... that she may have been my birth mother."

He expected this statement to cause some disturbance, some shock perhaps or a confused stare. But instead, Professor O'Connell immediately got up and came over to Matt. She stood very close to him, studying his eyes intently. "At long last!" she exclaimed. "The lost child, found!"

It was Matt who was now wholly put on the defensive. She knew? "The lost child?" He couldn't control the tumble of his thoughts or words. He'd never thought of himself as lost, and he hadn't been a child for decades. "The lost child? What do you mean?"

"She was pregnant when I last saw her in London, late summer, 1952. Very pregnant." The elderly professor shook her head. "Then, the next I heard, she'd died on Christmas Day. It didn't seem logical that she'd died in childbirth. And anyhow, she was too pregnant for that when I saw her."

Matt sat stock still as the elderly professor leaned in even closer. "Let me look at you again," she said. "Yes, you have her perfect robin's-egg-coloured eyes. Tell me about yourself. About your life."

It was strange being studied so closely by someone he didn't know. "I grew up in Winnipeg, Canada," he stuttered. "I now know my father remarried and that the woman I believed was my mother, Beth, was actually his second wife. I know nothing about my birth

SHADOW LIFE | 109

mother other than her existence and her name, which I discovered only recently."

"Misled all these years," Professor O'Connell said, shaking her head as she moved back to her chair. "In the dark about who you really are."

"Worse," said Matt. "I attended this very university. I attended classes in this very building. I thought about taking your course, but I knew nothing of Ireland and didn't think I'd be able to keep up."

"Well," Professor O'Connell said, "I wouldn't have been able to pick you out of the crowd. Presumably, if you didn't know she was your mother, I wouldn't have known you were her son. Not at a glance." She stared fiercely at him. "Even with her eyes, those perfect blue eyes. What brings you to me, now, after so many years?"

"You wrote that if she'd lived, she could've been Ireland's Edward R. Murrow. It was the only reference I could find."

"Yes, yes," said Professor O'Connell. "I meant it. Perhaps I was a little carried away, but she was very good. Very damned good. And good so young — if only she had time, the years to hone her journalism. She even debated Murrow in London about the Cold War and the Arms Race. No written record, sadly."

Matt felt a sudden anger course through his veins. "I never knew her," he said harshly.

Professor O'Connell fixed him a harder glance. "You feed that anger with your own ignorance, young man. Norah didn't want to die. She didn't set about to desert you or your father. She had an enormous talent. She pursued her journalism. Have you read anything she wrote?"

Matt shook his head. "The back editions of the *London Times* aren't available online. I haven't been able to obtain anything she wrote."

"You better do so before you condemn her. She had a passion

for life and a passion for journalism, for her country, and for this planet. She was half a century ahead of the environmental movement. She cared about the health of the planet long before almost anyone else did," said O'Connell in a rush, standing again as if a human exclamation mark.

She went to the office door. For a moment, Matt thought he was being thrown out for his impudence. Instead, the professor summoned Colleen.

"Please make young Matt here a copy of all of his mother's writings, Colleen. You will find them in a file marked Norah McCarthy."

By the time Professor O'Connell turned back to Matt, she seemed tired, spent. She sat back down in her chair, her countenance now showing concern, her richly lilted voice now sounding deeply persuasive.

"You need to keep an open mind, young man. I don't know what happened to you. Your mother was a wonderful writer and journalist. Learn who she really was and what happened to her before you let your anger overwhelm you."

Matt nodded, a little embarrassed by his burst of anger. "I understand."

When Colleen returned with the articles, Matt immediately began to rifle through them, unable to resist the temptation. He knew he was being rude, that she should give his undivided attention to Professor O'Connell.

"When you're going through them, you might want to look carefully at her interview with Dr. Oppenheimer," she said, smiling, clearly understanding the pull of his mother's words for him. "Norah really got to him. She may have even pushed him over to the peacenik side. After that interview, he lost his security clearance. They hounded him to an early death. I don't think anyone did as tough an interview as that, for a decade, maybe two decades, afterwards, not until Oriana Fallaci."

Matt had read Oriana Fallaci, the Italian journalist who changed the face of twentieth century journalism from the Second World War through the following decades. In fact, Matt had read pretty much everything Fallaci had translated into English. To have his lost mother compared to Fallaci by this eminent Harvard professor took him aback. "Really?"

He was confused, torn, and experiencing an anger towards his mother for dying before he could know her, but starting to be intrigued and curious. He looked at the copies. He'd need his reading glasses to make a dent in these.

"Her pieces on the smog are good, too. I believe that's what brought about her end, getting those pieces on the London smog. Being out there in that damned pea-souper too long," Professor O'Connell said, shaking her head in genuine sorrow.

"Pea-souper? Smog?" It wasn't something Matt knew about.

"The Great London Smoke Fog of December 1952. The harbinger of man's destruction of the very air we breathe. It killed 4000 Londoners, lately revised to 12,000," O'Connell said.

This was more information than Matt had prepared himself to absorb.

"And one last thing. It may turn out we're distantly related."

This was another curveball in a morning full of them. "Pardon? How? What do you mean?"

"Patrick McCarthy, your great-uncle, was a first cousin of my late father, Ginger O'Connell. Ginger was the General and Commander of the Army of the Irish Free State. It was my father's kidnapping from our house on Upper Leeson Street that touched off the civil war for the Irish Free State."

Matt knew some of Irish history of the period from his research, but he didn't remember a kidnapping. "So, your father was kidnapped by Michael Collins and his forces?" he asked, tentatively.

"No," Niamh replied, abruptly. "No, not at all. The O'Connells and the McCarthys were with Collins. They were always against de Valera. It was de Valera who sent Collins off to London to negotiate. It was de Valera who gave him the impossible mission. If there had been a win to be had, de Valera would have gone to London himself. Instead, he sent Collins on a suicide mission. It was de Valera who got him killed, as surely as if he had been on the grassy knoll himself."

She paused to breathe, before continuing her passionate tirade. "When I was a very small child, they hid the tommy guns under my bed in our house on Upper Leeson Street. Hid them under all of the children's beds. We slept atop the fight for Irish independence."

"Tommy guns?"

"Tommy guns — the first machine guns that were smuggled in from America to support the Irish Republic," said O'Connell. "The British searched our house many times, but they never looked in the children's beds."

"And how am I related?"

She smiled broadly. "You see, you should have taken my course. If you had, you would know this essential Irish history and politics."

It was such a kindly smile that Matt felt permission to be relieved, permission to shrug his shoulders, wave his arms and say, "I have much to learn. Would you give me the reading list for your course? Perhaps that's somewhere I could start in becoming a better Irishman after all these years. Over fifty years without knowing."

She smiled back. She was pleased with his response. It was a kind of progress. "I could also get you access to the Widener Library stacks."

"Thank you so much," Matt said. "I've done well enough in the world financially that I can probably afford to own these books, if the campus store has them."

"Yes, of course," she said. "The COOP will have copies of each and every one still in print. For the others, you'll need to visit Widener. My list hasn't changed very much over the years, but some of the books have gone out of print. Colleen will give you the course reading list. You're going to want to come back and see me when you have more questions."

She paused before continuing. "We weren't close friends, but I knew her. We went through University College together. Well, not really together, more properly at the same time. We were with different crowds then. She was eager to get to London and into the world. And I was eager to stay in school and get as many degrees as I could. But we came from the same soil. She was a true patriot." She looked at Matt with that direct, unblinking, blue-eyed stare of hers. "And when are you going to Ireland?"

It wasn't a *whether* question, it was a *when* question.

"I'm not sure," he said, a little stunned. "I need to read a lot before I even know what I'm looking for."

"You're looking for your mother," Professor O'Connell said. "And you'll find much of her there. Call me before you go. I can give you some names. Don't wait too long. The few that knew her are not young. You should try and see Garrett."

"Garrett?"

"Garrett Fitzgerald. The Taoiseach. The Irish Prime Minister is called the Taoiseach. He knew her slightly through her school class-mates. He also knew your uncle Patrick. Garrett can help put some of the pieces together."

She rooted around her desk for a minute, came up with a speech given by Fitzgerald. "Read this. You're up against a formidable chal-lenge if you're going to try and understand Irish history. Your mother's Uncle Patrick used to say that he barely understood it and he'd lived through it and helped to make much of it. He spent forty years in the Dáil."

"The Doyle?"

"The Irish Parliament spelled D-á-i-l, but pronounced, Doyle, actually." Professor O'Connell smiled at Matt. "You had better get in touch with that inner Irishman now that you have discovered he's in there. You really should have taken my course."

Matt thanked her, realizing only as he stood to shake her hand, the full impact of what she'd had to say. Before he was fully aware, he was descending the steps of the Littauer Building into a driving rain. He was barely aware of it until the water began to run down his forehead, and then he panicked, rapidly tucked the papers inside his jacket and wrapped it tightly around him to protect the precious clippings.

His mind reeled. This woman, this revered professor, had known his mother. Had known that a baby existed. *The lost child*, she'd called him. The lost child now a sixty-year-old man apparently of Irish descent. Amid the wonder of discovering this part of his identity, he worried if his excitement was a betrayal of Beth, the mother who had raised him.

He looked at the note Colleen had tucked into his hand when she bid him farewell. To Matt's mild disappointment, it was not her telephone number. Instead, written on the slip was a room number and *10AM tomorrow*, along with a note. *Professor O'Connell will give her first lecture of the course. You are invited to attend. JFK Presidential Library afterwards. Professor O'Connell has directed me to escort you*, Colleen had written in her careful penmanship. *There is a special exhibit on JFK's 1963 visit to Ireland.*

He hugged the file folder with copies of his mother's writings. *My mother's writings*, he thought. *I didn't even know she really existed until today*. Anxiety grew alongside his intense desire to read them. He wanted to know more about Ireland before he tackled the articles. He didn't want to bring only his ignorance to bear on this one connection to his lost mother.

He remembered there had been a movie about Michael Collins. *Liam Neeson*, he thought. It took him only a few minutes to walk to the Harvard COOP. "Do you happen to have the film, *Michael Collins*?" he asked the young woman at the information desk.

She rapidly typed on her keyboard. "Julia Roberts, right?" she said.

"Liam Neeson?"

"Him, too. You could just watch it on Netflix."

Matt felt every one of his sixty years. "I'd rather get a copy, if you have it."

"You're lucky," she said, without looking up. "We don't carry many DVDs anymore, but there's one copy. Third floor, look under drama."

"Thank you," Matt said, but she'd already moved on to the next customer.

Matt never travelled without his Apple laptop; and so it was on this later, propped up on the end of his hotel bed, that he foreshadowed Professor O'Connell's lecture on Irish history. For nearly three hours, he watched Liam Neeson as Michael Collins, striding across the Irish landscape, larger than life, fighting the British for Ireland's independence, through what he had to acknowledge would now be labelled terrorism, creating the conditions that forced the British to the negotiating table.

Collins was indeed sent to London as the sacrificial lamb by Éamon de Valera. He returned not with the Irish Republic but with the Irish Free State and Partition, the separation of the twenty-six counties of the south from the six counties of the north. This was the deal that, although supported by a majority of the Irish, split the nation, split Collins from de Valera and set in motion the Irish Civil War. This schism also set in motion Collins' own assassination.

After the movie ended, Matt sat for a time. Then he opened the file folder Professor O'Connell had given him and spread the copies of the yellowed clippings on the bed. In addition to the yellowing of the paper, there were grey and grainy markings. But the typeface allowed clear reading. There were nine articles, all from *The Times of London*.

The first one he picked up to read was titled "Lethal Flooding in Lynmouth."

The small coastal town of Lynmouth in Devon was devastated last night by a catastrophic flood. The flood carried large boulders and rocks towards the town. It was a scene of extraordinary destruction. Terror gripped the people of Lynmouth. The flood struck in the night while they were in their beds. Many died. Homes were destroyed, bridges and roads torn away. We could not get into Lynmouth due to the destruction.

The Minister of Defence refused all comments on speculation about experiments in the making of rain by the seeding of clouds. This must have been one of the most beautiful places before the flood. Apparently, for two hundred years it had been a Devon seaside resort and celebrated thusly. Now it is ruined, and the lives of those who live there have been ruined as well.

She wrote with sparseness and passion, he thought. The next article he picked up was titled "Smoking Linked to Lung Cancer." He stared at the date: December 14, 1952. He was surprised to see this story dated so early. It was a detailed account of the work of Richard Doll published in the *British Medical Journal*. Doll had started out to research the impact of diesel fumes on human health. His data took him a different direction — the first conclusive evidence that smoking could be linked to rising cancer rates in London — data that wasn't much written about until later in the twentieth century. The power of Big Tobacco reigned supreme.

The third of the articles described the death of the King and the preparations for the Coronation of Queen Elizabeth.

King George died today of lung cancer. It is a terrible burden to be thrust upon one so young. It seems somehow unfair that she would have to bear a lifetime of these rituals for the nation. I expect she will perform her duties with grace and style. Despite the vast, unspeakable horrors the British have inflicted on the Irish over the centuries, I cannot hold this twenty-five-year-old woman, now Queen, responsible. I hope that she has compassion in her heart, not only for the Irish but for all the other people who the British have wronged through the centuries in their quest for Empire.

His sleep that night was filled with dreams of Tommy guns under the bed and of the mother he never knew. He slept fitfully, tossing and turning in the grip of these powerful dreams. There was too much new information for his dreams to trammel up in a single night.

CHAPTER THIRTEEN

REMEMBERING STUDENT DAYS

MATT STOOD ON THE flat stone plaza that served as the entrance of Harvard Chapel, directly across from the seventy-two steps leading to the entrance of Widener Library. He noted the full name carved in stone above the pillars and portico: Harry Elkins Widener Memorial Library. As he stood thinking about his first visit to Widener in over thirty years, a tour guide arrived behind him with a group of visitors in tow. The guide wore a bright green T-shirt and spoke loudly, not a shout but a booming Southie Boston voice, pointing out the Widener's broad steps and magnificent facade and pillars.

No r's, Matt remembered. When he'd first arrived as a freshman, he had difficulty following conversations. *Beer* was "beh" and *car* was "cah." *Harvard* became "Hahvahd" in the vernacular.

Matt walked slowly up the seventy-two steps. He felt eighteen again, alive with his whole life ahead of him. A true homecoming. He remembered so clearly, although it had been thirty years, that one had a choice going up the stairs at Widener Library. The stairs were constructed in such a manner that if one climbed up one stair at a time, it was a dull, slow shuffle, unsuited to anyone but the elderly. Going up two at a time was not a normal step. It required a certain bounding. Matt figured the step design might have been twofold: To encourage the elderly scholars to move at a safe gait on their way to that sanctuary for learning. On the other hand, the double bounce gave students an air of energy and forward drive, and all those things that shouted intensity — the intensity Harvard so valued.

Tucked carefully inside Matt's Harris Tweed jacket was a letter on Harvard stationary from Professor O'Connell, addressed to the head librarian of the library. Matt imagined that he wouldn't actually meet with the head librarian, but it seemed a nice touch on the elderly professor's part to personalize it by addressing it that way. And, he thought, this should scare the bejesus out of anyone on the front desk, likely some student earning the funds necessary to help pay for such a princely education.

There had been a good deal of renovation to the library over the thirty years since Matt had last passed through its portal. He also noted that security, always significant, was massively strengthened. He felt better about the letter in his pocket. The only way in required Matt to swipe a Harvard identification card, which he did not possess. He showed the letter and his passport for photo identification. After a remarkably short period of time, Matt was ushered into the famed stacks of Widener Library.

Stacks — shelves that sit on their own foundation — had revolutionized the architecture of libraries. They didn't require the enormous weight of the books to be borne by the walls. There was no way in the world that Widener Library — when he was a student, the fifth largest library in the world — could have contained the materials it did, if the shelves had to be supported by the outer walls of the building. The stacks were really a building within a building enclosed by the building's shell of walls and roof but structurally independent.

As he walked further in, Matt thought about the several stories — legends, really — that were told to young Harvard students about the building. The great library's origins lay in the tragic fate of a Harvard student, Harry Elkins Widener, who graduated from Harvard College in time, supported by his wealthy family, to make the Grand Tour of Europe. Sadly, he caught the maiden voyage of the *Titanic* to return to New York from London. His swimming skills were not well-developed; Harry Elkins Widener drowned less than twenty yards from a lifeboat in the icy waters of the North Atlantic, as the *Titanic* sank beneath the waves. His book collecting interest, however, was sufficient to spur his family to make an enormous bequest in his name to establish the library.

The first awareness of Widener Library for a freshman Harvard student is its great imposing columns, its oddly spaced steps and its magnificent stacks. The second awareness of the Widener's bequest and its peculiar conditions was a notice in Matt's freshman kit, ordering him to report to the Harvard pool. This was not a voluntary activity. Each freshman was required to report to the Harvard pool, and swim one length of the pool, some twenty-five yards, unassisted by any flotation device or other student.

Once this small task was completed by Matt, a tick mark went in the appropriate box and he was spared any further time in the rather ancient, dogged, and slightly foul-smelling pool. If Matt had not been able to swim the twenty-five yards, swimming lessons would have ensued. This was not the result of some fanatic Harvard swim coach determined to identify the best swimmers, nor was it the American Red Cross Water Safety Program. No, this ability to swim twenty-five yards in order to graduate from Harvard had been imposed upon the university by one of its greatest benefactors, the Widener family. According to the legend, if one student graduated from Harvard who could not swim the requisite twenty-five yards, the Widener family was entitled to take back their bequest and their library with it.

Matt had no idea if the legend was true, but he remembered doing his lap of the pool, and he remembered telling and retelling this story to all those who visited him during his time at Harvard. It was the kind of story you told standing in front of the Chapel, looking at the magnificent front pillars of Widener Library, a story that caused your visiting younger brothers and sisters from Winnipeg to be suitably impressed, more impressed than just by the building but by the reality that a single family had caused it to come into being, and that single family had been galvanized by a singular tragedy.

Matt manoeuvred through the stacks to seek a place he might park his briefcase, before going in search of the books on Professor O'Connell's reading list.

Once settled at a desk, Matt began to work his way through the stack shelves. One of the tricks he remembered from his student days was once he'd found a book that he was looking for, it was well worth looking at all of the adjacent books, since they were organized by detailed subject index. This way, he found a great deal of material on the Irish and The Troubles, as they were called in Ireland, from the Easter Uprising to the Statute of Westminster, and all the ins and outs, between, around, before and after, on several large shelves. He was selective and carted back at first eight or ten books to his carrel so that he could go through them carefully.

One of the documents he discovered early on appeared to be a speech by Garrett Fitzgerald. Professor O'Connell had mentioned Fitzgerald when she referred to him as Taoiseach, the Prime Minister of Ireland, the head of its government. Matt puzzled over the dates. The speech had taken place at University College Court in April 2003. Garrett Fitzgerald, former Prime Minister, would now be nearly eighty years of age, and still speaking.

Matt read the speech, "Reflections on the Foundations of the Irish State," with interest. It began with the line, *The foundation of the Irish state is a vast subject*, and referenced a book, *Reflections on the Irish State*. The speech was as complicated as the situation; the tension, the back and forth among the factions. It was clear that Desmond Fitzgerald — the father of Garrett Fitzgerald — along with Patrick McCarthy, whom Professor O'Connell had said was Matt's great-uncle, had played major roles. Michael Collins's death by assassination was a seminal event, as had been the break between de Valera and Collins that brought it about.

Garrett Fitzgerald quoted W.T. Cosgrove on the nature of the government of the day. There were no real politicians and he was especially critical of Fitzgerald's father Desmond, who was too busy arguing about theology with Father Cahill and Paddy McCarthy, and who wouldn't go to Cork for a meeting. *Somewhere along the lines*, Matt thought, *these people shaped up and turned into real leaders.*

He reread the paper a few times and began to get a sense of some parts of it. It was the conclusion that brought it home for Matt: *But the survival of the democratic Irish state through a most turbulent period is the greatest achievement of those who founded our state. We owe this to the selfless patriotism, and toughness of the members of that first government. I am proud to have been the son of one of those men.*

Matt also found a lecture from April 1999 given by Lord Irving of Lairg, the Lord Chancellor of England. In it, he said, *I'm honoured to have been invited to visit University College Dublin. If, as I am told, I am the first Lord Chancellor to have done so, all that I can say is that it is high time. The college is, of course, best known in the wider world as the institution of learning founded by Newman and immortalized by Joyce, but it is also of real distinction in the legal world. I know that it has educated most of those who have made up the Irish Judiciary since Independence. History reports that Patrick McCarthy, the first Dean of the Law Faculty, was as Irish Foreign Minister in 1931, one of the major architects of the Statute of Westminster, a major staging post of the progress from our old colonial empire to the modern commonwealth.*

Matt knew that Ireland had gained its independence and that, over time, the British Empire converted into the Commonwealth with its colonies becoming independent states. Exactly how this happened was not a subject he had studied. What was the Statute of Westminster? Of what exactly had Patrick McCarthy been an architect? Matt felt a mixture of immense curiosity and at the same time, a certain hollowness. Why couldn't his mother have lived? Why couldn't he have asked her these questions? Why couldn't he have grown up Irish?

Immediately, his inner Canadian took over. He almost apologized for having the thought. "Irish-Canadian," he said to himself. "I would always want to be Canadian. That's who I am, but it would've been nice to know before age sixty about the Irish bit."

What was it? His fingers traced from the book to another stacked in front of him. It was pride, Irish pride. Matt was beginning to be proud of a heritage of which he'd known nothing a month ago. It was a puzzling, almost exhilarating development.

CHAPTER FOURTEEN

HER LECTURE: A TERRIBLE BEAUTY

MATT TOOK A SEAT in the top left corner of the lecture hall ten minutes before Professor O'Connell's lecture was to start. The large room filled quickly, in a rush, just before the appointed hour. From his position, high up and at the back, they all looked far too young, younger than his own children.

Professor O'Connell came out five minutes to the hour and placed her papers on the lectern. The lecture hall was one that Matt remembered from his own student days. Although, clearly it had been recently renovated. The rich wood panelling was preserved, as were the ornate cornices on the pillars around the room, but in place of the blackboards of Matt's memory there were flat screen displays. And, in stark contrast with her age and dress, Professor O'Connell clipped a small lavalier microphone of modern wireless design to the lapel of her tweed suit jacket before she began to speak.

Matt caught her gazing up in his direction, but she gave no sign that she recognized him. Moreover, given the distance, he was not certain that she would be able to see him sufficiently clearly. The lighting in the room was subdued. There were perhaps a hundred students. Matt remembered from his own student days that one had two weeks to decide about courses, so the first two weeks featured a scramble as students sought out the most interesting courses or the easiest, or the courses that met their requirements for graduate school.

At precisely nine o'clock, Professor O'Connell cleared her throat loudly enough to silence the room. This was the first lecture of the course, the first lecture of the semester. It brought back a flood of memories. The better professors, the ones who could hold a room transfixed for an hour, made him regret the end of their lecture. James Kurth from Political Science, Michael Walzer in Philosophy, Albert O. Hirschman and Edmund Clarke in Economics, and the Radcliffe librarian; these were the dynamic speakers who returned to his memory.

Professor O'Connell began calmly, in a straightforward way. "This is the first meeting of the course, *Twentieth Century Irish History, Literature and Civilization.*"

The course number followed. Matt tried to remember the number sequence, but her next sentence caught his attention.

"We have here with us today a direct descendent, a great-nephew, of Patrick McCarthy, one of the most important figures in the creation of the Irish Free State, or the Irish Republic, or more properly, the Republic of Eire. I would like anyone in the lecture hall who can tell me one or more contributions of Patrick McCarthy to Ireland to raise their hand."

Matt noted that no hands were raised, including his own.

"I won't embarrass him by asking him to stand up, but I should let you know that he only recently became aware of his Irish roots, and so knows little more about his own great-uncle, Patrick McCarthy, than the rest of you present. Today, in outlining the origins of the Irish State, in the early part of the twentieth century, I will make an extra effort to situate Patrick McCarthy, to help our new friend connect to his roots."

Professor O'Connell continued, "He was a great Irish statesman, later a cabinet minister who led the negotiations on the Statute of Westminster. He brought in the Shannon Scheme for hydro-electricity.

When he was Minister of Finance, he brought John Maynard Keynes and his thinking about economics to Ireland."

Matt closed his eyes. The professor's Irish brogue had the wonderful ability to enhance the telling of the story of Ireland's history, lulling him into a magical place. He imagined that it was his mother's voice; the voice that he'd never heard. He was a child, and she was sitting by his bedside, telling him the story of her native land, with its seven-hundred-year struggle for independence. Its bloody history, its terrible beauty.

Somehow, Matt had fallen asleep. He awoke to hear Professor O'Connell weave into her narrative of early twentieth century Ireland. She spoke not only of its political leaders, not only of its battles, but also of its most prominent literary figures. She captured William Butler Yeats's magnificent poetry and his passionate and unrequited love for Maud Gonne. She quoted the start of James Joyce's *Ulysses*. She captured the magic of *Finnegans Wake*, the poem, the song — its juice — as a metaphor. In her rendition of it, it wasn't the dead Finnegan rising from the bed, being splashed with Irish whisky at his own wake; it was Ireland, Ireland rising from centuries of domination, Ireland rising from the bed.

She even paused magnificently while quoting the lines of the song, "And shillelagh law was all the rage". She leaned down and brandished to the class a gnarled stick, ugly and menacing in its proportions. "This," she said, "is a shillelagh."

Throughout her lecture, she would pause, look at them, and the room would go still.

"The Dáil I am speaking of is the Irish Parliament. D-Á-I-L. Write it down. We'll be spending a good deal of time on it. And the Taoiseach is not some form of flavored lollipop. The Taoiseach — T-A-O-I-S-E-A-C-H — is the Prime Minister of Ireland. Write that down, too."

Professor O'Connell was at times a tyrant with this class, and other times, a magnificent polemicist. Driving them on, driving them through the pages of history. Ireland's history came alive in her voice, and because of that, in the imaginations of her students. "It was," as Professor O'Connell explained, "Maud Gonne who had introduced a reluctant Protestant Yeats to Irish nationalism. But it was Yeats who became bewitched with Gonne's beauty. He said many years later, 'When I met Gonne, the troubling of my life began.' And yet, Maud Gonne, the beautiful and dynamic Irish nationalist, co-founder of Daughters of Erin, revolutionary women's society, inspired Yeats. He wrote of her, *When you are old and grey and full of sleep, and nodding by the fire, take down this book, and slowly read, and dream of the soft look. Your eyes had once, and of their shadows deep; how many loved your movements of glad grace and loved your beauty with love false or true; but one man loved the pilgrim soul in you and loved the sorrows of your changing face. Bending down beside the glowing bars, murmur, a little sadly, how love fled and paced upon the mountains overhead, and hid his face amid a crowd of stars.*

The room erupted in applause with this dramatic end to the lecture. It was the best lecture Matt had ever heard.

Matt now knew, from his afternoon in the Widener stacks, that Gonne's husband, John MacBride, was executed as a leader of the Irish Rising of 1916. She herself was jailed by the British in 1918 and in 1923 she was imprisoned by the Irish Free State government, without charge. Gonne led the first hunger strike — herself and ninety-one women — against the Irish Free State. And the Irish government, understanding how hunger strikes devastated support for the British, folded within twenty days.

Maud Gonne's marriage to John MacBride was a short and unhappy one. As Matt would later learn, Sean MacBride, the son their union produced, would go on to be one of the founders of Amnesty International, a man whose work Matt had greatly admired. And in 1974, Sean MacBride was awarded the Nobel Peace Prize. Yeats was long dead, as was Maud Gonne, but his words captured the realities. *Everything is changed, utterly changed. A terrible beauty is born.*

After the lecture, Professor O'Connell was surrounded by young students clamouring for her attention. They had questions about the course, the exam, the reading list and all the other urgencies of student existence. Matt, not wishing to intrude, kept his distance and made his exit at the back of the hall, moved and shaken by what he had heard.

The film, *Michael Collins*, reminded him of Professor O'Connell's last line of the lecture. In Yeats's poem "Easter 1916," he struck the most powerful chord in this turning point of the emerging Republic of Eire, modern Ireland:

I write it out in a verse —
MacDonagh and MacBride
And Connolly and Pearse
Now and in time to be,
Wherever green is worn,
Are changed, changed utterly:
A terrible beauty is born.

After the lecture, Matt sat alone in his hotel room. The ghosts of Éamon de Valera and Michael Collins and Tim Finnegan and his own mother swirled about in his head. He slowly sipped a large tumbler of Jameson. When he'd been at the Harvard COOP buying the books and Michael Collins DVD, he'd also picked up a CD of the Clancy Brothers singing the song "Finnegan's Wake." Now, Matt played it, singing along at the conclusion so loudly he feared he might bother those in the neighbouring room. "Timothy rising from the bed, says, Whirl your whisky around like blazes, Thundering Jesus! Do you think I'm dead?"

His Irish mother was certainly long dead. She was dead almost as long as Matt had been alive. Was he dead or just deadened? Could this insight revive him or was it one more unravelling? Eventually the whisky and sleep overcame him.

CHAPTER FIFTEEN

DUBLIN

THE LETTERS ARRIVED FROM Australia with a note from David Podger. His father, Phillip, had died shortly after Matt's visit. Before dying, he told his son about Norah's letters and insisted that David locate them and send them on to Matt.

He read and re-read the first letter, which proved to be a challenging task. His late mother's handwriting ranked as the most appalling scrawl he'd ever encountered. She liked to write; he wondered if there were many other letters out there, other than the ones she'd sent Phillip Podger.

Then there was a phrase she'd used in one of the letters that stuck in his mind — *when I write my day*. At first it seemed to Matt a journalist's way of saying, "Now I have to file my copy. Now I have to write my article."

But gradually, it dawned on him that this might not be the right way to understand the phrase. A journalist files to a deadline. His mother would file her story before writing letters to friends. And so, he began to reread some of the literature of the time, looking for writers who used the phrase. Finally, he found solid proof that "write my day," was an abbreviation of "write my day in my diary."

Did his mother keep a diary? And if so, where could it be? Had it survived the intervening decades?

Any letters beyond the ones sent by Phil Podger would be scattered in the hands of her family, her friends, her lovers. A diary would be even harder to find. Perhaps lost, perhaps destroyed. His mind raced ahead. If it existed, he had to find it. Where might she have hidden it? London? Dublin? A safety deposit box? Who would make payments on such a box? How would she have arranged it? No, not a safety deposit box. Who was still alive today that would have been an adult in 1952? Where on the planet earth would Norah hide her diary? Did her family have it? Who in the family would she have trusted enough to pass her diary on to?

As he read through the rest of the letters Phil Podger sent, with Norah's frequent references to "writing her day," Matt became increasingly convinced that his ghost mother, who'd begun to take shape in her writing, had also kept a diary. Given her profession as a journalist, he expected the diary could yield up a great deal about what kind of person she had been, what she had thought, perhaps what she had thought of her child.

Would it still exist after more than fifty years? As far as Matt knew, he was her only surviving direct blood relation. If this diary had survived, would she have left it with her husband? It hadn't been amongst Daniel's possessions. In one of the letters written very close to her death, Norah had written to Phil: *You must help Daniel find a new love and forget about me. It will be very hard for him, but he will not be able to raise the baby alone. He needs to move on and put me behind him.*

Norah could not have left the diary to Daniel, Matt reasoned, because that would have kept her alive, a ghost to haunt his father. The burden of Daniel's loss would not have lifted; burdened by the existence of the diary nearly as much as he was burdened by the child.

Where else could she have sent the diary? Not Phillip; there would have been far too many private thoughts. Matt reasoned through the options as if his life depended on it. Who would the diary have value for? Perhaps she wanted her son to have the diary.

He went back over each of the letters again. He knew, in his heart, that he'd missed something — some clue as to the whereabouts of the diary. There was reference in several of the letters to Uncle Tody. He hadn't probed too deeply over this at first, didn't question who Uncle Tody might be. Sounded like a character, from Dickens maybe, someone who sat at the corner pub and quaffed Guinness. Perhaps a minor municipal politician — the name Uncle Tody conjured up the colour of local politics.

He reached out by phone to the only person who might be able to help to him: Professor O'Connell. He found her at her office at Harvard where Colleen connected Matt after a warm greeting and friendly exchange of pleasantries.

"It's Matthew Rice," he said. "From Canada. I have a question for you. It's going to sound silly, but I'm reading a letter that my mother sent to a friend. She mentions an Uncle Tody. Do you have any idea who that might have been?"

"Of course," Professor O'Connell said, immediately. "Uncle Tody, your great-uncle Tody. You don't … of course, you never could have known. He was your grandfather's brother. I mentioned him to you when you visited but not by that name. His proper name is Patrick McCarthy."

Matt thanked Professor O'Connell and put down the phone. He googled Patrick McCarthy. There was a great deal about Uncle Tody. His printer began to hum, printing the most important parts Matt found.

This was a formidable man. Patrick McCarthy had been a mainstay of Ireland's Parliament and its cabinets. Late that night, Matt discovered a reference to the Statute of Westminster in one Irish text — the statute that had given Ireland its independence from Britain, the statute that in fact created the Republic of Eire. It was referred to as McCarthy's Charter. It turned out Uncle Tody had negotiated it with Britain and gone on to serve as Minister of Finance, Attorney-General, and later, in his declining years, had taught at University College. He remembered some of this from the professor's lecture but seeing it in print invested it with greater weight and certainty.

Matt slept little that night, and was back at his laptop early the following morning, pursuing an intricate maze connected to Patrick McCarthy, a very common Irish name. Every lead, every variation of the name, every site at University College, every something, until he thought, as the sun came fully up, to google University College itself, and the Law Library.

And there it was, listed in the Archives of University College, Dublin. Professor and Dean Patrick McCarthy, twenty-one boxes of his papers lodged in University College library. Twenty-one boxes! Matt read carefully how they were described: papers from his parliamentary time, cabinet papers that had been released from the official Secrets Act of Ireland, his correspondence, two boxes of personal papers. Surely there had to be some clue, some link to his lost mother — Uncle Tody's niece — in those dusty boxes.

Goddammit, he thought, through the tiredness. *I'm going to have access to the legacy of Patrick McCarthy — twenty-one boxes of his papers.*

Matt found a description of his great-uncle as Finance Minister, in a book by Tim Pat Coogan, *Ireland in the Twentieth Century*:

"In a Cabinet room of dull, earnest and dutiful plodders, Paddy McCarthy was an intriguing and polished anachronism. When he entered a room, always late, with five or six three-inch-thick briefs under his arm, we all had to curb an inclination to stand to attention, the 'headmaster' had arrived. McCarthy impressed people with his sharp-edged Derry accent and the seemingly limitless range. of his dialectical and intellectual skills."

It was suddenly crystal clear to Matt where he had to go next: Dublin, Ireland's capital and his mother's home. He had a powerful sense he would find what he was looking for. This Uncle Tody was someone Norah looked up to. An important figure in Dublin. A man to be trusted. The boxes of personal papers might well hold a clue.

In an act of prudence, he booked himself an Aeroplan ticket for the next morning on Air Canada to New York, then splurged on a business class ticket from New York to Dublin on Aer Lingus. He liked the idea flying with the Irish carrier — plus the plane would be filled with New York and Boston Irish voices to accompany him on his first visit to Ireland. Matt booked a room at the Clarence Hotel in Dublin. The travel websites said that Bono owned the hotel; that seemed a sufficient reason to stay there.

On the flight to New York, Matt attempted to distract himself from his usual fear of flying by putting on earphones and listening to the music provided. Shortly after the plane finished its ascent, he scrolled his way through Neil Young's live album from his Massey Hall concert of 1971.

Matt was alone with his music and thoughts on the flight. Everything altered for him after he changed airlines to Aer Lingus at JFK. Business class was his treat to himself for this historic journey. It was grotesquely expensive, but he didn't care. How often would he search Ireland for his lost mother? Surely only this once.

Matt prayed silently as the Airbus climbed out of the clouds over JFK, higher and higher, turning north and towards Ireland. *Alas*, thought Matt, *I am a late twentieth century man. My existence is affirmed by journeys through the turbulent airs of the jet stream. I race across the Atlantic, the Pacific in jet aircraft. The air currents terrify me. As a sailor I understand them, but at 30,000 feet, they are capricious, savage, and inexplicable.*

Matt's calm analytical gaze deserted him. He was naked with his fears. He was drawn back to his father and his father's fisherman friend, Joe. These memories consumed him, haunted by the waters of his youth, the fishing, his father, and Joe.

Bouncing across Lake Wabigoon in the fourteen-foot Lund aluminum fishing boat, Joe was an icon, a power, possessing a serenity beyond that of the Pope. The outboard eighteen horsepower Johnson roaring, Joe rolling a cigarette, minding the tiller with a nudge of his knee. Commanding it. The bow slicing through the waves. His father Daniel moving back to the middle seat.

Matt bounced across the north Atlantic in fourteen-foot Lund aluminum fishing boat at sixteen kilometres altitude and eighteen hundred kilometres per hour. He imagined the air currents clutching at his soul. Joe and Daniel were long gone, now fishing with St. Peter.

As Matt clung to his memories and Scotch, the aluminum boat of his mind's invention bounced by Greenland and drove toward the Irish Coast. The Rolls Royce jet engines hummed more powerfully and quietly than their eighteen horsepower Johnson predecessors. The air currents cut through his soul, exacting their price. The plane bounced harshly to remind him not to take the air currents for granted. There are only stays of execution in this life.

In his memory, the Johnson changed pitch. Joe and Daniel were there, in the dark, just beyond his window, united in their resignation about the world, in their faith that fish inhabit the next reef, the next shore, the next pool beneath the mossy rock.

There was no mercy, only memory. Their loss compounded the foul grasp of the air currents. The Scotch dulled him, but its relief was ultimately overcome by adrenalin. Sleep would evade him so long as there were more bumps from the turbulence the captain was advising was the reason to fasten all seatbelts.

The events of the past few months and his discovery of a truth he had not been prepared to find fully hit home. He wept and blamed the Scotch. He wept at the happy memories of his family that now all seemed suspect. He wept at the trial and the little girl's death, which still haunted almost his every dream. He wept at the birth mother he couldn't remember. The ghost mother he had never known. He knew he desperately needed to understand her. Yet the thought terrified him. Beth had raised him. She was his real mother. Would this ghost mother displace his real mother? Matt knew he could not allow that to happen.

Matt was shaken awake from his fitful sleep by a brief but fierce buffeting of stormy weather over the Irish Sea as his plane descended through the dark clouds and rain into Dublin's airport. Despite his fatigue, he made his way carefully through Irish Customs and Immigration.

"Where to?" the taxi driver asked, after Matt, escaping the drizzle, flung himself into the back seat.

"The Clarence, Dublin," Matt replied.

"I know where it is."

"The Clarence or Dublin?" Matt replied.

"Both." His driver wheeled the cab between the parked taxis.

"Good." Matt settled deeper into his seat.

The driver went silent, sullen. Eager to share a story but deprived of an audience. Matt had hoped to doze, but the speed on the wet road restarted his adrenalin. By the time they arrived at the Clarence, it was a late Sunday. There was little he could do but let the transatlantic fatigue take him swiftly into sleep. He would have to wait until Monday morning, when he could present himself at University College at the Law Library and seek access to the twenty-one boxes. Patrick McCarthy's legacy, where he hoped the next clue to his mother might lie.

When he arrived at University College early the next day, it was an hour before the Law Library opened. He read the *Irish Times* over coffee. He had with him, in his briefcase, an obituary he'd pulled off the internet from the *Times*. An obituary for Patrick McCarthy, his Uncle Tody, although not described as that. A very flattering obituary that had run sixteen years earlier on the front page of the paper.

Patrick McCarthy, lawyer, politician, minister. He had never been Prime Minister; he hadn't sought the job, but instead was content to serve as Finance Minister, as Minister for the Shannon Hydro-Electric scheme, and later in his life, as Attorney-General. The obituary reinforced the Patrick McCarthy Professor O'Connell had described and about whom he'd found much on the internet. His great-uncle, the great-uncle he'd never met, the great-uncle whose existence had only recently been revealed to him. Perhaps that's where his real interest in politics had come from. Perhaps politics was, in fact, genetic.

When the Law Library opened, Matt was the first one through the door and to the counter. He explained to the young librarian that he wished to access the papers of Patrick McCarthy. He wasn't sure whether this would be easy or hard, to gain access to the papers. He was a little taken aback when he was asked to fill out a special form required specifically to access the papers of Patrick McCarthy, and even more surprised to find on the form, in addition to his name, address, and reason for wishing access, the question, *Are you a blood relative to Patrick McCarthy?*

He'd answered the question carefully, writing, *I am the only son of his niece, and therefore, Patrick McCarthy was in fact, my great-uncle — although we never met.* He felt pressured by the specificity of the form to throw in something they hadn't asked, just for the sake of completeness.

Half an hour later, the young librarian led him to the office of the head librarian of the University College Law Library: a very severe-looking older woman, Mrs. Barrymore. She stunned him by producing a letter, from a very old file that seemed to contain a number of legal papers, establishing the terms on which Professor McCarthy's papers would be donated to the Law Library.

"I knew your great-uncle," Mrs. Barrymore said. "I was young when I started here. It was before he came back from politics to teach, but I was here when they negotiated the conditions for the papers. Your great-uncle was a powerful man, and very particular in the things he did. He was said to be the best legal mind on our faculty. He was certainly the most detailed. My instructions are very clear. I am to give you this letter and you are to take this letter to the law firm of O'Connell, O'Conner, and O'Conner. You are to take it to the senior partner of that firm, Martin Daniel O'Connell."

"What about access to the papers?" said Matt, fixating on one detail as his mind reeled to take in the rest. "Don't I get to see his papers?"

The head librarian stared at him for a moment. "First you must go to the law firm," she said firmly. "If you like, I can call and let them know that you are coming. You will meet with the senior partner of that firm. Martin O'Connell is old now, quite old, not retired, but very old. He will tell you what it is your great-uncle intended."

Matt took the letter and left, but not before asking Mrs. Barrymore to call ahead for him. A meeting with Martin O'Connell was arranged for the next morning.

Only later, as he sat on the bench in the wet green grass of University College's courtyard, did he really question how extraordinary these events had been. It was as though someone, presumably Patrick McCarthy, his Uncle Tody, had known that he would come, or that he might come, and instructions had been left for that eventuality. What was this with the law firm? What could that possibly mean? Why wouldn't they let him see the papers? What could be so secret? His great-uncle been privy to secrets of the state, but all of that was so long ago now. All of these questions seemed beyond his reach at that moment.

Matt called his friend Don when he got back to the hotel. It was much earlier in Winnipeg, but the ever-reliable Don took the call. They had been friends since high school. He rambled on for ten minutes, repeating the questions that were haunting him. Don was reassuring. "Get a good night's sleep, Matt. The answers will come tomorrow."

SHADOW LIFE | 139

They talked for a few more minutes and then hung up. Matt was grateful that Don had been there through thick and thin; through the tough moments after his jury duty; through this side-voyage of discovery he was now on. Matthew considered calling his children but knew they'd ask questions for which he didn't yet have the answers. He made a note that he wouldn't call them until he was home, in Toronto, with all the details of his trip arranged in an orderly manner and prepared to explain that he was and wasn't the person they knew.

The next morning, he found himself in an ancient metal cage elevator riding to the top floor of O'Connell, O'Conner, and O'Conner to meet with Martin Daniel O'Connell. He did not doubt that one of the O'Conners served in the administrative function of managing partner, but O'Connell, as counsel, had his name at the top of the list of lawyers in the firm. Likely he had been the managing partner until age pushed him into the prestigious counsel position. Power could not be fully read from office directories, but they provided excellent clues.

As he waited in the reception area, Matt began to realize that they had taken him at face value when he came into the law firm. No one at the library yesterday had asked for his identification. No one asked for a passport, no one asked for a driver's licence.

Martin Daniel O'Connell's secretary came to fetch Matt. She wore a tailored, elegant suit, and, as Matt followed her down the corridor, he guessed her age to be in the early seventies. He couldn't help but steal a long, lingering glance at her well-formed legs. She was impressive. She moved fast. He had to stride to keep up with her. He was thinking these thoughts when she turned abruptly into a large dark wood-panelled office.

An elderly man rose from behind a large desk, which appeared to date from 1916. He walked around the dominating obstacle and gestured to two leather chairs facing each other in front of a fireplace that appeared functional. Logs were stacked beside the fireplace. All the brass necessities for building and maintaining a fire gleamed. Between the two chairs stood a small table. On it was a faded document of about the same vintage as the desk. Although well preserved, it had no markings that would allow Matt to identify its contents.

Martin Daniel O'Connell did not immediately shake hands with Matt. It was not rudeness, as Matt discovered, but a protection for his gnarled, arthritic hands. He gestured for Matt to sit in one of the armchairs; only then did he seat himself. There was a sternness about him, what would have passed for standard formality in an earlier time. He was no friendly Irishman in the pub. And yet he seemed unburdened by the weight of the world, comfortable in his own aged skin. Matt was relieved that he had not faced Martin Daniel O'Connell in a court of law in his prime.

Matt handed the elderly lawyer the request form he'd prepared to access the archive of Patrick McCarthy. Martin barely looked at it; he waved his own copy of Matt's request, sent by the chief librarian. "You say here, in this form, that you're the grand-nephew of Patrick McCarthy."

"Yes," said Matt. "I believe I am."

"Believe, or can prove?" Martin Daniel O'Connell demanded, his voice strong and a bit fierce.

This challenge took Matt aback. He fished in his own briefcase and produced several documents. First, his Canadian passport, which gave the date of his birth, but did not mention who his parents might have been. He also handed over a sheaf of letters written by his mother to Phillip Podger.

Martin O'Connell studied the letters carefully for what seemed like fifteen minutes, but probably wasn't. He said not a word. When he was done, he looked up at Matt. "Terrible handwriting. How have you come to be in Dublin, to seek access to these papers, and why? Take your time. We are not in a hurry here."

And then Matt began to tell his tale, the tale of his search for his lost mother. The letter, his journey to Sydney, Australia, the possibility of a forged birth certificate. It all came pouring out.

"You were raised in Canada by your father?" Martin inquired.

"And by my stepmother, Beth," Matt said. "Although I wasn't aware she was my stepmother. I always believed her to be my birth mother. It was only recently that I came to know the truth."

"What is it you hope to find?" the lawyer asked.

"I'm trying to find my mother — who she was, what she did, what she believed."

"And you've come here on a search for your mother?"

"I also believe that she may have kept a diary," said Matt.

"Yes, the diary."

Matt was startled. Did he hear the aged lawyer correctly or was his mind playing tricks on him after the fatigue of travel? He hadn't said *a* diary, he had said *the* diary. Clear indication that the diary existed.

Matt did not want to presume that the old lawyer's language might not be what it should be, might not be as exacting as he was parsing it out to be. "Is there a diary?" he asked.

"You came looking for it, didn't you?"

"But I don't know for certain that it exists," said Matt. "Mine was a speculative search. I inferred from her letters that she kept a diary, but I came because I didn't know where else to look."

Martin Daniel O'Connell stared directly at Matt, dark green eyes alert but not unfriendly. For the first time, his tone shifted from interrogation to explanation.

"I knew your great-uncle well. Patrick McCarthy was a wonderful man, a grand Irishman. When they speak of the Good and the Great, Patrick McCarthy fit the definition. He was my professor. He was old when he taught me. I was young then, though I am very old now. Before he died, he came to see me. I was the youngest partner, only in my late twenties."

Martin paused for a moment. A lawyer's pause. For emphasis.

"The other lawyers here believed I was made a partner because of my father, who was managing partner at the time. After several decades, I came to understand that it didn't matter. I became managing partner because of what I was able to do, not because of my father, and not because of my name."

He said this forcefully, as though expecting opposition that Matthew was not about to provide. Clearly, Martin Daniel O'Connell brooked no quarter on this point.

"Your great-uncle, Patrick McCarthy," he continued. "He was a very careful man, a very detailed man. He made very particular arrangements, because he thought someday, the son of his lost niece, his favourite niece, might come looking for some answers. He made those preparations with me because I was the youngest partner. He set trip wires like the form at the Law Library to direct you to me. Patrick said he didn't know if this young man would come in the adventure of his youth, or in the turmoil of his middle years, or not at all. But if he — you — came, I was to do everything possible to help you find your mother and to understand who she really was."

Daniel Martin O'Connell's disquisition was a little too cat-and-mouse for Matt. Such a learned counsel to the firm had earned the right to take his time, but there was a need to come to the point He'd waited decades for Norah's son to come, not in the adventure of his youth, but indeed in the turmoil of his later middle years. Matt wondered what proof he could offer him.

But the lawyer was ahead of him. "The proof of this, the proof of who you are, lies in who your father was. You were raised in Canada. Your father was Canadian. What was his occupation?"

"He was an orthopedic surgeon."

"Ahhh," said the lawyer. "And what was his name?"

"Daniel Harry Rice."

"And what was he doing in London?"

"I'm not entirely certain. He was studying surgery," Matt said.

"When did he meet your mother?"

"I know they married New Year's Day, 1952. I learned from one of her letters that they had two chambermaids as witnesses and Phillip Podger, a friend, was there as well."

The lawyer smiled for the first time. "Yes," he said. "Imagine your great-uncle's shame. His favourite niece, married, with chambermaids as witnesses, in London, to a Canadian. That story has stuck with me through all these years and the detail of the chambermaids as witnesses. There is a diary. You're entitled to it. As her only living heir, you're the only one entitled to it. Your great-uncle made some other arrangements as well. He hoped, perhaps, you had, somewhere in your character, an interest in your mother's side of the family. You're not a surgeon, are you?"

Matt shook his head. "No, I didn't follow in my father's footsteps. My career has been in public service."

"Good, public service is a noble calling," the lawyer said. "I have, along with the diary, something for you. A special letter. Arrangements were made by your great-uncle, after your mother's death. These arrangements, while extremely difficult for mere mortals to make, were not difficult for the Attorney-General of Ireland. We have been retained, by your great-uncle's estate, to ensure your eligibility for an Irish passport, an EU passport, in the hope that someday you might turn up and find such things useful. I expect the passport may prove more useful to you than the diary."

"There is a diary, and I want it. That's what I came for."

"Be patient, Matthew," Martin replied. "This diary has waited a very long time for you. You can wait for it a few minutes longer. It's only because Patrick McCarthy flew to London for your mother's funeral that you have the diary." He paused in sorrow before continuing. "When he returned from London, Patrick McCarthy was distraught. He told my father that the tragedy had overwhelmed him. Your father, you as a baby, Norah dead. Horrible." He drew a breath. "Norah had been their shining star. The Irish girl who made it as a journalist in London, in the heart of the British Empire. Suddenly she was gone."

"How did my mother die?" Matt asked.

"She died after your birth. Norah had gone to cover the hydrogen bomb test in the South Pacific. She was exposed to radiation. That was what lead to her death.

"Patrick told me that your father said he'd take the baby and return to Canada. Your father wouldn't look at Norah's desk. Patrick packed up her papers, her books, the diary. He packed up your mother's clothes and took them to the Charity Board. With respect to your mother's diary, Patrick took the responsibility for it in the belief that you would at some point in your life come looking for it. Daniel insisted that there was to be no effort to reach out to you."

Martin paused, shook his head. "Patrick told my father that Daniel was struggling to go on and wanted nothing beyond you — the baby — to remind him of Norah. He told him, 'I have my son, what more is there?'"

The elderly lawyer pushed a small button, under the lip of the table, which summoned his secretary. When she appeared, he simply nodded, and she returned with two items: the diary and a wrapped package.

Martin passed the diary to Matt with a sense of great ceremony. He was passing more than just the book. He was passing Matt the heritage he had not known was his. Matt dared not open it right then. It would shatter the moment. He resolved in that instant not to read the diary in Dublin, nor on Irish soil. The only place he could imagine properly reading his mother's diary was on Quarry Island, his place of refuge and safety.

When Matt placed the diary on his lap, Martin presented him with the wrapped package. It appeared to contain four books. These had arrived after Norah's death. Patrick had arranged sixty years ago for mail and parcels to be forwarded to the law firm from London.

Matt took notice of the old lawyer's hands as he took the package from him. The liver spots betrayed his true age, where the leanness of his face peeled twenty years off. Matt began to unwrap the package. Feeling awkward, he looked uneasily at the lawyer, who nodded, giving him permission to proceed. "I collect books," Matthew said, almost as an explanation for his movement away from the question of the diary to the package of books.

Martin replied, "A wonderful hobby, book collecting."

When he looked down at the unwrapped books in his lap, he saw a familiar title. John Steinbeck's *East of Eden*, published, as he knew, in 1952. Instinctively, as any collector would, he opened the mint condition volume to the copyright page. It was a first edition, a true first, a pristine, perfect first. For a brief moment he was a pure book collector; his nascent connection to his mother disappeared.

As he unravelled the rest of the package, he could see two more titles. Anne Frank's *Diary of a Young Girl*, and Hemingway's *The Old Man and the Sea*, both also published in 1952. The fourth book puzzled him, not the author's name, as Gwendolyn Brooks was well known to him, but the cover was one he hadn't seen before. It was, in fact, a first edition of her first book, as he discovered on further examination.

The books were all in mint condition. With them was a statement of account from Foyles, the Grand Dame of the Charing Cross Road bookstores. In 1952, it would have been exactly where his mother had her account. The first editions, he realized, were not evidence of her as a book collector. No, it was evidence that she read the newly published, important books of her time. His hand trembled; it was as though across sixty years of ignorance, a hand reached out. He felt closer to her than he had felt up to this moment. *How remarkable*, he thought. He'd spent thirty years pursuing the collection of books and there she was, his birth mother, harvesting these first editions as they came off the press. Not to collect them, just to read them.

Matt had a sudden thought. What if his mother was one of those people — hated by all book collectors — who wrote in the margin of books or underlined key passages, thereby destroying their value? Even though he knew that she had never touched the books he was feeling as her lost son that if there had been notes, what insights might they provide into his mother's thoughts? He leafed through the pristine passages. There was no underlining. Matt felt relief, tempered by regret. He was in all likelihood the first person to hold these books since the clerk at Foyles had wrapped them sixty years earlier.

East of Eden was seen possibly as Steinbeck's best book. *The Old Man and the Sea* had a uniqueness to it among Hemingway's work. Anne Frank's *Diary of a Young Girl* kept alive not only the existence of Anne Frank, but the existence of evil in the world — the war, the Holocaust, the capacity for man to visit unforgivable violence upon his own species. Gwendolyn Brooks had become the poet laureate of the United Sates in 1985. She was the first African-American to win the Pulitzer Prize — in 1950. Matt examined the volumes carefully. They were pristine, in mint condition. They were mint, as a bookseller would describe them — no chips, marks, dust jackets in perfect condition — but not mint because his mother had actually never read them. What kept them in mint condition was that they'd been sealed in brown paper and stored very safely for sixty years with the firm of O'Connell, O'Conner and O'Conner.

Instead of shaking Matt's hand, Martin held both his hands gently in his own aged ones before parting. "I'm so glad you finally came. I'm pleased to have rendered this final service to your late, great-uncle and through him, to your mother and to you."

Still holding Matt's hands, he imparted an old Irish wish, "And may the road rise up to greet you."

"Thank you," was all Matt could muster.

The elderly law partner escorted him first to the office door and then after a moment of confusion on Matt's face, down the corridor to the ancient elevator. At their parting, Martin hesitated, as though there were something important left unsaid. Matt waited, fearful the elevator would leave without him.

"I would like to show you the Dáil," Martin offered. Then, uncertain that this Canadian would yet know what the Dáil was, he added, "The Irish Parliament."

"I know about the Dáil," Matt said, pronouncing it correctly. "I'd be delighted."

"One o'clock this afternoon, then. Where are you staying?"

"At the Clarence Hotel."

"Ah, the Bono hotel," O'Connell muttered. "If money isn't a consideration, you should try the Shelbourne next time. Much better. No matter. I'll fetch you at the Clarence at one. You can bring Bono along if he is unoccupied and lurking about the foyer," he added, with a smile.

"I will," Matt laughed. "We can both get his autograph."

Matt walked back to the Clarence. His route took him along Ormond Quay on the north side of the River Liffey. Lost in thought about his mother, her diary, the events of the morning, Matt noticed nothing at all. His arms firmly cradled the package containing the diary and his four precious first editions from his birth mother.

CHAPTER SIXTEEN

THE DÁIL

AS GOOD AS HIS word, Martin Daniel O'Connell appeared in the lobby of the Clarence Hotel at precisely one o'clock. Matt was in the high-ceiling, oak-panelled reading room just to the left off the lobby, reading the *Financial Times*. He looked up, saw Martin, stood, and walked to him.

"Ready for a bit of Irish political history?" Martin enquired.

"Yes, I am," Matt replied.

The aged lawyer glanced around the lobby, making a show of looking for something.

"Bono couldn't make it."

"Too busy saving the planet," Matt said, a bit cavalierly.

O'Connell looked at him severely. "Don't like his music, but I respect his work in Africa and for holding the politicians' feet to the fire. Good for him, rose-coloured glasses and all. He is a genuine hero to me."

"I agree completely," Matt replied, suitably chastised. "Sorry."

The air cleared. Martin resumed chatting in a friendly manner. They exited the hotel together and walked along Wellington Quay. Before they'd advanced fifty feet, the lawyer stopped and drew Matt's attention to an official notice attached to the corner of the building immediately west of the Clarence.

"Development Application," he muttered. "They are planning

to tear down several buildings and build a colossal hotel and casino complex."

"Are they tearing down the Clarence itself?" Matt asked, suddenly concerned. "I haven't been here long, but I'm convinced it's a lovely hotel. The woodwork is superb."

The old lawyer held up his hand. "A beautiful building stands only a fair chance of surviving the pursuit of what the Americans call the almighty buck. The fall-out from the 2008 financial crash badly impacted this country, but not Dublin real estate development. That never seems to cease for too long. They are always eager to tear down history to build something shiny and new."

As they threaded their way through the cobbled, narrow streets of the Temple Bar area, Martin told the tale of how this special neighbourhood of historic buildings had narrowly escaped the wrecking ball.

"Expropriated, condemned. All slated to be knocked down for a massive bus terminal," Martin stated, a strong note of disgust in his voice. "Look at these magnificent buildings. A bus terminal!" He shook his head.

They strolled down a street teeming with life: bars, restaurants, small art galleries, street musicians with guitars. History reborn, rejuvenated. Hardly the ideal spot for a bus terminal.

"Truly and ironically, the bus terminal scheme has been abandoned." The approvals took so long that they had to rent out the buildings on short-term leases. These bars and restaurants moved in. The Temple Bar became a smash success. Architectural treasures saved by the Irish passion for the drink."

They continued their stroll towards the Irish Parliament. When they arrived, Martin was greeted by name by a white-haired guide. The man was older than Martin, with a broad accent and a friendly smile. He introduced himself as Kevin. Their tour had clearly been prearranged by O'Connell or his efficient secretary. As they climbed the stairs, the guide began to outline Ireland's political system. A storytelling duel commenced between O'Connell and Kevin as they toured the impressive rooms of the Dáil.

Kevin explained the origins of the names of political partners. "Fianna Fáil literally translates as 'Soldiers of Destiny,'" he began. "Seán Lemass wanted to call the new party the Republican Party." He paused. "But de Valera wanted greater Gaelic symbolism, and Fianna Fáil it became. The main opposition party was named Fine Gael, or 'Family of the Gael" — a name considered and passed over by de Valera."

By the time the tour concluded in the lobby of the Dáil, Matt felt a bond had emerged from the storytelling duel of O'Connell and the guide. Each time one would gain an edge with a particularly compelling story, the other would trump him with an even better story or more obscure trivia of Irish political history. Matt delighted in each exchange. There was a mutual admiration between the elderly lawyer and the white-haired guide. No real animosity, but a genuine competition in the exchange of tales.

After climbing a deeply carpeted set of stairs, Kevin opened a magnificent, large wood and glass door. Beyond the door was a spectacular chamber. "The Senate Chamber," the guide said. "Before I tell you the history of this room, let me mention the notables who have occupied seats in the Senate."

"William Butler Yeats," O'Connell volunteered.

"How is your Senate chosen?" Matt inquired. "In Canada, the Prime Minister appoints all senators."

"Very much more complex in Ireland," Kevin said. "Some are even appointed or elected by Trinity College. That's how Yeats came to be in our Senate."

As they moved from portrait to portrait, Kevin and Martin continued their duel. Kevin was circumspect when describing the prime ministers, his words careful. Matthew could gauge his views by his tone.

O'Connell's views were presented directly and forcefully, although tempered with humour.

"When did Ireland fully break its ties with the United Kingdom?" Matt asked, trying to think back to the books he'd skimmed at the Widener Library.

"The story that's told is that in 1950, Taoiseach Lemass was seated at a dinner in your country in Ottawa," the guide replied. "Next to him was a truly obnoxious British Embassy official. The Taoiseach was allegedly so furious at the official's condescending comments that he declared, that very evening, that Ireland would cut its final ties to the British Crown. He announced formally the next day that Ireland would become fully an independent republic."

Daniel Martin O'Connell smiled broadly and looked at Matt. "There is another version," he began. "In this other, darker version, the Taoiseach had a great deal to drink at the very same dinner and declared Ireland's independence to all present. The next morning, the story reached Ireland on the news wire. Jubilation greeted the announcement. Although a sober and reflective Taoiseach was relieved to let the bravado of the dinner pronouncement fade, the die was cast. Popular demand cemented his resolve. If there was to be a parade for full Irish independence, the Taoiseach would lead it."

"Which version is generally accepted?" Matt asked his two mentors.

Silence descended over the two men. Finally, Martin spoke. "Probably a measure of truth in each version."

Kevin nodded, agreeing with O'Connell's compromise.

Before them, encased in glass, was the banner of the Fighting Irish, donated by John Fitzgerald Kennedy, twenty-third President of the United Sates — the first of Irish descent, and the first Roman Catholic.

"The Irish who went to America became policemen, firemen, and soldiers long before anyone let them be senators or the president," the guide said.

Matt remembered the Canada Loves New York rally two months after the tragedy of September eleventh. Canadians, many embarrassed by the tepid response of their own federal government, flooded New York. Thousands came by air, by train, and some, from the Yukon, spent five days on a bus. At the rally, Matt had stood in the packed, sweaty Roseland Dance Hall beside a tough, white-haired fire department superintendent. When Mayor Rudy Giuliani spoke, he talked not about the three thousand lives lost, he talked about the ten thousand lives saved. The veteran Irish-American fire commander, standing next to Matt, wept openly. He was not alone.

Later, Matt learned that twenty-three of his fellow firemen, all Irish, all sons of firemen before them, had run into the collapsing towers, trying to save more lives, and had lost their own. Matt thought then that this is who the Irish are: they run towards burning buildings, towards the danger.

"The Fighting Irish Regiment first fought in the Civil War for the Union. They have been in every single fight since. Vietnam, Korea, and Iraq. Kennedy chose well. The Irish fought with passion for their adopted land. Kennedy was himself a fighter in World War II, and his own brother, Joe, died in the war when his plane was shot down."

Irish blood for Irish-American success, Matt thought, but didn't say it.

Next to the banner, an enormous photograph dominated the wall. The entire Dáil and Senate had crowded into the Chambers for Kennedy's address a scant few months before his assassination.

Martin pointed at the back of a white-haired head. "That's Paddy McCarthy in the front bench." He turned to the guide. "His great-uncle and my father's best friend."

"Patrick McCarthy, quite the statesman," Kevin said. "In the Dáil for forty years."

Matt, uncertain of loyalties and allegiances, looked at Martin. "So, your family was for de Valera not Collins?"

"Quite the contrary," he replied, somewhat brusquely, as though Matt had asked an impertinent question. "We were always Fine Gael. My father believed that Dev was on the grassy knoll when they shot Collins. Never forgave him."

Kevin nodded gravely. It became clear that he favoured Séan Lemass as Ireland's greatest recent Taoiseach. It also became very clear that neither of them liked de Valera.

Matt imagined de Valera as an Irish Mackenzie King, the enduring leader. Not loved, but a necessary piece of the fabric. Kept on for decades for the power he had wielded in earlier days. So skilled at governing by endless Canadian compromises was Mackenzie King that, when he died, the poet Frank Scott wrote scathingly of him, *His greatest ambition was to pile a Parliamentary Committee atop a Royal Commission. Nothing was done by halves that could be done by quarters.*

The tour concluded back in the lobby of the Dáil, where it had begun. Kevin pointed out an enormous clock, at least nine or ten feet tall. It dominated the wall on which it had been placed with its rich, dark mahogany case and its brass pendulum.

"Donated to the Dáil by Roddy Fitzpatrick," Kevin explained. "One of Ireland's wealthiest new businessmen." He paused. "Pharmaceuticals."

"It's a magnificent clock," Matt chimed in, trying to be supportive. Although as he spoke, he noted broad grins on the faces of both his companions. They seemed to be sharing a silent moment of irony at his expense. Matt was so certain of this quiet conspiracy that he blurted out a single-word question, "What?"

Kevin and Martin exchanged glances. Kevin nodded to Martin, encouraging him, giving him permission to tell the final story, to have, in effect, the last word.

"Well," Martin began, "our newly rich pharmaceutical tycoon — 'the drug baron,' as the newspapers dubbed him — did not take the time to fully examine his clock."

"After he paid fifty thousand euros for it," Kevin added.

"Yes," repeated O'Connell. "After he foolishly paid fifty thousand euros for it at an auction in London. It plays songs. Well, just two songs, really."

The guide's grin gave way to a low chuckle.

"The donor, Mr. Drug Baron, had no idea, until the day of the presentation, when his new American wife, half his age and well-endowed below the shoulders, piped up, 'It plays songs.'" O'Connell paused for breath. "Apparently, she'd been instructed in the detailed workings of the clock by the auction house. In particular, the great clock's musical talents." He smiled, savouring the yet-to-be-delivered punch line. "With the Taoiseach, half the Cabinet, the Archbishops of Dublin and Galway, the Lord Mayor of Dublin, and fifty other notables of the Irish Republic present, she reached in and yanked the appropriate lever. And this great clock began to play a tune."

He paused, a twinkle in both his eyes and Kevin's as they each savoured the story's conclusion about to come. "Yes, the pride of the Republic of Eire, the passionate defenders of all that is holy Catholic and Irish, stood transfixed in place, as the great clock chimed 'God Save the Queen.' As the dignitaries' faces reddened and the insult of it sank in, the doomed American wife tugged on the lever again, desperately trying to halt the anthem. Instead, this second pull moved the great clock to play the only other tune in its repertoire: 'Rule Britannia.'"

They laughed. Matt, taken at the outstanding irony of it, laughed longest.

"It's rumoured that the drug baron was so embarrassed by his bride's actions that he briefly contemplated divorce. He even consulted learned counsel."

"Would he really divorce her over a tune, even 'Rule Britannia'?" Matt enquired, still laughing.

"Not likely," O'Connell replied. "His carefully constructed American prenuptial agreement wouldn't survive an Irish court. A divorce would cost him half his vast fortune."

"Rule America," Kevin added.

At this, they shook hands. The tour was over. In a final act, Kevin presented Matt with a yellowed replica of the Proclamation of Irish Independence. It began with the bold declaration of the Provisional Government of the Irish Republic. The six who signed the proclamation were all put to death by the British along with others who supported the 1916 Easter Uprising. To Matt's newly awakened Irish eyes and ears, the phrasing rang with clarity, history, and hope: "Irishmen and Irishwomen: In the name of God and of the dead generations from which she receives her old tradition of nationhood, Ireland, through us, summons her children to her flag and strikes for her freedom."

Martin O'Connell encouraged Matt to sit down in the lobby of the Dáil, after the tour guide took his leave, then sat down beside him. "There's something I need to tell you, Matthew." His tone had become serious, even grave. It contrasted sharply with the humour of the tour's end.

Matt was instantly apprehensive. Had he done something to offend the elderly lawyer? Was a dark family secret to be revealed?

"We've spoken a great deal about your great-uncle Patrick McCarthy," O'Connell began somewhat formally, "but your mother's father, your maternal grandfather, was not a great man like his brother." O'Connell paused. "He drank too much. He played at the IRA, and not in a good way. He ran up debts that his brother paid. He abandoned your grandmother. He ran off with another woman. He was truly the black sheep of the great McCarthy family. Your grandmother was a saint, a genuine saint. She deserved far better. She taught school for nearly fifty years. She raised three daughters including your mother, without a husband."

Matt had feared something much darker. An errant and unknown grandfather struck him as a mild tragedy. But the gravity of O'Connell's tone and his seriousness caused Matt to adopt a grave tone. "Thank you for telling me," he replied.

They sat in silence for a few moments.

"I experienced something much darker," said Matt. "Earlier this year I served on a jury." He paused.

"What sort of case?" inquired Martin.

"Murder," replied Matt. "The murder of a young child by a stranger."

"A truly terrible crime."

"Worse still. It was a hung jury. I was foreman, but could not get a unanimous verdict. The accused went free. He killed again. Another young girl."

"Truly dreadful."

They sat in silence for several minutes. Neither one knowing how to begin again.

They had each imparted dark news.

O'Connell decided to move to better ground. "Quite a story, that clock," he muttered.

"Rule America," replied Matt.

They shared another laugh at the drug baron's expense.

And they parted, with a shared certainty that their paths would cross again. Matt felt deep down that some force or event would cause their lives to be further intertwined.

CHAPTER SEVENTEEN

WILLIAM BUTLER YEATS

MARTIN DANIEL O'CONNELL TOOK his leave, walking slowly but steadily through the black wrought iron gate. Matt stood for a long time in the courtyard just south of the Dáil. On his right was the National Library of Ireland. Scaffolding obscured its façade. A renovation appeared to be at its mid-point with the old paint scraped away but not yet replaced by the intended new coat. To his left stood the National Museum. Matt chose to visit the National Library.

His mind still reeled with the political stories from his tour of the Dáil. As he entered the white door of the library, he chuckled again at the story of the impertinent British clock and its hapless donor. The lobby of the National Library offered a special exhibition on the life and works of Matt's favourite poet, William Butler Yeats.

As he stepped into the first exhibit area, Matt heard a recorded voice, one that he never expected to hear. A reading of the exhibit description confirmed what he already suspected. It was the voice of Yeats's early and, some would argue, only true love, Maud Gonne. Matt was struck by the drawn-out character of her accent. To Matt's ear, more a British than Irish accent.

Turning, he stared at the first glass exhibition case. There, arranged in pristine glory, was an assemblage of Yeats's early books. These were jewels. Any single volume was far beyond an amateur collector's dreams. There was Yeats's first published book, *The Wanderings of Oisin and Other Poems*, from 1889 and next to it his second book, simply titled *Poems*, published in 1895.

Arrayed in display cases were the first editions of Yeats's writings. In large wall displays and on television screens were presentations of each of the periods of Yeats's life. Interviews with Yeats scholars played on screens in alcoves. The display was moving, powerful.

Staring at the first large poster of Yeats, Matt shifted slightly sideways to get a better perspective and bumped jarringly into a younger woman beside him. He had been completely unaware of her presence until his shoulder collided with her. They both jumped back.

"Excuse me — sorry," Matt muttered. "Completely distracted by hearing the voice of Maud Gonne."

"Me too. I didn't know she had ever been recorded," the woman replied, with what Matt thought was a Boston Irish accent. More prominent than her accent, was her long, dark red hair. Dressed in faded blue jeans and a rich dark green wool sweater, her beauty gave Matt pause.

"Are you from Boston?" he asked, immediately regretting the question as a verbal equivalent of the inadvertent bump.

"Boston Irish, single, journalist, Harvard Lit major, thesis on Yeats. Now writing for *Fortune* magazine." She grinned broadly. "And you?"

"Harvard alumni — economics, not lit — Canadian, divorced, recently discovered to be of Irish descent. Long lost Irish birth mother just revealed." Matt held out his hand. "Matthew Rice. Matt, actually."

"Mary Louise Patricia O'Reilly. Mary Louise, actually. Pleased to meet you, Matt actually."

They shook hands quite formally, though both were laughing. She had a firm, strong grip that suggested a sport. She was perhaps four inches shorter than his own six feet. Her smile lit up the room.

"Do you know Professor O'Connell at Harvard?" Matt asked.

"Of course. She's my thesis advisor. I went back to do my PhD after working as a journalist for fifteen years. Forty and in school again! I still take the occasional assignment as a journalist to keep my hand in it."

Matt felt completely trumped. "She commanded me to visit Ireland to discover who my mother was and who I am," he said.

"She ordered me here to truly understand Yeats and Ireland. Luckily, *Fortune* magazine also had an assignment in Ireland for me."

"She is truly a remarkable woman. I wonder if she also commanded us to collide."

They laughed again in shared affection for their remarkable Professor and began naturally to walk through the exhibits together. As they toured, Mary Louise regaled him with numerous stories, each of which cast the legendary professor as a brilliant but complex character. Mary Louise proved far more knowledgeable about both Professor O'Connell and William Butler Yeats than Matt, but she did not insist on trumping his every comment.

The exhibition's structure was chronological. It set out to detail the journey of Yeats's "pilgrim soul" from his early poetry of the 1880s through his death in 1939. Four films were included in the exhibition, with tiny viewing rooms scattered throughout the exhibition. Only six people could sit to watch each film in the small space, but there was standing room. As they settled next to each other on modest plastic chairs, Matt was fully intoxicated by Mary Louise. Her perfume lingered elusively but sweetly amidst the musty smells of the dried paper of the National Library. Mary Louise struck Matt as the kind of woman men fell in love with swiftly and without remorse. He wondered who loved her and whether she loved any of them in return. He shook off these unusual feelings of near instant intimacy to focus on the film and to try to keep up his end of the conversation about the great poet.

"He was so handsome," declared Mary Louise, gazing at the young Yeats on the screen. "How could Maud Gonne resist him?"

"Apparently she preferred other men who treated her poorly to the one man who truly loved her," Matt replied.

"Not recovering from a recently broken heart, are you?" Mary Louise enquired.

"No, not recent. But I am mindful of the continuing affection we all have for unrequited love and the consequences. What about you? Is Yeats filling in for a lost love of your own?"

"I am without significant other at this time," Mary Louise declared, with a broad smile.

"Are resumés being accepted?" Matt asked, returning her smile.

"Love isn't found through resumés."

Matt felt chastened. "I know."

"You are, of course, a romantic or you wouldn't be sitting here lamenting the pain Yeats suffered at his continuing rejection by Maud Gonne."

"Guilty as charged." He paused. "The pain of unrequited love never seems to go out of fashion."

"Never," Mary Louise retorted. "It will never go out of fashion among the Irish. Not in a thousand years."

"Perhaps I really have an inner Irishman after all."

"You know that Yeats proposed several times to Maud Gonne? The last time she refused, he proposed to her daughter, Iseult, with her blessing. Iseult also refused him."

"Two strikes and you're out!"

"They remained friends."

"That's three strikes. The third for allowing her to turn love to friendship."

"And that's a bad thing?" Mary Louise demanded.

"Not bad. Just quite normal. I believe we wisely spend much of our lives converting lovers to friends when the passion has fled."

By now they'd moved to the next exhibit featuring Yeats and

his family. At the final display was a larger-than-life photograph of Yeats's tombstone, as well as a manuscript heavily edited in his own hand. Here, Matt could see where Yeats carved his final words to the world and honed them before they stood as his ageless monument:

Cast a Cold Eye
On Love, on Life
Horseman Pass By

The words resonated as a final brilliant poem, almost haiku in its phrasing; his permanent message to those who might seek out his final resting place.

All that eloquence silenced, Matt thought, staring hard at the tombstone. He was surprised to hear the words out loud.

Mary Louise was studying him. "Did you know Yeats said that James Joyce was the only Irishman with enough intensity and passion to be a novelist?"

"I did not know that," Matt replied, puzzled that Yeats himself wrote only poetry and plays. "I collect first editions and I would dearly love to own a Yeats first."

"Come with me," Mary Louise beckoned, as they exited the National Library together. "I know just the place, Ulysses Books. But be forewarned: they are quite expensive."

"I can imagine," Matt replied, with considerable bravado.

The bookstore stood off Grafton Street at 10 Duke Street. Not large, the bookshop was a single room on the main floor with another smaller room below in the basement. But it was magnificent. In glass cases, the high spots were exhibited in a near museum-state of pristine beauty. Here, a case filled with James Joyce. There, another resplendent with first editions of Yeats. As they roamed slowly through the store, Mary and Matt's eyes scanned each title.

After examining several Yeats's firsts, Matt settled on a beautiful volume. The cover was pristine — a glorious, black art deco design. Although a later work, he felt it gave him a direct connection to Yeats. He held the slender, black volume carefully in his hands. He opened the volume carefully to read its title, *The Winding Stairs and Other Poems*. The publication date, 1933. It contained Yeats's 1928 poem "The Tower." The price, a staggering 1500 euros (over $2,000 USD Matt quickly calculated), was a third of the others. It would be his most expensive book purchase ever.

"It's gorgeous!" Mary Louise exclaimed as he held it out for her to examine.

Matt read aloud the tipped in description. The volume was one of only 2,000 printed in 1933.

"A fine book," the cashier assured him as she skillfully wrapped both that book as well as a first of Nuala O'Faolain's novel, *A Dream of You* that Matt bought as well. "Would you like to join our mailing list for catalogues?"

"Yes, please."

"Me too," Mary Louise added.

Over a dark Guinness at the pub next to the bookshop, he presented *A Dream of You* to Mary. "You might enjoy O'Faolain."

"I would enjoy the Yeats!"

Her grin was infectious. Matt smiled back. "But we're only acquaintances — it would seem a bit forward of me."

"Only a bit forward," Mary Louise laughed. "Thank you for the Nuala O'Faolain. I haven't read her, but I hear high praise for her writings from wise people."

They left the pub after a single Guinness. "I feel full," Mary Louise said. "Let's walk."

They strolled across St. Stephen's Green. "What poem of Yeats is your favourite?" Matt asked. He half expected her to dismiss the question with an "impossible to answer."

"Easter 1916," she immediately said. "It'll endure forever. Not only is it his best poem, I believe it may be one of the best poems ever written in the English language. Although I understand, of course, other contenders would challenge for that title."

She recited the poem from memory and with real passion, from the opening line, *I have met them at the close of day*, through its powerful concluding stanza, *Everything is changed, utterly changed, a terrible beauty is born.*

"Do you understand Yeats's brilliance and how much of a journey this poem was for him?" she demanded.

Matt tried to sound knowledgeable without setting himself up for a fall. He failed. "I understand most of the poem. The Easter Uprising. The sacrifice."

Mary Louise rounded on him. "Who was MacBride? Why was he a drunken vainglorious lout?"

"Married Maud Gonne," Matt replied.

"Not a good marriage."

"No."

"John MacBride married Maud Gonne, the true love, the unrequited love, of Yeats's early life. MacBride beat her in his drunken rages. Yeats risked his reputation in the Irish courts to free her from the marriage in the straitjacket of Catholic Ireland." She paused for breath. "MacBride was a drunken, vain lout until the uprising. Then, as with Ireland, Yeats went on to say, 'has had done most grievous harm to one near my heart ... he was changed, utterly changed, and made glorious.'"

She paused again. "How it must have tormented Yeats to write those words. His honesty, his integrity as a poet, must have forced him to tear out his heart — the heart he had given in its entirety to Maud Gonne."

By now they were seated on a park bench in St. Stephen's Green, just across from the Shelbourne Hotel. The late day sun weakened and a cool breeze emerged.

"Two of the leaders of the 1916 Uprising, Pearse and Connolly, are speaking in a garden," Mary Louise began to speak again. "The

garden of which they spoke was Ireland. And the uprising watered the roots of the dream of the Republic with the blood of its
dreamers and patriots."

She paused, then recited from memory the poem in its entirety:

O words are lightly spoken,
Said Pearse to Connolly,
"Maybe a breath of politic words
Has withered our Rose Tree;
Or maybe but a wind that blows
Across the bitter sea."
"It needs to be but watered,"
James Connolly replied,
"To make the green come out again
And spread on every side,
And shake the blossom from the bud
To be the garden's pride."
"But where can we draw water,"
Said Pearse to Connolly,
"When all the wells are parched away?
O plain as plain can be
There's nothing but our own red blood
Can make right a Rose Tree."

Matt paused for a moment, letting the passion of Mary Louise's
recitation linger before he spoke. "Extraordinary. For me, 'The
Second Coming' was always the one. But recently I found another,
darker poem. One closer to a recent event in my life."

"Which one?"

"*What hour of terror comes to test the soul / And in that
terror's name obeyed the call / And understood, what none have
understood / Those images that waken in the blood.*" Matt stopped

for a breath. "'Hound Voice'. That's not the whole of it. Just the fragment that sticks in my head."

Mary Louise nodded. "It's a fine poem. Much darker than many of his others. Blood is a recurring theme in his work."

Matt was certain that he could not match Mary Louise's stunning performance of "The Rose Tree" from memory, but his competitive spirit had him in its grip. He thought for a moment. "He wasn't a poet, but I always loved Teddy Roosevelt's speech about the man in the arena." This, Matt knew by heart. He was fond of quoting it to young public servants during his years of government service.

"'It is not the critic who counts; not the man who points out how the strong man stumbles, or where the doer of deeds could have done them better. The credit belongs to the man who is actually in the arena, whose face is marred by dust and sweat and blood; who strives valiantly; who errs, who comes short again and again, because there is no effort without error and shortcoming; but who does actually strive to do the deeds; who knows great enthusiasms, the great devotions; who spends himself in a worthy cause; who at the best knows in the end the triumph of high achievement, and who at the worst, if he fails, at least fails while daring greatly, so that his place shall never be with those cold and timid souls who neither know victory nor defeat.'"

Matt finished with a flourish, instantly knowing that, in his own recent life, he had drifted towards becoming one of the timid souls "so fearful of defeat that victory was foreclosed to him." The thought struck him suddenly and forcefully. He needed to move on before a dark mood overcame him.

"What dark event brought you to 'Hound Voice'?" Mary Louise asked.

"That is a longer, more difficult telling."

"Perhaps a telling over another drink?" she asked.

"Another drink would be most welcome."

"Have you been to Dublin's famous Horseshoe Bar?"

"No, where is it?"

Mary Louise pointed at the grand hotel across the street. "Just there, in the Shelbourne Hotel."

"I'd be delighted to become acquainted with the fabled charms of the Horseshoe Bar."

They negotiated the traffic to reach the Shelbourne's front entrance. "I am reliably informed that if money is not a consideration, this is the place to stay," Matt said.

"Of course. Where are you staying?"

"At the Clarence." He tried not to sound defensive.

"Trying to finagle an autograph from Bono, are we?"

Did the entire population of the city of Dublin, as well as visiting American journalists, view the Clarence as solely the chosen residence of shallow, autograph-seeking Bono groupies?

"Is Bono staying there as well?" Matt asked.

This netted him a less-than-gentle punch on the shoulder. "Don't play innocent with me. You must know he owns it. That is the only single fact known about the Clarence Hotel by any non-Dubliner!"

Over drinks in the Horseshoe Bar, Matt told Mary Louise the story of his jury duty. He spared her none of the horror of failing to convict and the aftermath, the murder of the second child. He wept and she put her arm around his shoulder to hug him.

"Your quest for your lost birth mother. Please tell me that story."

Relieved to let go of his trial memories, he told her in detail of his search for his mother's identity. He concluded with the delivery of her diary into his hands that very morning. The telling of his long voyage of discovery exhausted Matt. Mary Louise reached over and held his hand in hers. It was a spontaneous gesture of support, of sympathy. Matthew wiped away what he hoped weren't tears. She bestowed a gentle but lingering kiss on his lips.

"Weep not," she said gently. "You have found your way home."

Mary Louise suggested dinner that evening at an Italian restaurant in the Temple Bar. Matt was grateful for some time to pull himself together. "It's called Trastevere," she said. "It's very good. It's near the Clarence. Seven PM. You can even bring Bono if you come across him."

Matt admired the beautiful Mary Louise as she swept through the lobby. He walked back to the Clarence, thinking of little else but her. Tired from the time zone changes and burdened by his newly acquired knowledge of his mother Norah, Matt felt strangely alone and unsettled, even as he was looked forward to spending more time with this captivating woman.

At dinner, Matt recounted his tour of the Dáil. Mary Louise laughed heartily at his description of the tour of the Irish Parliament. "Imagine that!" she exclaimed. "Two old Irishmen competing to impress the naive Canadian. Do you believe that even half their stories were actually true?"

"I'm wounded by your cynicism," he replied. "I actually believed every word." He looked somewhat stricken by the suggestion that he'd been conned by these wily old gentlemen.

Regret showed immediately on her lovely, open face. "I'm sorry if my cynicism wounded you, but two Irishmen with such a golden opportunity. Certainly, they are a pair of like-minded scoundrels. How could they not take a chance with the truth? How could they resist the temptation to have fun with a newly discovered Irishman?"

"I admit that the beautiful Baroness who gave birth to nineteen children seemed a bit farfetched," Matt replied, eager to salvage their previous happy mood.

"Actually, that one is true," Mary admitted, somewhat chagrined. "I suppose Irish history and politics need very little embellishment." She leaned in towards him. Her warm smile gave them back their agreeable intimacy.

Matt devoured every morsel of his succulent veal scallopini;

Mary Louise was equally thorough with her seafood risotto. *A woman with healthy appetites*, he thought, mesmerized by the way her red hair swayed as she spoke, how her dark green dress matched the colour of her eyes and displayed ample cleavage. Mary Louise drew furtive but admiring glances from other men in Trastevere, yet she seemed oblivious to her own beauty and the effect it was having on the men in the restaurant.

The waiter arrived with espressos and small glasses of grappa. Mary gave Matt a lascivious grin as she leaned across the table to stroke his cheek. "You are very funny," she said. "Am I violating your personal space?" she inquired teasingly.

"I am more than willing to have my personal space violated," he said, working to contain his breathing. "Violate away!"

Mary came quickly round the table, she rewarded him with a passionate, probing, lingering kiss. Then she went back to her chair, kicked off her shoes, and put one of her feet not so gently on his groin. "Still willing?" she grinned.

"And able," Matt replied, as her foot accomplished her objective. "So able, that it may shock the other diners."

"You can hold a hat over it," Mary laughed, enjoying the effect her foot had produced.

"Did anyone ever tell you that you are very naughty?"

"You can spank me if I'm so naughty." Her eyes narrowed and brightened in anticipated pleasure. "Can we go to your hotel? Now?"

The next morning, Matt awoke to find Mary wearing only one of his shirts, propped up with four pillows. She was reading his prized first edition of Yeats.

Mary looked over at the still sleepy Matt. "Now that we are more than acquaintances, I am examining my new book." She laughed at his immediate discomfort. "Carefully!" she added.

Mary reached under the covers, assessing Matt's state of readiness for more passion. "Well, I've certainly earned a read, if not ownership. Would you like me to read you a poem or arouse you in some other fashion?"

Her hand rested on him beneath the covers. Matt stirred. "A terrible beauty is born," she declared enthusiastically, and placed the Yeats gently on the bedside table.

"A terrible beauty, is it? I thought the proper Irish greeting was, 'May the rod rise up to meet you!'"

"That's *road*, not rod," Mary Louise Patricia O'Reilly giggled.

"Either way, it's rising up to meet you."

"I won't let you take liberties with the folk traditions of Eire," Mary Louise declared firmly. "But I intend to take full liberties with you."

To Matt's delight, she did just that.

CHAPTER EIGHTEEN

LAST FLIGHT

MATT BARELY MADE DUBLIN airport in time for his plane to New York. While the cabbie drove fiercely in the bucketing rain, Mary Louise and Matt hugged each other tightly in the back seat. Matt worried little about the flight to come. He did not know whether he would survive the cab ride. As he held Mary Louise, he wondered if it was possible that he could love someone so soon. His defences came up before he could answer his own question.

Then Matt, with Mary Louise at his side, dashed through the Dublin airport towards security. They ran past the banners with portraits of Ireland's four Nobel laureates in literature: George Bernard Shaw, Samuel Beckett, William Butler Yeats, and Seamus Heaney. He admired the achievement of this island nation of less than four million, producing four Nobel Laureates in literature. James Joyce was honoured with a banner although he never received the Nobel Prize in Literature, an affront the Irish chose to ignore, as well might the rest of the world.

A young woman thrust into his hand a pamphlet advocating the banning of Irish fur farming. He tucked the leaflet in his briefcase, not wanting to offend the earnest young protestor by discarding it. As they parted, Mary Louise kissed Matt passionately. She presented him with a wrapped gift which had the look and feel of several compact discs. He tucked it into his briefcase to open later when he wasn't rushing through security to make his plane.

"Usually, I read magazines," he told her. "I need to keep much of myself available to will the plane to keep flying, to hold the wings on, and, of course, for prayer."

"Liar, atheist," she'd replied, laughing. "You'll probably read a tedious thousand-page history of Ireland up there, and drink too much Scotch."

"You know far too much about me already," Matt said. "At nine thousand metres above sea level, I become a devout Catholic. I'm only an atheist while on solid ground."

"Just promise me you'll listen to the first twenty minutes. Then you can drink too much and flirt with the stewardess."

"I'd never do that," Matt replied.

"Liar again. Just listen to the first twenty minutes. Now kiss me and get on your damned plane."

As the Aer Lingus Airbus 340 carefully navigated its way from the gate to its assigned runway for takeoff, Matt tore the wrapping off his gift from Mary Louise. The cover of a colourful CD audiobook package read, in bold yellow letters: Jonathan Harr, *The Lost Painting: The Quest for a Caravaggio Masterpiece*, read by Campbell Scott. Matt flipped the box over in his hands as the Airbus thundered down the runway to the east, out over the Irish Sea, and began a long turn towards the northwest. Matt discovered six compact discs, six hours of unabridged listening.

Matt did as instructed. Now, reading the cover copy, he said a soft, "Got it," to himself, when he realized that the Lost Painting of Harr's book was the very same *Taking of Christ* that she'd taken him to view that very morning in the National Gallery. *The artist Caravaggio, the master of the Italian Baroque, was a genius, a revolutionary painter, and a man beset by personal demons*, it read.

The Italian van Gogh, Matt thought. *Hopefully without the self-mutilation. Four hundred years ago, he rose from obscurity to fame and wealth, but his rage finally led him to commit murder, forcing him to flee Rome, a haunted man. Today, Caravaggio scholars estimate that between sixty and eighty of his works are in existence. Somewhere, surely, a masterpiece lies forgotten in a storeroom or in a small parish church or hanging above a fireplace. There it hangs gazed upon by unknowing eyes mistaken for a mere copy.*

Matt also read the brief biography of the author, Jonathan Harr, and learned that his book *A Civil Action* had won the National Book Critics' Circle Award for Non-Fiction. Clearly that, plus being a staff writer at the *New Yorker* and the *New York Times Magazine*, suggested Harr could write powerfully and clearly and tell a compelling story.

Matt looked out the window as a subdued bell notified passengers that the seat belt sign had been switched off. They were above the rain-filled clouds, now smoothly heading west in a brilliant blue sky, flying toward the sun. Engrossed in the copy on the CD box, Matt had completely ignored his usual climb-out anxiety. Had it been bumpy? With this to encourage him, he pulled out his laptop and sound-dampening earphones and started to play disc one of *The Lost Painting.*

It began with an elderly British art historian, Dennis Maughan, dining in a small restaurant next to the Pantheon in Rome. As he listened to the fascinating story of the search for the lost Caravaggio unfold, Matt wondered about his own quest for his lost mother. This magnificent painting, *Taking of Christ,* lost for hundreds of years, shipped from nation to nation, dismissed as unimportant, had been finally restored to a place of reverence. He considered the restoration of his birth mother to a place of importance in his life.

The Airbus bumped gently across the edge of some invisible confluence of air currents. Matt was calm, almost unaware of the plane, as the story of the search for Caravaggio's lost masterpiece drew him further from his own reality. He was in a café in Rome, in a villa's archives, plunged into the mysteries of Caravaggio's patrons. Campbell Scott's voice flowed over him in a compelling, gentle torrent.

When Matt slid in the first CD of the six in the case Mary Louise had given him, he had been skeptical. *I'm not really a fine arts major type*, he thought. Still, the Caravaggio, the *Taking of Christ*, in the National Gallery, had a power, a force beyond any other painting in that gallery. To Matt's astonishment, over five hours later, he was still listening intently to the story of *The Lost Painting*. The pilot slowed the Airbus. They began their descent through innocent white clouds, to JFK in New York. Matt still had disc six to hear. He also had a one-hour flight to Toronto. And he had the diary.

Matt spent two impatient hours at Kennedy Airport before boarding an Air Canada CRJ for the last leg of his journey. He decided against listening to the last disc of *The Lost Painting*. It had to be savoured at leisure, not on the up-down flight of ninety minutes. After a completely uneventful flight, his Air Canada plane descended through the clouds and bumped onto the north runway of Toronto's Pearson airport. Matt was back home in Canada — and alive — again.

BOOK THREE

RETURN TO THE WORLD

Bidden or Unbidden
God is Present

Carl Jung, over his door while he lived, on his tombstone after his
death.

It has been said, time heals all wounds. I do not agree. The
wounds remain. In time, the mind, protecting its sanity, covers
them with scar tissue and the pain lessens. But it is never gone.

Rose Kennedy who endured the death of her son Joe in World
War II and the assassinations of both her son President John Fitzgerald Kennedy and her son Senator Robert Kennedy.

CHAPTER NINETEEN

NORAH'S DIARY

MATTHEW RETURNED TO QUARRY Island, his Fortress of Solitude, where he could read his ghost mother's diary in peace. My Book of Dreams. That was the name Norah had given her diary. The title appeared in her dreadful scrawl on the first page. When it was first placed in his hands in Dublin, her Book of Dreams felt heavy in Matt's grip. Weighty as it began, it seemed to grow heavier with each passing day as its unfilled dreams communicated their burdens to Matt.

What was it Langston Hughes, who had written about dreams, had said? *What happens to a dream deferred? Does it drop like a raisin in the sun? Or does it explode?*

Matt's dreams grew darker and heavier. Slowly, it dawned on him that the dreams were about his future and not his past. This obvious reality had been obscured by the tenacity, vigour, and restlessness of his search.

He opened the diary only to be confronted by a familiar and favourite poem. His long-departed ghost mother had begun her diary by writing out, in her impossible hand, William Butler Yeats's poem "The Second Coming" in its entirety. Matt's eyes teared as he read it. His spine tingled. Over the years, Yeats had surpassed all of the others to become Matt's favourite poet. Eliot, Hughes, Whitman, even Pound, had held sway, but as the years went by, it was Yeats who revealed his strength and staying power. Among all of Yeats's poems "The Second Coming" was, for Matt, his most powerful. And here it sat, as the preface to her diary, written out in her nearly illegible handwriting.

Turning and turning in the widening gyre
The falcon cannot hear the falconer
Things fall apart; the centre cannot hold;
Mere anarchy is loosed upon the world,
The blood-dimmed tide is loosed, and everywhere
The ceremony of innocence is drowned;
The best lack all conviction, while the worst
Are full of passionate intensity …

He read through the rest of the poem slowly. As Matt laboured through the diary entries, his eyes and mind adapted to the cramped writing. He struggled to read each word as it slowly unfurled itself in his mind's eye. Occasionally the trial and its aftermath poked through his memory. He was haunted by the girls who died and the murderer his jury had failed to convict. He locked the painful memories away in his mind and continued to read.

DECEMBER 29, 1951

Travelled to Dublin to see my sister and mother for Christmas.
Daniel stayed in London to study for his examinations for the
Fellowship in Surgery. Only in Ireland for four days but felt
suffocated by it. So glad to be back in London with Daniel and
at work. I know now that I could never return to live and work
in Dublin. It is a parochial small town compared to London. My
family barely accept that my work is important. Except Uncle
Patrick who sat next to me at Christmas Day dinner. He reads
everything I write and was very encouraging. Uncle Patrick is in

the government serving as a Cabinet minister. He told me good journalism is as important as his work. I made a secret journey to see my father who is estranged from our family. Felt like a spy travelling across Dublin by taxi and changing taxis several times. If my sister finds out, she will banish me from her home, the family, and the country. I would miss Uncle Patrick more than the others.

JANUARY 1, 1952

Today Daniel and I were married. We did not get married in a church. It was New Year's Day. We had the licence and we didn't want to wait another day. We convinced two chambermaids to serve as our witnesses. We got married in the Registry Office. Phillip joined us, although I know he would rather have been the groom than the best man. My beloved Daniel had operated on the son of the Register, so he had agreed in an instant to come in on the holiday to marry us. I am happier than I ever remember being. I love Daniel with all my heart. I know he loves me with his whole heart. He looked so handsome in his new suit from Austin Reed Tailors.

Matt began to imagine his mother sitting across from him in the screen porch of the Quarry Island cottage. He imagined her as she must have been in London at twenty-eight years of age. He imagined her and heard her voice in the diary. In Matt's imagination, Norah wore a colourful green-and-blue tweed suit. She had blonde bangs. She did not speak, but Matt began to read her diary entries aloud to give voice to her words.

FEBRUARY 2, 1952

Strange filing today from our correspondent in Havana, Cuba. Tropical storm in February. Earliest ever recorded. Is something odd happening to our planet's climate? Is our weather changing? Why would it change? I am resolved to learn far more about the weather. Apparently, the science is properly called meteorology.

"What are you reading?"

Harris stepped up to the outside deck and peered through the screen at Matthew.

"Sounds like a diary."

"It's my birth mother's diary. I was given it in Dublin. Her uncle arranged that it be left for me to find many years ago."

"Need your privacy?"

"No, actually. I'd like some company if you can bear a few more pages of her diary."

"Absolutely. Let me pour myself a glass of wine."

"Gin and tonic on the kitchen counter. And some lemons if you prefer. I'll have another one if you're pouring."

"Much better, two gin-and-tonics coming up."

When they appeared, grasped tightly in Harris's large hands, they were mostly gin with a substantial slice of lemon and a modest splash of tonic.

"Thank you. Here's her diary entry about her interview with Dr. Oppenheimer from 1952."

MARCH 14, 1952

Interviewed Dr. Robert Oppenheimer at Perro Caliente today in the desert of the southwestern United States after a very long and exhausting journey from London. He is a likeable man but difficult interview. He has spent so many years in the science of the atomic bomb, it is his conscience that has now come to the fore. It will not go well for him as he begins to oppose the last of the generals for a bigger bomb.

A maid served us tea. We sat in a strange garden in the desert. Flowers blossomed on the prickly arid cactus plants. At first, the dryness of it, the sharp plants with their jagged thorns thrust in all directions, struck me as harsh, almost ugly. After an hour, the shapes seemed more abstract. Picasso in nature. The brilliant flowers became small miracles.

Oppenheimer agreed to our interview reluctantly and with conditions. The most onerous condition was his insistence that I interview him at this ranch. I learned from his secretary that Dr. Oppenheimer had leased it in the 1930s and finally purchased it in 1944. We spent five long hours on horseback, me and my guide, Bill McSweeney, the owner of Los Pinos. Eager as my editor was for this interview, my poor thighs were chafed raw by the long ride. My nausea from the early stages of my pregnancy made for a difficult journey.

I allowed him to speak to me off the record for a time. His voice grew more emotional, less careful, and his passion focused and propelled his words. The most chilling of his insights into the second arms race, the hydrogen bomb race, was this: "We may be likened to two scorpions in a bottle, each capable of killing the other, but only at the risk of his own life."

I begged him to let me use this powerful image, but he firmly declined. "Not yet," he declared. "Not yet. Not while Senator McCarthy still reigns."

Matt said to Harris, "My mother would never know, that a year later, after her death, in a speech in New York, Oppenheimer used this analogy. It would be five more long years, in his inaugural William James Lecture at Harvard, four days after the death of Senator Joseph McCarthy, that a frail but still angry Robert Oppenheimer walked to the blackboard in the massive Sanders Lecture Theatre." Matt paused. "Silently, he wrote in chalk: R.I.P. No explanation was needed. McCarthy's ugly reign had finally ended. The tyrant senator was finally dead. And Oppenheimer was finally free to express his full views."

Harris nodded. "McCarthy. Ruined a lot of lives."

APRIL 3, 1952

I was given a new and exciting assignment. I am to travel to interview some of the rumoured frontrunners for this year's Nobel Prize. Most interested in tracking down Albert Schweitzer in Gabon. Author François Mauriac for Literature; Selman Abraham Waksman for Medicine; Felix Bloch of Stanford University in California and Edward Mills Purcell of Harvard University for Physics; and Archer John Porter Martin of the University of Harvard and Richard Laurence Millington Synge of Scotland for Chemistry.

What a glorious assignment. America, England, France, and Africa. If only Daniel would or could come with me. He is so consumed by his studies that he can focus on little else. His final exams are coming up soon and he is determined not simply to pass but to have the highest marks.

APRIL 10, 1952

Albert Schweitzer in London. Interviewed him in the ward of St. Bart's Hospital. He's the Missionary surgeon and founder of the Lambar Hospital in Gabon. A gentle but determined man with a philosophy, a concept of ethics he calls Reverence for Life. He seemed at home at St. Barts amidst the urgent activities of the hospital. Likely he's most at ease in his familiar hospital setting.

APRIL 23, 1952

Selman Abraham Waksman of Rutgers University in New Brunswick, New Jersey. He discovered streptomycin, the first antibiotic effective against tuberculosis. Daniel says this discovery is important to treating tuberculosis. He says millions of lives will be saved.

JULY 7, 1952

Today, I rode the last London tram. It was driven by John Cliff, deputy chairman of London Transport (LT), who began his career as a tram driver. Car number 1951. I took the full tour, which turned out to be some three hours in length. We were greeted at the New Cross depot by LT chairman, Lord Lathom, who declared, "In the name of Londoners, I say, Goodbye, old tram." It seemed a fitting obituary.

They all treated me very well. I am getting large. The pregnancy has made me awkward, but everyone made a fuss and found room for me to sit.

JULY 25, 1952

Today I arrived in Helsinki to cover the opening of the Olympic Games. It is very exciting to see so many athletes sporting their national costume. It proved to be a smooth flight of nearly four hours.

The Helsinki Olympic Games are now underway. For the first time Israel and the USSR are participating. Israel was only admitted to the UN three years ago. The Soviets insisted on their own Olympic Village. The Finns, a pragmatic nation with the Soviets armed to the teeth at their border, thought a separate village to be an excellent idea. No doubt much vodka was consumed in its consideration of this demand and the negotiation of terms and conditions.

Harris asked Matthew, "Did you know any of this?"

"Nothing. Until we capsized the catamaran, I believed Beth was my birth mother. I had no idea that my birth mother was Norah McCarthy."

He continued to read the diary aloud.

JULY 26, 1952

Today in the Village, I met the remarkable Hungarian marksman, Károly Takács. What a story. My editor promised me page one after he read it.

Károly's story begins in 1938. He was a member of the Hungarian national pistol shooting team. At twenty-eight, Károly was already ranked as an outstanding marksman. He was expected to win gold at the 1940 Olympics. But he was unable to participate. While serving as a sergeant in the Hungarian army, a defective grenade exploded in his pistol hand. The force of the explosion shattered his hand beyond any repair. The month of hospital recovery deepened his depression. The world darkened for everyone, not just Károly, as World War II forced cancellation of both the 1940 and 1944 Olympics.

In the spring of 1939, when Károly turned up at the National Hungarian Pistol Shooting Contest, his former competitors all offered condolences. Their presumption that Károly had come to watch was short-lived. Károly refused to be defeated by the loss of his shooting hand. Shooting with his left hand, Károly won the championship.

Nine years later, in London, Károly met the reigning world champion, Carlos Enrique Díaz Sáenz Valiente (what a name). He asked Károly why he had come to London. "To learn," was his reply.

After Károly beat Valiente for the gold medal, they met again on the podium. Valiente, wearing the silver medal, said to Károly, "You have learned enough."

Now, in Helsinki in 1952, Károly, at age forty-two, is competing again.

Harris said, "I wonder if Sophie knows this story. She's Hungarian. If she doesn't know it, she'll really like it."

AUGUST 17, 1952

Just returned from visiting the small coastal town of Lynmouth. It was devastated two nights ago by a catastrophic flood. The flood carried large boulders and rocks towards the town. It was a scene of extraordinary destruction. What terror must have gripped the people there? The flood struck in the night while they were in their beds. Many died. Homes were destroyed, bridges and roads torn away. We could not get the Minister of Defence to admit it, but there were unofficial sources indicating that the ministry had secretly carried out experiments in the making of rain by the seeding of clouds. This must have been one of the most beautiful places before the flood. Apparently, for 200 years it had been a Devon seaside resort and celebrated thusly. Now it is ruined, and the lives of those who live there have been ruined, as well. When I saw the town, I prayed, which I do not do very often, for all those who had lived within it.

AUGUST 18, 1952

Daniel and I fought. He was angry that I had put myself and our unborn child at risk by going to Lynmouth. I am too weary to argue. Daniel respects my right to work. He told me he doesn't want a stay-at-home wife just a stay-alive wife. He checked his anger when he saw my tears.

SEPTEMBER 1, 1952

Interviewed Picasso today. Oddly charming but difficult man. Flirted with me although I am over eight months pregnant and as large as a lorry. Picasso, sufficiently moved by events, has painted a Peace painting, half of his War and Peace pair. In his painting, the inversion of birds and fishes has the fish bowl containing birds and the birdcage is filled with fish. I found myself oddly compelled by its power.

"My God," remarked Harris. "She even interviewed Picasso. What an amazing time she had."

"Until she died at a very young age."

SEPTEMBER 23, 1952

I watched the young woman descend the gangplank of the Cunard ocean liner, the Queen Elizabeth, with her husband, Charles Chaplin. Their four children followed them at a pace. No longer the thin little tramp of the early movies, Chaplin had thickened and filled out into a white-haired man. I knew that this was his fourth marriage and Oona O'Neill's first marriage. He was 54 and she was 17 when they married. Of Chaplin's four wives, Oona was only the third youngest. Two of her predecessors were 16 when he married them. I watched Oona O'Neill with a mixture of curiosity and envy. At 28, she is exactly my age. Oona O'Neill wore a spectacular hat for her arrival. It sported the most astonishing peacock feather that glittered in the morning sun.

Very difficult for me to move about. Very pregnant and eager for the baby to come.

Matt put the diary down on a side table. "I think my drink needs refreshing."

"Agreed. Mine, too. Would it be too much trouble to augment the drinks with a little food?"

Matt nodded his agreement before collecting the glasses and taking them to the kitchen. Harris followed him inside, talking the entire time.

"I wasn't one for Chaplin's humour," Harris said. "Or his taste in young women. But I admired his opposition to Nazism. Did you ever see his film *Modern Times*?"

"I don't think so."

"Brilliant satire. You have to remember it was a time when many

American corporations such as Ford and IBM were profiting from the Nazi regime. American politicians for the most part wanted to keep America out of 'Europe's war.'"

Matt started to put together a plate of cheese, bread, and cold cuts. "He got on the wrong side of Edgar Hoover too, didn't he?"

"Not to mention the US Attorney General at the time, James McGranery. By revoking his reentry permit, McGranery stripped Chaplin of his ability to travel back to the United States. It wasn't until a year later that the US finally came to view Nazism as clearly as Chaplin had. And then only because of Pearl Harbor. It's a shameful history. Took them twenty years before they allowed Chaplin back in."

"I remember in the seventies when the Academy gave Chaplin a special Oscar. And the Queen knighted him. He was an old man by the time vindication finally came his way."

"Watch who you're calling old," Harris jokingly harrumphed.

Matt smiled. "To think that at the time my mother was watching Oona and Chaplin descend that liner in 1952, the family of nations was beginning to heal their wartime wounds. Germany and Japan had been accepted into the International Monetary Fund. Reparations were being paid to Israel. The United Nations building started in New York City. But under the surface, horrible things too. The arms race. The Cold War. The hydrogen bomb. My mother saw the best and the worst of the world at a pivotal time."

Matt went silent.

"What are you thinking?" Harris said, concern in his voice.

"If only my mother had lived to share those reminisces with me. And so much more."

Harris picked his drink, nodding at the door. "Should we go outside?"

"Yes."

"Tell me, Matt, how are you doing?" Harris said, as they headed outside. "Reading your mother's diary entries, it has to have an impact, emotionally. What is your impression of the woman who's being revealed in these pages?"

"She was a remarkable and determined journalist. She had passion for life, and for Daniel. I wish I'd known her." Matt paused, jumbled thoughts crowding each other. "Beth was a real mother to me. For Norah, I wonder if her work would always have come first."

"You don't have to choose between Beth and Norah," Harris replied.

Matt said, "It's a challenge to know someone who has been gone so long."

"Time heals wounds. Give yourself time to absorb this newly revealed dimension of your life."

"Thank you." Matt picked up the diary again. "I'm struggling but working to find my way."

SEPTEMBER 25, 1952

Our beautiful baby son was born at 10 AM. Daniel was with me for the birth although his presence upset the matrons. They tell me the baby is large at 10 lbs, 6 ounces and healthy. We will call him Matthew. Now, I must sleep to regain my strength.

"This is you being born! That's amazing," Harris said. "Quite odd to read about one's own birth, especially in a sixty-year-old diary."

NOVEMBER 1, 1952

I have glimpsed the end of the world. Today, the Americans detonated the first hydrogen bomb. It is vastly more powerful than the atomic bombs that were dropped on Hiroshima and Nagasaki. It is a terrifying weapon.

I am on a small Japanese fishing vessel, the Daigo Fukuryu Maru, near the Marshall Islands, with only the fishermen and

*my journalist friend Oshi, who works for Yomiuri Shimbun in
Tokyo. Oshi arranged this trip. Although the fishermen stick to
their nets and the hard work of fishing, I would not be here
without Oshi, nor would I feel safe as a woman alone on a fishing boat. But Oshi is my guide and protector. Oshi reported on
the horrors of Nagasaki and Hiroshima. He is passionate about
avoiding nuclear war.*

*I fear for my baby, who is already 36 days old. Daniel is very
upset that I accepted this assignment from The Times. But I
must tell this story. The hydrogen bomb will take our world
back to war. It will not make us safe.*

*Oppenheimer believes his bomb is dreadful. He did not want
it to be built.*

*The explosion came early. Not long after dawn we witnessed
an enormous fireball, like the sun exploding. It appeared above
the western horizon.*

*After the fireball, silence descended. At seven minutes there
came a dull rumbling sound like distant thunder. We had witnessed the detonation of the world's first hydrogen bomb. These
few fishermen had witnessed a bomb Dr. Oppenheimer forecast
to be 1000 x more destructive than the atomic bombs dropped on
Hiroshima and Nagasaki.*

*White dust began to fall on the deck of the Daigo Fukuryu
Maru eight minutes later. At first, the white dust was mingled
with a light rain, which grew heavier. At the worst moment, the
rain and dust became so heavy that we could not breathe easily
or see. After nearly three hours, it stopped falling.*

*When it stopped, the crew swept the white sludge into the
sea. Later that day, most of the crew became ill. Some vomited.
Others were so fatigued they were unable to set their nets or to
haul them back in. Ulcers appeared that same night on the skin
of several of the fishermen.*

Matthew paused. He now realized why his mother died a young woman. He looked at Harris. "Norah died of radiation poisoning." After a few moments, he collected himself and continued.

I have not had a skin reaction. My long-sleeved blouse covered my arms, but I am nauseated and exhausted. It will be four days before we reach port. The fishermen are all very sick from the radiation. I am made more ill by the thought of how our species has uniquely gained the ability to end all life on earth. Are we mad with our lust for destructive power?

I am so many thousands of miles from home and my baby. Will I live to see my husband? My son?

NOVEMBER 2, 1952

I have never experienced nausea as severe as this. I kept convulsing and retching. Am I dying?

Matthew stopped. They sat quite still and quiet.

"Your mother was a remarkable woman."

"I was given a number of clippings, in addition to the diary," Matt said. "She interviewed some pretty impressive people, including Richard Doll."

"I'm afraid I don't know who he was."

"Richard Doll published the first paper in the *British Medical Journal* that proved smoking cigarettes caused lung cancer," Matt replied.

"Did this woman, Norah, your mother, did she smoke?"

"Everyone did."

"Did you?" Harris asked.

"No. You?"

"Started in high school. Continued in university. Stopped when I graduated law school. I think it's time for me to go, Matt. Thank you for sharing the diary with me. Remarkable document. More remarkable was the woman who wrote it, who turns out to be your mother."

After Harris left for his cottage, Matt read an interview with Sir Richard Doll on the BBC news website. The discussion ranged over his entire life and work. Much of the interview confirmed what Matt already knew from his mother's diary. Doll began by noting the rapid increase in the incidence of lung cancer. His first idea of a cause had been vehicle exhaust, but then he turned his attention to cigarettes. His path-breaking study of 1950 suggested the link, and the 1954 study confirmed it.

"The thing about lung cancer was the mortality was increasing at such a rapid rate. At the beginning of the twentieth century, it had been a rare disease, and between the 1920s and the 1950s, the mortality from lung cancer had increased more than 20 times. Something was happening."

What took Matt's breath away was the final question from the BBC interviewer: "What worries keep you awake at night now?"

Sir Richard Doll's answer stunned Matt. Here, at ninety-two, was what kept him awake at night. Not his own mortality, not regret, not even pride, but "global warming is the most important and worrying issue scientifically. I can't over-emphasize the importance of that. We really aren't doing enough to control it. It's CO_2. It's burning fossil fuels. No question about that."

And so, thought Matt, *the scientist whose early career focused on uncovering the perils of smoking tobacco ended his life worrying about global warming. He's been right a second time.*

The next morning Matt became absorbed reading his mother's interview with Robert Oppenheimer. He also became obsessed with her subject. Before he could understand his lost mother's interview, he needed to know more about this man, who led the creation of the atomic bomb and witnessed its destructive power. When he opposed the development of the hydrogen bomb, he was hounded from his post as a traitor.

Matt was particularly taken with a comment by journalist and historian, Priscilla McMillan. "The story I tell is an old one. The story of what happens when some institution, a church, say, or a government, decides to rid itself of someone that's becoming an annoyance or threat to it. Or that wants to change course without saying so openly ... The case of Robert Oppenheimer, the deviations from what we consider basic rules of our democracy, were so egregious, that even today, half a century later, the story still stirs our consciences. Makes us wonder what it was all about. It was about many things. One of them was our government's decision to move to a new and deadlier level with the nuclear arms race without telling the American people."

The sheer magnitude of the atomic arms race staggered Matt. By the mid-1950s, atomic testing released vast quantities of radioactive isotopes into the atmosphere. Between the Russians and the Americans, over fifteen hundred bombs were detonated. By 1960, the United States and the USSR each had thousands of atomic weapons. Strontium 90, an isotope, began appearing in baby teeth of children. Voice of Women and other peace groups began collecting mother's milk for testing. Protests against bomb testing in the atmosphere accelerated, but a test ban treaty took many years to achieve. Matt remembered that Beth Rice had been deeply involved in the peace movement when he was a very young child.

Matt's optimism, nurtured through his childhood by Beth, who protected him from Daniel's growing cynicism, was ebbing away. His fear of the fragility of life threatened to overwhelm him. *The little girl in the park, wearing pink. Are we all that little girl waiting to be carried away by evil?* The darkness consumed him.

CHAPTER TWENTY

SECURING THE ISLAND

STUNNED BY THE ONSLAUGHT of events and the discovery of a mother he did not yet fully comprehend, Matt returned to his calming routines of preparing for survivalist isolation on Quarry Island. Norah's diary had been set aside. He had read it, but stopped short of the final entries. He wanted time to reflect on who she had been before he read of her final days. What would be her meaning for him, in his life. He thought of calling Mary Louise. He thought about her often and with great affection, but he could not bring himself to make the call. He didn't want her to hear doubt and defeat in his voice.

Norah's diary had set in motion an emotional undersea tsunami. Quietly, without alerting the island neighbours or alarming his children, Matt went about preparing the cottage for winter and for the Armageddon that might accompany the breakdown of industrialized society: climate change, rolling disasters, and the subsequent panic.

Matt ran a copper wire through the water intake line, a hundred and fifty feet of barely buried plastic pipe that ran down to the beach well. The copper wire snaked through the full length of the intake line within the plastic pipe itself, a small electric current to keep the water in the pipe from freezing. He took pride in having been particularly clever. Instead of wiring the current through the main breaker box, he'd purchased a solar-powered battery charger from Canadian Tire and hooked it up to a battery.

He had six back-up batteries and six back-up solar panels. As long as the sun shone — something that could be counted on, despite Armageddon — the batteries would be charged and he'd have running water. Matt replaced the old pump with a new, smaller, electric pump that could be run either from the main-line current, as long as that lasted, or from the sequence of batteries. Running water, the foundation of a civilization, as the Romans had known two thousand years earlier, would continue to be his. Not as clever or as long-lasting as the vast stone aqueduct of the Roman Empire, but functional. The Romans didn't have to countenance minus twenty in the winter.

At the annual Green Living Show in Toronto, Matt found a manufacturer of solar-powered hot water tanks. One thousand dollars and a day's labour later, solar panels adorned his cottage roof. They were hooked up to a very well insulated tank in his basement. The solar system provided an abundance of hot water. He left the previous hot water tank hooked up to the main breaker panel — it seemed wasteful to discard it — but drained it and turned it off at the breaker. The old tank could be used to supplement the new solar-powered system if necessary.

Matthew wondered briefly whether Harris was watching his activities. He said nothing, if he was.

Other measures followed. His friend Don gave him a battery-free triple LED Torch. "It's really just a windup flashlight from Restoration Hardware," he explained.

The box promised *No batteries or bulbs to ever replace*. Apparently, the combination of LED lithium stage technology and a simple crank handle would create thirty minutes of illumination some five hundred times. Matt's skepticism eroded as the simple crank-it-up-light worked perfectly. He sought out Restoration

Hardware and bought a dozen more windup lights, two for each room in the cottage.

Food was much more problematic. But here, he made progress by installing a low energy freezer in the basement, wired to the solar back-up system and batteries. He filled it with a supply of basic staples that could carry him for a year.

He cut five cords of wood and stacked it behind the cottage. As winter approached, he intended to stack the wood in the screen porch which he would line with plastic before covering the screen windows with plywood shutters. A small, electric space heater would keep the wood warm and dry.

He updated his fishing gear. Fishing with a hook would be folly in times of desperate survival, so he purchased several nets with a small mesh opening. His plan was to tow them behind the sailboat — should gasoline be in short supply. The nets would scoop up enough fish to fill his freezer. He felt particularly good about this idea. He bought an ice auger, so he could carve a hole through the winter ice to fish.

The small shelf-lined room in the basement was his larder; he filled it with canned goods and staples, enough ground coffee for a year and enough Campbell's soups for two.

The one issue that bothered him a little was access to and from the island. With the stout twenty-four-foot Limestone, he could handle any weather, from spring break up to fall freeze-up. He had snowshoes and cross-country skis that would allow him to get off the island once the lake was frozen. There would be a period — and he'd discussed this with Buck at the marina — each spring and fall, where it was not possible to get on or off because the ice was too thin to walk on and yet too dangerous to sail in.

He fretted about this. That stormy season when the ice was too thin to cross would occur twice a year, probably for as much as six weeks, so there would be twelve weeks when nothing could reach him and he could not reach out. What if he had a heart attack or a critical illness? What if one of his children needed him? What if he ran out of some vital supply? He'd walked the entire island, thinking there might be a large enough open space for a helicopter to land, but there wasn't. There wasn't a single spot that met, as he recalled them, the ministry requirements of one-hundred square metres of clear space. In his day, they put helipads everywhere. But there would be no helipad on Quarry Island; there were simply too many trees and too narrow a beach.

Matt talked to the only person he knew who had seriously considered spending the winter on Quarry Island, Jim, the engineer, two cottages to the west along the beach.

"Maybe a small hovercraft could get you across the Bay in the bad seasons," Jim said, sounding unconvinced.

Hovercrafts were not only noisy, they were enormously consumptive of fuel, not to mention their price tags, which were exorbitant. Matt dismissed the idea. If he did indeed hunker down on Quarry Island, he'd just have to last through those inaccessible periods with the supplies he had on hand.

He reviewed his progress. He had, as long as satellites lasted, a way of accessing all the information in the world online. He'd converted most of his power needs to solar powered batteries and had laid in a large supply. He had secured the water on an all-season basis. He had, and he thought this was a particular detail to be proud of, enough Septo-Bac to keep the septic tank going for a decade. No one had ever bought a full case of Septo-Bac before. The hardware store, although not persuaded that he was in fact the operator of a church camp, still took his order and delivered the case.

On the more positive side, he contemplated his Scotch coup. He had cleaned out one last full case of eighteen-year-old Glenlivet from the Summerhill liquor store. It was all they had. He added it to the earlier stash — less aged, only twelve years — that he had garnered from the store in Honey Harbour. It cost him a modest fortune, but what use would money be after the power went down? At least he'd have his favourite Scotch. He had his twenty tanks of propane, his solar panels, his array of batteries, his cases of Scotch. What else did he need?

When he wasn't consumed by preparedness planning, inner voices nagged at him. He'd drifted over the years, gone from being engaged with the world to finding ways of cutting himself off from it. Of hunkering down on this island. His son had teased him, "Your survivalist phase, Pops."

"I just need a winter," he mumbled to himself. *A winter to heal, to find my way back.*

He stopped listening to the hourly news, once an obsession of his. He couldn't bear to listen to it. He read small, contained, snippets of the news online. The murdered girls continued to haunt his dreams. He was haunted by the image of a girl in pink in the park. On the rare times he went back to the city, he felt overwhelmed, afraid. He wondered what Norah would think of him. His mother had been so engaged with the world and its horrors, a world that killed her.

Would the struggle to survive winter on Quarry Island be enough to fully occupy his mind? Matt didn't know. He did know that he was running away from the world. It seemed the only safe refuge.

The ringing phone startled him. "Matthew Rice," he answered.

"Hello Matthew. It is Dr. Bergman. How are you?"

Matthew hesitated, "Unsettled. My trip to Dublin proved productive but troubling."

"Let's start with productive. Did you learn more about your birth mother, Norah?"

"Yes, I did. And I was given clippings of her work, she was a journalist, and her diary."

"Tell me about her."

"She was a journalist in London. Young, but a rising star. She met my father when he was doing his British Fellowship in the early 1950s. She travelled the world covering stories. They married on New Year's Day in 1952. I was born in September of that year."

"Have you read her diary?"

"Most of it. I have been dreading reading the final entries, but I will soon. I had one other thing happen in Dublin. I met someone."

"Who did you meet?"

"Mary Louise O'Reilly is her name. Met her at the National Library. There was an exhibit on the life and works of W.B. Yeats, my favourite poet."

"Someone who might be special?"

"Yes, she might be very special, but she lives in Boston and has a PhD to finish."

"Sounds like you're hesitating. Did she make you feel happy?"

"Yes, she did."

They spoke for the rest of the hour. Matthew said more than he intended about both Mary Louise and his plan to spend the winter on Quarry Island.

"Our time is up, Matthew. I'm reluctant to give direct advice. Generally, you must find your own way. I *will* tell you that when you speak of Mary Louise you sound happy and keen about life. When you speak about the winter on Quarry Island you do not. It is your choice, but in this matter I suggest you follow your hopes not your fears."

"Thank you, Doctor. I'm smiling and agreeing with your advice."

CHAPTER TWENTY-ONE

NIGHT JOURNEY

BEFORE HE CRAWLED UNDER the warm, soft blanket adorned with silly moose caricatures that covered his lonely bed, Matt closed all the windows around the cottage. He secured them for the coming storm. The wind already howled and the clouds were low and dark. There would be no moon or stars tonight, only a brutal storm from the west.

He slept fitfully. He heard noises. Not acorns dropping on his wooden porch; he thought he heard voices and then there was a pounding on his door. Maybe the wind and the storm waves had taken his boat off the mooring again. Another "unbreakable" line had given lie to its maker's claims, Harris was coming to tell him. That had happened before, only once, but he'd replaced the chain mooring line and the heavy cement anchor block, so it didn't seem likely.

But he got up and sat on the side of the bed. He looked at his watch; it was four AM. Now he could really hear voices over the crazy wind. One was urgently calling his name. With a start, Matt recognized it as Harris. He got up and pulled on his shorts and a sweater.

When he unlocked the sliding patio door, three people rushed inside, dripping rain. Harris, alongside a young neighbour and his six-year-old daughter — "the new islanders" everyone called them, unable to remember their names. They'd bought a cottage on Quarry Island months earlier. There was no visible wife and mother, rumours had her dead from cancer. No one wanted to ask. She was certainly gone.

The father sat and held his daughter, who was wrapped in a blanket. She moaned, clearly in extreme pain.

"Since when do you lock your door?" Harris growled.

"Since the trial," Matt mumbled. "What's going on?"

"The girl is very sick. You are the healthcare guy, so we came," Harris said.

I was a manager in health care, Matt thought. *I'm not a doctor.* But he reached out instinctively to put his hand on the young girl's forehead. She was on fire. Even with his own children's high fevers, he'd never felt anything like this. She was almost doubled over in pain. "How long has she been like this?" he asked her father.

"She got the fever earlier in the day. It got very severe after dinner and the pain ... I didn't know what to do. Gave her some Children's Tylenol. It was all we had. It helped for a few hours, but she's in agony now." He paused as he hugged his daughter closer. "She vomited everything up and now there's just bile."

Matt looked out past them at the waves crashing on the beach and towards the boats pounding against their moorings. He couldn't actually see the boats; he could imagine their struggle against the massive waves. The four of them huddled together in the cottage, the impossible weight of the storm upon them. Howling wind and crashing waves. Matt's attention came back to the little girl, not moaning now, but crying in pain. Small cries, almost animal-like. Her face twisted in agony.

He did what he always did when faced with a medical emergency. They all made fun of him in the family. His younger brother was a doctor. Matt always reached out to him, no matter what the time or occasion. It was an understanding they had across thirty years. Matt could do health policy, but if anyone was really sick, he called his brother James.

Now he speed-dialled his brother's cellphone. James was a family doctor in a small town, a full three days drive to the west. Matt called because he trusted his brother. In all those long years, with everything from poison ivy to cancer scares to heart attacks in the family, his brother had never let him down, had never been wrong. James had become an excellent and thoughtful doctor. And his brother's cellphone, like his own, was never turned off. Never. Nor was it ever far from reach.

He knew his brother was at the family cottage fifteen hundred kilometres away to the west, on the border of Manitoba and Ontario, near Kenora. He could see the cottage at West Hawk Lake. Matt could imagine his brother's cellphone echoing in the dark of the family cottage. His brother answered on the second ring. Doctors' training. The ability to countenance only shallow sleep. Two decades of emergency room call rotation and three teen-aged daughters. One slept shallow or not at all.

"Yes?"

"It's Matt," he said. "I'm at the cottage at Quarry. Sorry for calling so late. I need your advice."

His brother moved him along with a doctor's mumble. "It's okay. What is it?"

"It's a little girl," he looked at the father. "Six years old. She's in agony. She's got an extremely high fever."

"How long?"

Matt gave him as much of the detail as he could, and then put the father on the phone. The father answered a series of questions and then handed the phone back.

"You don't have very much time," James said. "It's her appendix. Sounds like it's on the verge of rupture or has already ruptured. She needs rapid surgical attention. You need to get her off the island."

Matt's thoughts instantly flashed to the waves he could hear crashing on the beach and the unyielding blackness of the night. He'd only tried to get off Quarry Island twice at night, once with a big moon, and the second time to pick up a guest who had come late. With a calm lake and a big bright moon, it had been all right. He could see the buoys that marked the reefs and shoals all the way round to the marina. And that had lulled him into the false sense of security that took him out on a night as dark as this, but without the wind or the storm. That night, he'd torn the propeller off, not on the last rock but the first one. He had savaged it beyond repair on the first easy rock that he hadn't seen, because he had no goddamned idea where he was in the dark.

That was the previous boat, the eighteen-footer. He'd had nothing on it to navigate, not even a depth finder. The Limestone had a GPS and sonar, but he'd never used them at night. He had been playing with it, rehearsing, thinking that someday he might actually need them to get off the island at night, but he hadn't done it. He'd worked it out. He had gone through the motions, carefully programming in all the buoys and the route. That would have to be enough tonight.

"It's 4:30 in the morning," he said to his brother. "What if we wait until the first light, wait until dawn?"

James was always careful with words. In his whole life, Matt had never heard his brother use the words *die* or *death*, even when their own father was clearly dying. He was a doctor always gentle with words, always understated. Professional distance, coolness. "I don't think that would be a good idea, the waiting." His brother's tone gave it all away.

Matt knew what that tone meant without asking. He asked the question anyway. He asked it even though the little girl's father stood right there. "How long do we have?" *How long does she have?* is what he really meant to ask. *How long before she's dead?*

"She needs to be somewhere really good in a hurry. In the next hour, hour and a half at the outside. Longer than that is not good." James didn't need to say it twice. Not good was what he said when their uncle was diagnosed with cancer. Not good was a life clock ticking away fast.

"I take it you don't mean the nearest local hospital," Matt said, taking care with his words in front of the father and daughter. One hour. Even if he could get her off the island, it was an hour and forty minutes to Toronto by road, and there was no ambulance waiting at the pier. This was the lake country, not the city. "Two hours?"

"Two hours is probably too long. You must do it in an hour and a half if she is to have a decent chance."

His brother had never been to Quarry Island. Had no idea how impossible the journey he insisted upon would be. Matt thanked his brother and hung up.

A step at a time, Matt thought. *Stay cool. Take it a step at a time.* He needed help now and he needed speed. He thought about a helicopter. And immediately remembered that even in daylight, there was no conceivable space for a helicopter to land on Quarry. The trees overhung the beach, which was too narrow. There was no clearing on the island. They needed to move the child by boat to Honey Harbour, and then rapid transport from there to a serious hospital.

Matt dialled 911. *No time*, he thought. *Not enough time.* Fear welled up in him. He didn't know who he'd be speaking to, but he did know they could patch him through, if he was persuasive enough, to the emergency medical dispatcher. To the Ministry of Health air force. To a fighting chance for this critically ill girl.

It'd been fifteen long years since Matt actually had responsibility for these things, but he still remembered how they worked. He could never really forget the heady days of real authority and real responsibility, the weight of it never fully lifted. He still remembered the voice he needed: a steady voice, not to show the fear, not to let the agony of the little girl and the terror in her father's eyes shake him.

He needed his own professional voice back. But he was nervous. He needed the voice of authority. He needed the voice that the trauma of the trial had stolen from him. Perhaps he could not find that voice again. There was a time when a single, plastic card in his wallet held all the key numbers at the Ministry of Health. The keys to the kingdom. In those days, the buck stopped with him. Ministers came and went. He stayed.

Matt got through the first hurdle. He told the 911 operator what was happening and where he was. Then he declined his offer to speak to Emergency Medical Dispatch on his behalf. "Let me speak to them," Matt said. Then he shaded a little bit. "I used to work there," he added.

On a normal operating day, he had been a long distance from Emergency Medical. On a normal day, he went to Cabinet committees' meetings with his Minister not to Emergency Medical Dispatch. But he was counting on someone there being old enough to remember. As he spoke, he realized that getting the child to the boat or the boat to the dock was going to be an extremely difficult task. He also noticed that Harris was gone from the room. The storm howled, venting its full fury on the swaying trees outside. The rain pounded on the roof and windows hard, violent, dark and ugly. Matt felt a rising terror. Part of his mind screamed, *You can't do this. You will die.* The other voice, the calmer voice, told him to take one step at a time. It told him that he couldn't lose another little girl.

His mind came back to the call and the voice he needed.

"My name is Matthew, Matthew Rice," he said to the emergency air ambulance dispatcher once patched through.

"Yes." The dispatcher had an older voice, its youth and vigour worn away by too many years.

"I'm on Quarry Island in Severn Sound in southern Georgian Bay with a critically ill young child. It is island 40 and we are Lot number 1822," Matt instructed.

"Yes." Again, there was a pause.

"How long have you worked there?" Matt asked.

"Twenty-three years."

"Does my name mean anything to you?" Matt asked directly.

And in that smallest of seconds, Matt heard the dispatcher's tone change. "Yes, Deputy."

You could leave the Ministry of Health — years could pass, decades could pass, most of a lifetime could pass — but for those who remained, those who had served with him, he would always be Deputy. He had never really left the Ministry of Health.

Now, Matt was deliberately vague. "I'm being told," implying by someone who would know, "this little girl needs to be on the roof of the Hospital for Sick Kids ninety minutes from now." Precision was essential. Authority flowed from precision. And calm understatement. These essential principles came back to Matt.

There was a pause. "Is there any place for a chopper to land on your island?" the dispatcher asked.

"No. Is there a helipad in Honey Harbour?" Matt asked.

"Just a minute," the dispatcher said, clearly hitting keys on his computer. "The nearest helipad is Port Severn, fifteen kilometres away." More clicking of keys, and a pause. "I've got good news and some not so good news," the dispatcher continued. "I've got a medivac chopper at the Royal Barrie Hospital, just dropped off a traffic accident victim. It's just about to be airborne empty back to Toronto. I could reroute it to you. And the not so good news, there's no ceiling at Port Severn. No ceiling anywhere north of Barrie."

No ceiling. The words hit him like a sledgehammer. The memory of no ceiling and its fatal consequences came back to him. It had happened fifteen years earlier, but he still remembered the inquest as though it was yesterday, every miserable hour of it. "Do you remember North Bay Memorial?"

The dispatcher had the same thought he did. "I testified at that inquest, Deputy."

It came back, all of it, every ugly moment. Eight-year-old boy crossing the street is hit by a car right in front of the North Bay Memorial Hospital. Three times Emergency Medical dispatched the medivac plane from its base in Sudbury, and three times, flight rules said the ceiling was too low and the plane was turned back. They never told the pilots the condition of the child because those are the rules. After the third attempt, the child dies. There's an inquest. Matt testifies, the dispatcher testifies, everybody goddamned testifies, but it doesn't do a bit of good, because the eight-year-old boy is still dead.

Why the no-tell rule? A decade earlier there had been another inquest. The pilots broke the ceiling rules. They had broken all of the rules because they knew a life depended on it. The resulting crash had killed everyone on that plane: two nurses, a doctor, two patients, and the pilots themselves. They had taken seven lives, including their own, by their actions. After that, the pilots were not told.

After the North Bay Memorial inquest, Matthew briefed his minister. In the interest of safety of the pilots and their patients, pilots are not to be told the condition of the patient, lest it encourage them to break flight rules.

No ceiling on this night would be a death sentence for the little girl, just as it had been fifteen years earlier.

Matt asked the dispatcher if there's been a change of the policy. He answered right back. "The policy hasn't changed since your day, Deputy. We don't tell the pilots."

A silence descended on the line. The howl of the storm came to the foreground, ugly and defiant. Matt knew he needed to break the rules. It was the only way.

Matt reached into his past for his own rule one: getting things done in the world. There were strict rules. There were always strict rules. All large organizations must have a forest of rules. And then there's always a way around the rules. But it was tricky; the organization only works, and the world is only orderly, if people follow the rules.

In governments, there are always severe penalties for rule-breaking. Careers end. Sometimes lives are lost. And there was always another inquest. The howl of the press, the pounding of the Opposition, and the public hunger for someone to be held accountable — a scapegoat for the reality that large systems fail and people make risky judgements There were also times when rules had to be broken. Times like these.

"I know this is out-of-the-box," Matt said to the dispatcher. "But would you patch me through to the pilot?"

There was a slight hesitation. Matt knew that the dispatcher was thinking that he was close to retirement and his pension, but there was no rule prohibiting patching someone through to the pilot. The rule says nothing about someone telling the pilot the condition of the patient. Or her age.

"Would you patch me through to the pilot?" Matt said again, pushing at the dispatcher's hesitation. "Take yourself out of the loop?"

Deference to authority, even to authority from long ago, won out. "Yes, I can do that, Deputy. Hold."

The line went not dead, but quiet. When it came back, there was the noise of the helicopter, the thump-thump-thump of the rotors.

Matt went first into the noise. "Is this the pilot?" he said, trying to imagine himself in the cockpit of the helicopter. He needed to convince the pilot to take a huge risk, a career-ending risk. Just as

Matt was thinking of the man, the pilot, to his surprise a woman's voice came on.

"Yes," she answered. "I'm on route to Port Severn, but if you have somewhere to put down in Honey Harbour, I'll head there."

"Have they told you about the ceiling?" Matt asked.

"Affirmative," she said, in a military tone, clipped almost mechanical. Then, more bluntly, "There is no ceiling."

"I need to tell you this little girl doesn't have —" He hesitated. He changed direction to the affirmative. "She needs to be on the roof of Sick Kids in ninety minutes."

There was a pause. "She has ninety minutes?"

"Yes," answered Matt, "at the outside." Then he asked, "Have you been with Emergency Medical long?"

"First year."

Damn, he thought. *Rookie*. This rattled him. His heart sank. First year people don't take chances. Whole career goes up in smoke. Long service people don't take chances. He needed someone in the middle. "And before?"

"I started with the US Air Force. The 53rd Weather Recon," she said. "Then Canadian Forces Sea Kings and then the North Sea, commercial choppers." Her tone was firm, strong, and military. No nonsense.

"Canadian Helicopters," Matt said, remembering who flies helicopters over the North Sea.

"Yes," she said. "Oil platforms, day and night, storm or not."

Matt's mind was still stuck on Weather Recon. The 53rd. Air Force. A faint memory. Then it tumbled out. "Hurricane Hunters. You flew the C-130s."

"In twenty-two hurricanes," the pilot replied.

"Only twenty-two?"

"Quite enough."

Matt knew in his soul that God was with this little girl this night. This was the right pilot, probably the only pilot, for this impossible night. "The pad is in Port Severn."

"I know," she said. "Fifteen kilometres from Honey Harbour. If there's a big enough space in Honey Harbour —"

"I remember," he said. And he did remember, forty metres by forty metres. This small detail had returned through the years. Government was about seeing the big picture while remembering the small details.

"If there's a big enough space in Honey Harbour and you can tell me how to get there, I will be there. Just find me that place." There was no maybe in her tone. No equivocation. It was a command.

Matt's mind raced. He was in Honey Harbour all the time to get papers and food, but he'd never explored the village. The road in front of the marina wasn't wide enough and there were too many trees. Up the road, there is the school. With a school yard.

"There's a school, maybe 100 metres from the marina, to the northeast. I have GPS on the boat. I can send you the exact coordinates when I get there. The school yard is large enough — they play soccer." He comes back to it. "And the ceiling?"

The pilot breaks off her coolness just long enough to let Matt hear her determination. "After the hurricanes and the oil platforms, I spent four years landing Sea Kings on moving ships," she said. "If you find me a place to land, I will land. Let me worry about the ceiling. We are already on route. I am not flying at cruise. I have the hammer down. You get that child there in the next fifteen minutes."

Nothing more for him to say. He gave the pilot his cell number so she could reach him. She repeated it loudly so her co-pilot could write it down.

The phone went dead.

He switched the cell to vibrate and buttoned it into his shirt pocket. He turned to the father. "We must to get your daughter to Honey Harbour. Now."

His mind came back to the treacherous trip across Georgian Bay from Quarry Island. The reefs, the shoals, the waves, the wind. Suddenly, he was full of fear again. Fifteen minutes. It took him a full twenty minutes on a calm sunny day. Fifteen minutes.

He took the big military flashlight that actually lived up to its billing. They rushed out the door into the storm. The poplar trees were bent to nearly ninety degrees in gale-force winds.

The boats were moored three boat lengths offshore. They headed down the path to the dock, running against the wind and fierce rain. Huddled in her father's arms, the girl cried in deep agony. The father was tearful and shaking but determined.

Matt now wondered about Harris. He'd disappeared while Matt was on the phone. Now he saw why. Harris had taken Matt's Limestone off its mooring. He'd moved it towards shore, to the end of his long dock. By himself. Matt could not believe this feat. In five-foot seas and a fifty-knot wind. Harris was over seventy, but a large and powerful man. He'd played football in university. Played tennis every day since. And he was now doing what Matt considered inconceivable.

A month earlier, Matt had nearly lost his boat, trying to bring it off the mooring buoy to the dock, in less than half this wind and sea. But Harris had brought the heavy boat in this storm near the dock and was holding it against the wind and waves. He was an oak tree standing against the fierce wind and sea. He was magnificent. The Limestone bounced up and down like a toy in the powerful waves, fighting him, but Harris held the boat exactly where it needed to be.

They raced to the dock and climbed into the Limestone. Matt believed half the dilemma was solved if they could get into the boat. But, getting into the boat wasn't getting off Quarry Island. Harris couldn't start the motor and let the props turn until they were back out to the buoys. It was simply too shallow. Although a sandy bottom, there were some boulders, and if the propeller hit just one, the mission would be over.

Two dozen yards of huge, savage waves barred their way. Matt saw the froth blowing off the cresting waves. He felt the force of it like rough sandpaper on his face. He felt cold fear stab his heart. Harris knew what needed to be done. Matt ran through his checklist: blowers on, bilge pump on, lights on, power switch on. The motor started. He turned his attention to navigating the treacherous journey.

He turned on the GPS, trying to remember how to start it. He'd missed a step. He was frantic. He had to reset it to fix the boat's location. It needed a starting point. He typed in the sequence of the buttons. The map came up. He could see where he was, and he saw the line he needed to follow. He got the motor going. It didn't warm quickly. If it stalled, they would be blown back on the beach and pounded to pieces. His hands shook from the cold and fear.

Harris was buying the time the engine needed to warm. Buying this little girl's life with every sinew in his exhausted back and legs. Buying it by holding the immense and violently bucking weight of the boat against the obscene fury of this storm.

Matt felt the boat rock as an exhausted Harris heaved himself off the dock and into the boat.

"Go!" Harris shouted, as he lay on the boat floor, gasping for breath.

Matt lowered the propeller, pulled the throttle out of neutral and then hard forward to engage the gears. He pushed the throttle forward smoothly but firmly, kicking the Limestone into gear and motion. The two-hundred-sixty horsepower Mercury engine spun the propeller shaft. The five-bladed aluminum propeller bit into the black water. He looked over, anxiously. The father still had his daughter wrapped in the blanket. They were huddled in the front of the boat behind the windshield. The little girl shook.

212 I MICHAEL DECTER

Matt looked up to the windshield. The wipers tried and failed to push away the torrents of rain. Harris crawled forward and stood beside Matt holding on to the seat, peering into the storm. The wind howled and there was nothing but blackness ahead of them.

Matt focused his eyes on the glowing green electronic screen. It was hard to do, as he was accustomed to using his eyes, looking at the horizon, looking at the water. But all he could do was look at the green display panel. The boat was the blip on the panel, the points were the buoys. He needed to keep the blip as close to the points as possible

They made the first buoy. He pushed the throttle forward, increasing speed. The speedometer in the boat had never worked but the tachometer did, so he ran it on the engine revolutions. He took it up to 3,000 RPMs. The bow came up. The boat was moving stronger now against the huge waves. He looked again at the little girl. Her father's arms trembled with her shaking. Fifteen minutes.

He pushed the throttle to 4,000 RPMs. He had never run the boat at 4,000 RPMs. He thought to himself, what if we hit something. And then he realized it wouldn't matter the number of RPMs. Minutes were what mattered now. There was no red line on the tachometer. Stops at 6,000. So, he pushed it forward to nearly 5,000. The bow came down; the Limestone was on a step plane. The throttle wouldn't go any further. Fifteen minutes. The engine roared and took on a deeper note. The boat slammed through other waves. The waves broke to the sides as the deep V-hull sliced into and through their rolling power. The blip was moving faster now on the screen. They were the blip. He thought to himself, *No damned hung jury this time. All in.*

Distracted by his thoughts, he cut the third buoy too close. The moving blip was right on the marker light. The bang was explosive as the fiberglass hull slammed into the buoy. Matt's heart stopped. Would it hit the propeller?

It did not. He'd need to replace the buoy if he survived, but the collision had not damaged the boat. He came around the point. Arced out, around the tip of Quarry Island, out around the treacherous shallow point of land. Huge waves pounded at the hull. Harris had the military flashlight. His light beam found the big green channel marker into the harbour. The marker bobbed like a toy in the heavy grey seas. It showed up as another point of light on his screen, and then the one, the one that marked the big rock at the entrance, the rock that took off a prop two years ago. He had to stay to the outside, around the corner. And now it was straight ahead.

Matt had a long, arching route to Picnic Island Marina through large green and red buoys bobbing violently in the channel. On the screen they were all greenish blips. The passage to Picnic Island was rough, but much calmer than the open lake. Two rocks that tower thirty feet above the lake guarding the entrance to Honey Harbour present a narrow passage. In daylight, it was an easy turn to make. In the dark, Matt could only hold the arc on the screen. One more turn. Hold the arc and pray that his chosen line would allow his propellor to clear the last rocks.

Matt looked up from his screen. Through the darkness he could see the lights of what seems to be a convention of OPP cruisers, lights ablaze. Their searchlights paved a watery path to the marina dock. Matt realized that the dispatcher had not abandoned them. He had not taken himself out of the loop. God bless him. The dispatcher only muted his sound and then he sent the cavalry.

It was not until the Limestone was nearly upon the marina dock that Matt noticed that the wake, at 5,000 RPMs, slammed every boat in the harbour into its dock, rudely awakening every inhabitant of the floating armada of big sailboats and large cruisers. His very real problem was whether he could slow in time to avoid putting the Limestone right up through the dock and killing them all. The boat was heavy and travelling very fast. The momentum of the Limestone was colossal; it was a waterborne freight train. He jerked the throttle back to neutral. The Limestone continued hurtling forward, its mass and momentum slowing its speed but not sufficiently. He threw it into reverse a little bit, a little bit more, and then he pulled it back hard. The engine reversed and roared against the wind. The propeller and engine shaft groaned. The entire hull shuddered. Finally, the boat began to slow.

He spun the Limestone as he got to the dock. Two burly OPP officers grabbed the side of what had once been their own boat. In an instant, father and daughter were in motion. One of the OPP officers had the trembling little girl in his arms. The other had his arms around the father's shoulders. They were over the side, onto the dock, and hurtling toward the light.

Matt dialled the pilot's cell phone. He read her the longitude and latitude off the GPS screen. He shouted the coordinates over the storm three times before he heard the pilot say, "Got them."

It seemed hopeless. Matt looked at Harris and they looked up the road towards the school, where flares lit all four corners. Then they both looked up together at the low dark clouds. The ceiling. There wasn't much of one. The storm clouds, grey-black, were right down to the tops of the trees.

"No ceiling at all," he said out loud. Harris nodded. There was certainly not enough ceiling for anyone following the rules. The chopper would hit the trees before the pilot could see them. There'd be another inquest.

Matt feared that his frantic dash across the lake had been in vain. He looked at his watch. From the time of the conversation with his brother, twenty-five minutes were gone. Not even the OPP, not with their fastest vehicle, not with their best driver, not on a sunny dry day could drive this sick little girl to Toronto in an hour. It was just too far. As they looked at the school grounds, he tried to calculate how long it would take a helicopter. He couldn't remember the speed of helicopters. Could they get from Barrie to Honey

Harbour, if she could even find Honey Harbour? He looked at the flares. He didn't believe that she could see the flares. The pilot certainly couldn't see flares through this depth of black cloud. *No ceiling.*

And then Matt thought he heard something. Was it hope playing with his ears or was there a real change in sound? Was it the triumph of the willful, hopeful imagination? It was faint, but that pocketa-pocketa sound came through the howl of the wind. And it got louder. And then he saw something in the bottom of the clouds — the white and blue bottom of a Ministry of Health chopper. Then the orange sides became visible. Never before had he been so relieved, so grateful to see that beautiful white, orange, and blue. It descended, not into schoolyard, but too far west. The chopper hovered for an instant over the marina, right on the GPS coordinates. The pilot finally saw the flares and spun the chopper, bringing it round into the wind and directly over the playground. The winds fought her below the ceiling. The chopper bucked. The pilot steadied her steed, then, dropped it like an elevator straight down the shaft, despite, what Matthew later learned, were crosswinds gusting as high as ninety knots per hour.

Much later, Matt read that these particular helicopters could not fly in a ninety-knot crosswind. Much later, an aviation expert assured him that no one, not even the best pilot could drop a helicopter straight down in that wind. The expert told him, "It is beyond their design characteristics. It can't be done." Much, much later, Matt read that above fifty knots, they grounded all helicopters in the North Sea. But now, this turbulent night, Matt watched in awe as the pilot planted the chopper dead centre in the schoolyard.

It was an act of courage, defiance, and skill. She kept the rotors going fast at a revving speed that severely shook the chopper, even though it was firmly on the ground. The thump of the rotors defied the howling winds of the storm.

The two OPP officers approached the chopper in a crouching

run, one holding the sick child, the other propelling her terrified father. Paramedics pulled them in. The door closed. Matt watched the pilot take the chopper up, back up into the black clouds and the fury of the storm. Then, suddenly, the rotor noise was gone. The OPP put out their flares. He sat in the boat. For a long time, he and Harris didn't say a word to each other. An exhausted silence descended upon them, in the midst of the storm, as their adrenaline began to ebb.

Finally, Harris said, "Maybe you could go a little slower on the way back. Try not to wreck the rest of Jim's buoys."

Matt realized he didn't want to return to Quarry Island in the dark and storm. He wanted to sit on the boat at the dock until the sun came up and lit their way. He said to Harris, "Why don't we just wait until there's some light."

Harris nodded.

They sat under the woefully inadequate shelter of the Limestone's flapping Bimini top. The wind howled and the rain drove across the water and under the top. They didn't care. They were already soaked to the skin. They huddled at the front of the Limestone, too exhausted to feel, their remaining adrenaline immunizing them against the cold and the wet.

One of the OPP officers came back down the dock. He handed two take-out coffees to them. "Quarry Island? They're saying you got her off Quarry Island in this storm?"

Matt and Harris nodded.

The OPP officer shook his head in disbelief. "You know you're madmen?" He looked out, into the storm, which was only now beginning to decline in force. "Thank God there are still madmen left in this world."

His statement invited no reply. He walked slowly back to his cruiser, shaking his head.

They sat on the boat and sipped their coffees in silence as they waited for the sun to come up. The coffee grew cold before they finished it. The wind continued to howl. Matt's cell phone vibrated in his shirt pocket. His fingers struggled to unbutton the pocket to take the call. He looked at the time on his phone. Thirty-eight minutes had elapsed since the helicopter left.

It was the pilot. "We're on the roof at Sick Kids. Her pulse is still strong."

Tears of relief welled up in Matt's eyes. "Thank you."

The pilot hung up.

An hour later, the pale light of the deep red dawn broke in the east. "Red sky at morn, sailors be warned," Matt muttered to Harris.

Matt took the Limestone slowly back out, around the markers.

Harris pointed. "You put a good-sized dent in Jim's third buoy, but it's still there."

Matt didn't take the boat above 3,000 RPMs on the way back. Dawn had brought further moderation to the fierce winds, but the huge rolling waves would not be diminished for another five long hours. They were both exhausted from the strain of their almost-impossible task, but were buoyed by the pilot's call and the take-out coffee. They moored the Limestone at the buoy, then waded ashore.

When he got to his cottage, Matt peeled off his wet clothes, and left them where they fell in a puddle on the hardwood floor. He took a towel from the bathroom and dried himself off as best he could, then he wrapped himself in a sweatshirt, pulling the hood over his head, and put on dry jeans. Still shivering, he put on thick, warm socks and a vest over the sweatshirt.

He knelt beside his bed, closed his eyes, and prayed for the survival of the little girl. He remembered the comforting presence on his left side, where Beth knelt when he prayed each night as a child. He finished with the Lord's Prayer. He imagined Norah joining him and Beth. There was something right about this, knowing that he had two mothers after all, one he knew well and one he still had much to learn about.

His hands shook as he built a fire in the fireplace. He made himself a large cup of coffee and put in two large shots of Glenlivet. He waited for the fire and the Scotch to warm him. He thought about the little girl, his own lost mother, his now adult children. His own nearly lost life. He couldn't order his thoughts. They washed over him in big, soft waves. Matt worked his way slowly through more Glenlivet and coffee.

Four hours later, his phone rang. It was the little girl's father. He started to talk, but was overwhelmed with emotion. He was crying. He couldn't get the words out.

Matt was terrified. Had the little girl died? Had their night journey been in vain?

There was a pause, but then the father began to sob. There was another pause, after which a calm, professional voice spoke.

"This is Dr. Langer. I believe the little girl is going to be all right. We were four hours in surgery. She came close to developing sepsis. She's still in intensive care, but I believe you got her here in time. She is one lucky girl."

"Thank you, Doctor." Matt hung up before any more could be said. Then he wept. He wept with relief because this little girl would live. When he stopped weeping, and regained his composure, he called Harris. "Talked to the surgeon and the father. The surgeon believes she'll make it."

"Thank God." Harris didn't say anything else, but Matt knew that his were not the only tears shed that morning on Quarry Island.

CHAPTER TWENTY-TWO

FINAL ENTRIES

MATT SAT IN FRONT of his fireplace with his mother's diary. He read the final entries.

DECEMBER 4, 1952

A strange yellow smoke fog descended over London overnight. They called it radiation fog. Londoners called it pea-souper. This pea-souper seems thicker and hard to breathe. I interviewed older people in the street who told me that it seemed thicker than other times. Visibility dropped to 150 feet. Heathrow Airport closed today and most roads as well.

DECEMBER 7, 1952

The smoke fog did not burn off this morning as predicted. It seems to have settled over the city like a ghostly yellow blanket. The elderly I interviewed were having trouble breathing. They coughed continually into their soaked handkerchiefs. A few were gasping and had great difficulty speaking. I asked for their addresses so I could visit them in their homes. The Stewarts seemed very ill but gave me their address.

219

DECEMBER 8, 1952

The smoke fog continues. The headline-writer at the paper abbreviated it to SMOG *today. My story made the front page above the fold. Mrs. Stewart was hospitalized overnight. Mr. Stewart was also in hospital. The hospital emergency rooms are overcrowded. Daniel is working day and night. The meteorologists say it is a temperature inversion that is caused by the formation of a static layer of cooler air close to the ground. I have trouble catching a decent breath when outside.*

DECEMBER 9, 1952

Mrs. Stewart died last night. Thousands of others are very ill. The air is hard to breathe today. My own coughing is worse than before. The city is covered in this poisonous air. The temperature inversion continues to trap the smoke fog. I wonder how many more Mrs. Stewarts will die from this terrible smog.

DECEMBER 10, 1952

The smog finally began to disperse. Hundreds, perhaps thousands, of older Londoners are very ill. Many have died.

DECEMBER 19, 1952

The estimated death toll is now 4000. *My breathing has worsened. I am very weak. Daniel is looking after his patients, as well as the baby and me. He looks completely exhausted. He moves like a ghost.*

DECEMBER 20, 1952

Daniel has moved me into the hospital where he works. He keeps bringing specialists to examine me — eminent professors of medicine. They never smile. They took away my cigarettes and gave me a tank of oxygen. Our friend Phil Podger is looking after Matthew during the day while he studies for the Australian Foreign Service exams.

Matt could read no further that day; he put the diary down. Oddly, as he did after Daniel's death, he took refuge in painting. As he applied the paint to the window frames of his house, both a peace and a world weariness came over him. He could only take it all in a little at a time, or he risked being overwhelmed. Rebirth took its own time.

DECEMBER 24, 1952

Christmas Eve. Struggling to breathe. Daniel seemed angry today when he came to see me. I asked him what he'd learned from the specialists. That seemed to make him angry, but he controlled his temper and put on his best soothing bedside manner. He said, "They tell me the pneumonia you have has been made much worse by the London Smog, by your smoking, and by the exposure to radiation when you were in the South Pacific."

The worst of these things, two of them, she knew, Matt thought. Decisions she'd taken — to continue to smoke, to go to see the hydrogen bomb test — decisions she'd taken over Daniel's angry objection. She'd done it anyway.

I've smoked what cigarettes I could get since I was 12. As many as I could get my hands on. In university, it levelled off at two packs a day. Daniel hates my smoking. He hates tobacco and is quite certain it makes people ill.

I say to him, "Give me some proof. They keep me thin."

Matt had never heard of the London Smog of 1952 until Professor O'Connell mentioned it. He put the diary down and went to his computer to google it. *A long-lasting temperature inversion trapped coal smoke along with fog for five days in London, England. Smog that took 4,000 lives, mostly the elderly and the infirm. See also 1948 Ecology and the Environment, 1963, Ecology and the Environment.*

Four thousand lives, Matt thought. *Four thousand lives. Including his own mother. Four thousand lives.*

DECEMBER 24, 1952

Sleepy now. Hard to breath. Must rest.

He turned to the next and final entry. He was startled that it read:

A Letter to My Son, Matthew.

This was his mother's last communication to the world and her only communication directly to him.

> *You will be three months old tomorrow, Matthew. Christmas Day. Also, your father's birthday.*
>
> *Your father is very angry with me. He will never know that all of my love, every morsel of it is for him and for you. I am very angry at the world. We are building fearful weapons. We are poisoning the very air we all breathe. God knows what awaits you, my beloved baby boy. Maybe the world will come to its senses. Weren't two World Wars enough? Do we need to race towards a third?*
>
> *I consign this diary to you my son, Matthew. Even if I am not alive to share it with you, I believe this diary will reach you someday. It must.*
>
> *Fight only for peace and justice, my son. Fight with your head*

and your heart. Fight with your true words and passion. Do not pick up a gun and join the next slaughter. No war ends all wars. Only peace can ever end war. Remember this truth. There is a Gaelic blessing, my son, that I wish for you:

May the road rise up to meet you.
May the wind always be at your back.
May the sun shine warm upon your face;
The rains fall soft upon your fields, and until we meet again,
May God hold you in the palm of His hand.

Tears welled up in his eyes and ran slowly down Matt's cheeks. There was no more of her diary to read. He had retrieved as much of his lost mother as remained. Mixed with his tears, Matt was comforted in his newfound understanding of who his mother had been and the knowledge that she'd perished fighting for what she believed in; peace, truth, and justice. And most importantly of all, he was comforted by reading the message she had left for him to find sixty years later. Matthew felt a gentle peace at last.

CHAPTER TWENTY-THREE

RETURN TO THE WORLD

MATT PUT DOWN THE diary and tried to catch his breath. He sat on a heavy red Georgian Bay chair on the sandy beach. His heart rate slowed as he gazed out at the pale blue of the Georgian Bay sky. He let it soothe him. He let the gentle breeze cool his face, still red from the sun and wind. He watched his Limestone 24, bobbing on its long white line from the orange mooring buoy. The ugly storm was gone. It had blown itself out. The resulting peaceful scene restored his tranquility.

He had read the final pages of Norah's diary and for the first time had experienced the loss of the mother who had slipped away from him sixty years earlier. He wept fresh tears for the mother he had lost — tears for the mother he could not save, the mother he knew only through her difficult-to-read handwriting.

"I found you," he said out loud, to himself, in a voice that surprised him. "I found you," he repeated. "We will never be apart again."

Matt was haunted by his lost mother. Perhaps not haunted. Possessed.

Norah had been headstrong. Matt learned this from her diary, but he was also aware of the formidable battles she would have had to face, being a young woman in journalism. Irish to boot. The Brits were not uniformly welcoming of a beautiful Irish lass. She must have been very strong to survive a young Daniel. Matt knew his father as a man of barely constrained anger. He railed against everything he encountered that would not bend to his will. This relentless drive and determination yielded only to his wife, whom he would not directly oppose. Matt had been aware since early childhood that his father's rage rarely boiled over at Beth. No one else was spared — not his children, not his patients, and certainly not his colleagues.

Matt watched the tiger lilies sway in the breeze. He marvelled at how they closed at sunset and opened in the early morning light. They would be here, every summer he returned. Someday, on this very beach, he would teach his grandchildren to swim, to canoe, and to sail. He would teach the great-grandchildren of Norah Patricia McCarthy to sail. He would also teach them how to run the Limestone at night through the reefs and shoals of Georgian Bay on the GPS and radar. And he would give them her diary to read, so that they would know, as he now knew, who their great-grandmother had been, what she'd done in the world, and what the world had done to her.

That evening, Matt returned to his big, red wooden chair, and watched the sun set, pink and red, over Beausoleil Island. His mind travelled a circuitous route. He re-read Yeats's poem "The Lake Isle of Innisfree." Yeats filled him with peace as did this island beach.

Matt listened to the lapping lake water. He now understood in the deepest part of his being that he could not run away from the world. Whatever ugliness and violence were out there. However isolated he felt. Melting polar ice caps. Raging wildfires. Extinction of species. Colony collapse of bees. Warming oceans. Beyond the rhetoric and the dire warnings, there was little concrete action underway. Treaties and protocols were the stuff of the public face of nations and inaction. Laws, regulations, funding of real programs — these all seemed slippery and elusive.

Matt's whole career, his entire waking life, had been about getting hard things done. Now, the hardest thing of all faced not Matt,
but every living inhabitant of the earth. And where was Matt?
Hiding in his cottage on his damned island. Matt knew in his heart
that he couldn't continue to hide. Norah had not run away. She
had faced some of the biggest challenges of her time and had paid
for it with her life.

Matt pondered the chain of life, his own genetic code, and how
Norah was a part of him. Although he remembered nothing of her,
he felt a bond, a deep cord of attachment to Norah. As he had
come to know her through her diary and the clippings, a bond had
been created. She had always been part of his flesh and blood and
of his soul, but unknown.

When Beth and Daniel had fought, the child Matthew would
run down the back lane to hide behind a brick wall at its end. He
was certain that he would be missed, and his parents would come
to search for him. But they never did. After a few hours, he would
trudge back home and rejoin his family. He believed that no one
would notice his hiding out on Quarry Island and his absence from
the world would achieve nothing. Matt knew with certainty that he
must rejoin the world and find his way back to return to the battle
for change.

Pacing the living room of his cottage, he reconsidered his survivalist plan. Later that day, he put up and attached the plywood
shutters covering each of the screen windows. He drained the water
system and the pump. He carted the food in the fridge down to his
boat. He built and lit a last fire in the fieldstone fireplace. He drank
some Scotch. He was gone at first light the next morning.

He left Quarry Island to rejoin the world, in his own way, to
do what he could in that world, just as Norah had before. And
perhaps he would also perish as she had in the struggle, but he'd
perish in the arena, not hiding on this island.

The Limestone carried Matt across the now-calm blue waters

of Georgian Bay. Carried him back to take up the struggle for a better world for his own children, for all children. His thoughts were not filled with the stirring ballads of Gordon Lightfoot. His lost and regained Irish mother drew him back to the poetry and life of Yeats. Not to a poem, but to the epitaph on his tombstone, the words that Yeats had carefully chosen for his final poetry.

Cast a cold Eye
On Life, on Death.
Horseman, pass by.

Matt was not done with this world yet. Not ready to cast a cold eye or have a cold eye cast upon him. There was far too much to do and far too little time to make a new start. He now understood he needed to be engaged with the world. He could not hide from that engagement on this island. He took the Limestone up to 3,000 RPMs and rounded the last mark to what lay ahead.

Before leaving the marina, Matt checked his email. He found a report from the chief financial officer of the City. It included pension arrangements should Matthew choose to retire. He put on his glasses to read the pension on offer. Matt surprised himself by saying out loud, "I'm free. I will return to the world. I will take up the fight for the better, more peaceful world my mother sought."

Life felt renewed. Perhaps the retrieval of his lost mother's diary. Perhaps the near-death experience in the storm. Perhaps, a renewed conviction that no matter the actual result, he ought to try to make a difference. He was filled with an energy and hopefulness that he hadn't experienced in many months.

Matt thought longingly of Mary Louise O'Reilly. What would she do if he suddenly reappeared in her life? He began to write a letter to Professor O'Connell in his mind.

His cellphone rang. It was Charlie from Finance at City Hall.

228 I MICHAEL DECTER

"We extended your leave by another six months and you are approved for the full pension if you so choose."

"Thank you, Charlie, for looking out for me. I got your email. I will be taking the pension."

"You'll be missed, boss," Charlie replied. "Get on with your life. Don't even think about rejoining this circus. Every week it just gets worse in here."

"I won't, Charlie. I'm going to take on some other challenges, ones that got away on me. Try to fix things from the outside not the inside."

"You on the outside pissing in? God help us all."

Matt waited several minutes before calling his children to arrange to meet them in Toronto for dinner. "I have much to tell you, my children. Good news, important news."

"Not planning to live on Quarry Island for the winter?" Sarah asked sternly.

"No," he replied. "Was I that transparent?"

"Yes," she said. "I'm really glad you changed your mind."

On an impulse, he dialled Professor O'Connell's office number. Her secretary, Colleen, answered on the second ring and connected him to the Professor.

"Professor O'Connell, it's Matthew Rice. I don't know if you would remember our conversation —"

"Of course, I remember," she interrupted. "Did you learn more about Norah?"

"I did. I am still working to make sense of it all, but I am making progress. Thank you so much for your help," Matt said. "I have a favour to ask. I'd like to take your course this fall, if possible?"

"Of course, Matt. Be in touch with my assistant, Colleen. The first lecture in the course is on September seventh. I expect to see your robin's-egg-blue Irish eyes when I look up from my notes."

"Thank you, Professor O'Connell. Better late than never!"

"Speaking of better late than never, I have a request."

"Anything," Matt replied.

"Call Mary Louise. She's been worrying about you."

He was taken aback "I will."

"Good. See you in September, young man."

No time like the present, Matt thought, looking up another number in his contacts list. Mary Louise answered on the first ring.

"Did you read your mother's diary?" she asked, straight away.

"Yes, several times. At least most of it. I struggled to read the entries just before her death."

"Did you find her in it?"

"Yes, I believe I really did."

"And did you find her in yourself?

Matt paused for a long moment before he answered. "Yes, I found her there too."

"Is your quest at an end?"

"Yes, although there's a new one just starting. Time for me to return to the world," Matt answered, surprising himself with the speed and directness of his answer. "Time to get things done."

"I'm back in Boston next month," said Mary Louise. "Perhaps your new road will rise up and meet me there?"

"I would like that very much."

"So would I, Matt. So would I."

"You may find me a burden," Matt continued. "I'll be taking Professor O'Connell's course."

"Outstanding, the professor will make a true Irishman out of you."

His neighbours on Quarry Island would be puzzled when they opened their cottage doors that morning. On each of their doorsteps were two canisters of propane and one bottle of Glenlivet. Except for Harris, where he had decided, all things considered, that it would be more appropriate to leave two bottles of Glenlivet, the eighteen-year-old, and only one canister of propane.

And while the cottagers of Quarry Island would chat, puzzled over this odd sequence of events — the rescue of the little girl, the sudden departure of Matt, the puzzling appearance of the propane and much-admired eighteen-year-old Glenlivet — Matt would be far away. Only Harris knew where Matt was headed. Matt imagined Harris smiling and sipping the very fine Scotch as his wife Sophie asked where Matt had gone.

He could almost hear Harris's reply. "Back to the world. Back to do what he can to save this bloody awful, wonderful world." And he hoped Harris had enough faith in him to know he would try.

ACKNOWLEDGEMENTS

Many thanks to Marc Côté who is not only the publisher of *Shadow Life* but also its insightful and intelligent editor. This novel is far, far better due to Marc's work.

I'm grateful also Sarah Cooper, Sarah Jensen, Tiana Trudell, and the rest of the Cormorant Books team.

Thank you to my determined agent, Beverley Slopen, who was convinced from the start that Cormorant Books was the right home for *Shadow Life*. Bev also provided many invaluable editorial suggestions in her positive, supportive way.

A special thanks to Anna Porter, my friend and mentor through the journey of a first novelist.

Other readers of the manuscript who provided both support and comments included Steve Kaszas, Maureen O'Neill, Sarah Miniaci and Rachel Thompson.

A big thank you to Sarah Miniaci and Isabella Kuscu for their marketing support in *Shadow Life*'s launch. As well as thanks to Rachel Thompson of Bad Redhead Media for all her assistance on social media.

Helen Walsh fully supported and encouraged my efforts to write a first novel. I am most grateful for her sage advice and assistance at every stage.

Two further sources of information about *Shadow Life* and

its author can be found at https://michaeldecter.com and https://www.cormorantbooks.com/shadow-life.

This is a work of fiction. Names, characters, places, and incidents are either the product of the author's imagination or are used fictitiously. Any resemblance to actual persons, living or dead, businesses, companies, events, or locales is purely coincidental. The author affords himself the full protection of all relevant, or irrelevant, reverent or irreverent statutes of law. All backward-looking statements should be taken for fiction or near fiction. All forward-looking statements are merely speculation. This is a work of pure imagination and intention.

For the sake of the story, a few historical events have been time shifted. For example, the crew of the *Lucky Dragon*, who were all fishermen, became ill due to radiation from the second hydrogen bomb test in 1953, not the first one in 1952. There was no Patrick McCarthy in Irish politics, but the enduring Patrick McGilligan spent forty years in the Dáil — but that's another story.

Other liberties have been taken under the broad protective cloak of literary licence. The author hopes that the reputations of good people who actually lived or still live have not been harmed in the telling of this story. Names have been altered to protect the guilty. There are no wounded for the press to pursue — only those who are healing. All those who believe they have been unfairly mentioned can avail themselves of the stated truth that this is purely a work of fiction. Or they can face Harris in a court of law. Harris is even better at libel litigation than he is at tennis or at moving heavy boats in a gale. Consider yourselves forewarned.

Michael B. Decter
Quarry Island, Georgian Bay
Lake Huron
Ontario, Canada

Michael Decter is a dual citizen of Canada and the Republic of Eire. He has lived most of his life in Canada and in Cambridge, Massachusetts. Michael has an Irish heart. Previous books include *Million Dollar Strategy* and a memoir of his father, *Percy*. He divides his time between Toronto, Quarry Island and the larger world.

We acknowledge the sacred land on which Cormorant Books operates. It has been a site of human activity for 15,000 years. This land is the territory of the Huron-Wendat and Petun First Nations, the Seneca, and most recently, the Mississaugas of the Credit River. The territory was the subject of the Dish With One Spoon Wampum Belt Covenant, an agreement between the Iroquois Confederacy and Confederacy of the Anishinaabe and allied nations to peaceably share and steward the resources around the Great Lakes. Today, the meeting place of Toronto is still home to many Indigenous people from across Turtle Island. We are grateful to have the opportunity to work in the community, on this territory.

We are also mindful of broken covenants and the need to strive to make right with all our relations.